OUT OF
NOWHERE

I Dani, unwaith eto

OUT OF NOWHERE

roger granelli

seren

seren is the book imprint of
Poetry Wales Press Ltd
Wyndham Street, Bridgend
Wales

© Roger Granelli, 1995

A CIP record for this book is available at the
British Library Cataloguing in Publication Data Office

ISBN 1-85411-120-5

*The publisher acknowledges the financial support of the
Arts Council of Wales*

Cover Illustration: Jennie Bowring

Printed in Plantin by
WBC Book Manufacturers, Bridgend

OUT OF
NOWHERE

ONE

The city lowered at him as he walked through its maze of tall buildings. Light was crushed, streets were cast in raw gloom, and each slim tower of stone outgrew its neighbour. When he saw the sky, it was rubbed grey with winter. There was just a glimmer of orange in it over the East Side: the echo of a sun lost. It was mid-November, and colder than he had ever known. Blowing on his hands he took a firmer grip on his case and heaved his sack onto his shoulder, sailor style.

Free of the customs check and anxious to save the money of a taxi fare, he had walked a long way from the docks. Yet he laughed at the cold his body felt, protected by the adrenalin that pumped through him. It was nineteen fifty seven, he was in New York, and he did not care about the temperature. Frank Magnani was here, in his Mecca, in the heart of cool. To play.

When his crude map failed him he took to asking people the way. One answered, 'that's way over town, buddy.' A few scuttled by, hands up to their faces in defence, or defiance, leaving a white breath of indifference in their wake. It was late afternoon when he found his hotel.

The Golden Age was a delapidated three storey building of brown sandstone, old by the standards of the city. In welcome a yellow cab doused him with water its tyres threw up from a leaking hydrant. As his cigarette crumbled in his hands he felt like a character in the old films he had seen: a man alone, and searching. Icy drips ran down his legs into his shoes, and his hands were numb from the weight of his things. And he still did not care.

An old man was slumped over a desk in the lobby of the hotel. A small, bald man, with a hooked nose which curved out of his face like an eagle's beak. He was reading a comic book, turning its pages idly, with his face almost touching the illustrations. From his mouth hung the remnants of a dead cigar, which he chewed on, as if it was an extension of his lip. He looked like a man tired of living, or one who had never lived. Without changing his position he glanced up at the new arrival.

'Yeah, you want a room, kid?' the man said.

'Yes. I've been given this address, for somewhere to stay.'

'That's us, a place where you can stay. If you got ten dollars in advance.'

He fumbled in a coat pocket and extricated his damp wallet.

'Not broke. Makes a change.' The clerk smirked at the puddle Magnani made on the floor. 'Got wet real good.'

This turned his mind to water and he cocked an ear towards the entrance. 'Jesus Christ, ain't they fixed that hydrant yet? What we pay taxes for, I wanna know.' He looked his new guest over again, this time with a spark of attention. His eyes rested on the case.

'Guitar player, huh?'

'Yes.'

'Get a lot of you dudes in here. Famous for it, I guess.' He turned away and spat yellow juice into a pail behind his counter. It resounded in the dull silence of the lobby. A stained checking-in book was pushed across the counter. 'Sign yourself in. What's that accent anyway? You a Limey?'

'That's right.'

'Don't see many of you in here. Had a blind guy in once, after the war. Piano player he was but he got money and didn't come back.'

The clerk laughed, a clucking sound that died in his throat, which he cleared with another spit. He handed over a key. 'Number twelve, second floor on the right. We don't have no bellhop, in between them you might say. You look like you don't need one.'

He waved a hand vaguely towards the stairs, and settled over his comic again. As the musician was about to climb the clerk called out to him.

'Say kid, we don't get a lot of white boys in here, mainly niggers, playing that new jazz, you mind that?'

'No.'

'Ok. Didn't know what a Limey might think of niggers. Some of them are pretty up these days, if you know what I mean.'

He had reached the fifth stair when the voice stopped him again.

'I'm part nigger myself, though you'd never know, huh? If you need anything, dames, dope, anything, ask me, Al. That's what I'm here for, I'm everyone's friend.'

He climbed to the second floor, passing sounds on his way. After the shabbiness of the lobby he was glad to hear signs of life. In one room a trumpet played, fat and sweet, and as full as a city night. It was better than anything he had heard back home. In room eleven forties' music was blasted out from a record player, old jump stuff that rolled through the door. Voices vied with it for control but were beaten. Inside he heard a woman laugh and furniture being moved around.

The door to number twelve yielded to his key. He entered a bare room, containing a bed, a chair, a hand basin and a faded print of

New Orleans on the wall. Paint the colour of tobacco flaked from the ceiling. A single heating pipe ran along the wall but it was cold to Magnani's touch. Someone had scratched 'Jesus loves Marty' on the back of the door. It was a bleak welcome.

From the window he looked down on 52nd Street, the famous street with its clubs. They were starting to come alive in the dusk. The neon sign of one spluttered into life. A crackling, hesitant pink at first, it surged to a deep red glow, announcing its presence like a cheap whore. Magnani's spirits rose when he saw the names up in lights; it was hard to take it in, that he was here and about to merge into all this.

He tried to open the window jammed by a generation of dirt and paint, then lay on the bed, wrapping the sheets around his wet and fully clothed body. The mattress was thin and none too clean, but he accepted its bony touch. In the room he felt the cold more. He listened to the sounds of the great city, making music out of what carried up to his window. It was a habit. Somewhere out on the river a tug hooted. It competed with a siren he guessed must be a police car. Next door the woman screamed and was told to 'cool it babe'. The room emptied and he heard the clatter of its occupants on the stairs. He was grateful for his childhood diet of American films, the language was familiar and he felt less of an outsider. He struggled out of his wet things before sleep took him.

Waking, he searched his sack for a crumpled shirt and his coolest red tie. It was wide and the colour of wine, with a motif of musical notes running down it. He tried the wash basin. The pipe rumbled a complaint and the water coughed out in intermittent gobs. For a moment he thought it might be warm but it proved as cold as the room. He threw some dank water on his face, ran a comb through his hair and resolved to complain about it in the morning. But tonight he wanted music. It beckoned him, its hands around his future.

He heard the closest club start up, a combo playing a fast standard. Even with the window shut he could hear it: he was hypersensitive to sound tonight, addicted to it. Before sliding his guitar under the bed he opened its case and was comforted by the warm glow of its red interior. It caught the lights of the street and shone. Fortified, he went out into the American night.

The area around the Golden Age Hotel was full of life. He thought of his home, tired and dull, a monochrome hangover from the war, where good times were rationed with the food. He had seen few black people, just the ones he had caught in London clubs, and the G.I. who had pressed gum into his greedy boy's hand. Here they were everywhere. They represented what he loved in music, what he tried to play, and what he tried to be. 'Only black musicians play black music' he had been told, but he wanted to disprove this. It was the colour inside that counted, he told himself.

He found the club he wanted, paid the two dollars cover charge and went down its steps, running his fingers over the money in his wallet as he did so. The notes were few and work would have to come quickly. The club was a basement with a low ceiling. Bare bulbs gave inadequate light and it was a quarter filled with early people trying not to look eager or bored. A few checked him out as he went up to the bar, noting an outsider.

'What'll it be, mac?' The barman thrust his face at him, white teeth flashing in an ebony face. 'Whisky,' he said, as cool as he could. The bar was tiny, just large enough to get a drink and move away from it. The tables were a similar scale, wooden circles that served only as drink stands. He found a corner where he could watch the stage and soak up the atmosphere.

Already the club was full of smoke. A collective steel-grey pall hung under the lights. Everyone, it seemed, sucked on a cigarette in this country. Around him assorted night people came to life. There were hustlers, a few hookers looking for an early evening score, some whites from uptown, musicians not working-he recognised these by their hungry eagerness. The place was seedy but vibrant with its own identity. It was confident, expectant, arrogant and its people moved with the night's promise. The musician in him enjoyed it, this was his milieu and he was a ready participant.

There was a ripple of applause as the combo came on. He recognised the sax and trumpet players immediately. Magazine photographs were animated in front of him, ready to blow the sounds of his records. His fingers ached for his guitar, and he wondered if he could ever play with the likes of these. His thoughts were impatient and anxiety warmed in his gut with the whiskey, but he knew he had worked hard for his chance, and it was very close now. He was here to prove himself.

The club filled as the combo played. A brilliant rhythm section attacked the first number, the drummer crashing through the changes and pushing on the two men in front: they were all hot. The alto played a well known melody and the crowd played along with it, alert and straining to go with the music, to take it, use it, and be part of it. The players controlled their world. Hugging his horn close to him with his shoulders hunched and his eyes closed to slits, the alto player exploded into a series of tricky figures. Each chased the one before, daring and inventive. It was a soaring, hard, sweet sound, yet as delicate as running brook water. There were no stray honks or squeaks, the man was in his prime; he gained the great heights for which he reached. Magnani followed his every move and thanked God he was not a horn player.

The number built to a crescendo. The drummer attacked his kit, but was always in control of his chaos. He rode his drums like a man possessed, eyes rolling upwards to another world. Cymbals crashed, exhorting still more from the frontmen. Near to the stage a woman screamed to her idols to go on, to go higher, to find more: she invited a climax. As the whisky slammed his empty stomach he wanted to join in her screams but he kept quiet, and wondered.

There was a break. The musicians disappeared backstage, apart from the sax player, who pushed his way over to the bar with admirers hanging from him. A god in this small world, he was unknown outside. He was large, somewhat paunchy, and puffy around the eyes: thick jowled from fast living, he was a picture of ill-health but tonight strength poured from him. He had power. Magnani would see different nights.

He drank more whiskey and stayed until three, when the music ended and the crowd spilled out into the street, laughing and shouting its way home. He spilled out with them and staggered along the sidewalk with a vague fear of violence, but no-one approached him. In his room he threw up in the wash basin, a thin bile of drink and hunger, then fell into the bed. He was completely happy.

A knock on his door roused him in the morning. At first he could not remember where he was, and the rumble of the street hammered at his head. He heard a whirl of traffic and calling voices, and smelt cooking drifting up from below. His stomach leapt like a salmon. He answered the door shakily, shivering with the cold. A well-dressed black man stood in the corridor, blowing air into his cupped hands. His wide smile depressed Magnani.

'Man, it's a cold one. Slept in your clothes, huh? You Magnani, Frank Magnani?'

He nodded. 'Yes. Who are you?'

'Coleford Johnson, at your service. Cole to my friends, and that's everyone, man. They told me to look you up, down at the local, our union, dig. Said a white guy was coming over from England. Ain't never seen one before.' He stared at Magnani with mock wide eyes.

'Yeah, I can see you arrived last night.' Johnson walked himself into the room. 'Sheet. Place never changes. And cold too.' He went to the wash basin and ran a tap. It chugged reluctantly. 'Don't ever drink this stuff, man.'

Magnani stood in the doorway, not knowing what to do.

'I can see you are completely underwhelmed by my arrival Frank. Tell you what, use some of this swamp water on your face and meet me downstairs. We going to breakfast, boy.'

He slapped his hands together and Magnani knew he was a drummer. Johnson left, his clicking fingers in the corridor announcing his presence to the other rooms. Someone shouted to him and he answered with a laugh. The place went back to sleep.

Magnani braced himself against the ice of the water and washed quickly, too hung over to risk a shave. He kept the same shirt on and left the collar open. His topcoat was too thin so he trapped it close to him with a scarf that matched his red tie. He adjusted the coat in an effort to look smart but failed miserably. There was a shout from outside, Magnani realised his name was being called. He peered down to the street to see Johnson playing an imaginary guitar. 'Bring your axe down man. I forgot to tell you, you playing today.'

Magnani was too muzzy-headed for nervousness, but there was a quick stab of anticipation. In London they had told him he was ready, but he had dismissed the talk. When the Americans he had met in Paris said the same he began to take notice. He pulled out his case, opened it and checked over the guitar, giving it a quick polish with his rag. He had worked years to get it. It was an American full bodied model with two pick-ups, handbuilt and favoured by the best. A dark tobacco stain lightened to soft orange as he rubbed. He clipped the case shut again, flicked back his dark hair and put on his one hat, tilting it for maximum effect. He clapped his hands together, like Johnson. They were too large for his frame, a worker's hands, strong and fat-fingered, unusual for a musician.

The cold air smacked him as he pushed through the hotel entrance. Johnson grinned, immaculate in a herring-bone over-coat, brown fedora with satin band, and gleaming leather shoes. Magnani rubbed his own on the back of his trousers.

'Man, you are smart,' Johnson roared. And you are loud, Magnani thought, I'll have to get used to you. 'Come on, heave that axe over the street, we'll go to Nina's deli. It's good.'

Nina's was bustling with people on their way to work, or musicians stopping off before bed. They had jammed together since their official early morning finish and now ate as if their lives depended on it. Magnani was amazed at the amount of food piled on their plates. His own eating habits had been shaped by a childhood of wartime rationing which he thought would fit in well with the pawnshop existence of the jazz musician. Perhaps he was wrong, for here they ate like kings, it seemed.

'How much money you got man?' Johnson asked, guiding him to a table.

He knew enough to say 'not much'.

'Uh huh. You like us already.' Johnson nodded and waved to people as he passed their tables.

Nina served them herself. She was huge, her black dress could not disguise her bulk. When she talked she shook a little. She beamed at Magnani, hands on hips, rocking back slightly on her heels.

'This here is a Limey, Nina,' Johnson grinned his pearly grin. 'He ain't had real food before. Show him all you got.'

'You'll be a novelty here, honey, that accent of yours will open doors. Just don't take this lowlife through 'em with you.' She feinted a swipe at Johnson, who widened his grin.

'How do you like this smile Frankie?' Johnson said. 'It's my special Jim Crow de-luxe, look at the happy nigger smile. Honkeys feel comfortable with that. Pops has gone a long way on it.'

Magnani nodded.

Johnson ordered for Magnani and charged both meals to him. They ate platefuls of scrambled eggs and rolls called bagels, with side plates of crisp bacon. It was a day's food for Magnani but went down easily. Copious cups of coffee cleared his head and he felt better. Johnson became more serious.

'So Frank, you made it over here. We been hearing about you, you been spotted, you might say. The boys who've been across the water, hey, they said, there's this ofay over in London Town, well they all ofays over there, but he can play man. Get him over, they say, see if he can cut it here. Ain't too many guitar players in this game.'

Magnani guessed what an ofay was and was flattered by Johnson's words. He fumbled with his collar and looked around him. Nina's had soaked him with warmth, it mingled with the sweat of his hangover. The solid breakfast pushed it out of his pores.

'The hotel,' Magnani said, 'is it the best I can get, for the money?'

'Hell yes. There's plenty worse, man. If you play and folks like you, you can get somewhere better. But I tell you brother, not many dudes earn much. A few of the older guys, the Duke, Pops, those kind of guys. Bird did for a while, he was good for us, put us on the map. Everyone wants be-bop now, shit, it's respectable man. But there's still no money in it. Better learn that now.' Magnani already had.

He brooded for a while, wondering how he would fit in. His other trip abroad, to Paris, had been smooth and easy paced. Magnani had gained his first real contact there. An old American soprano player from the days of King Oliver had told him he was good. 'So be good, man,' the old man said, 'go to New York and be good, or you'll have never done it.'

Jazz sifted through Paris naturally: it went with the smell of coffee on the streets, the burr of French whispered between numbers, the easy intermingling of races. Now he was in a shouting melting pot of a place. His first night had been one of shouts, the combo shouted its music, the crowd shouted back its identity. Even now, at breakfast he felt the surge of New York life. It was exciting, but it might be dangerous.

Johnson brought him out of his thoughts. 'Okay, Frank. I've arranged a little session for you. We checked around the guys and found a few willing to stay awake. We got three pieces for you, drums, bass and piano.'

'No-one known?'

'Are you kidding? Don't look so worried. You're no-one here, dig? You got no reputation but you might be getting a hoist up quick: not bad for your first day. People would kill to come here and get a chance right off.'

'I know.'

'Come on then. It's two blocks over. Pay Nina first.'

Johnson hustled him through the streets. Magnani's eyes were everywhere and the city looked kinder now that he knew someone. He took in its sights and smells, and looked in the stores they passed. There was a startling mix of races on the streets. Magnani saw the many clubs of fifty-second street, crowded together in a shabby unity, each trying to attract a share of the small jazz public. Johnson pointed out Birdland and Magnani looked up at its sign with a sigh. Musical gods returned his stare, haughty faces of men who had reached jazz pinnacles. For ten years they had been his encouragement, their triumphs his inspiration, the spur that led him to master his own instrument. Now they had drawn him to them.

Johnson took him to a club just like the one he had visited the night before. Its cold emptiness ached for people. They went down some steps past an ancient janitor who acknowledged Johnson and waved them inside as he swept. The musicians waited at the far end of the room, the bass player plucking out a few notes, the others drinking coffee. Johnson greeted them and ushered Magnani in front of him.

'Fellas, this is the guy from England.' He pronounced it Engerland. 'We had the word on him from a few of the dudes and now he's here.'

Magnani saw tired, disinterested faces. He had arrived at his first proving ground with the smell of the ocean still in his head, and a queasiness in his guts. Sweat moistened his hands.

'Hello, glad to meet you all,' Magnani said.

The drummer shrugged, 'How you doing, brother?' The others were silent.

Johnson faded away towards the bar, leaving Magnani alone. He took his guitar from its case, put his coat on a chair and took another to sit on. He tuned the instrument to a note from the pianist and tried to fill his head with music.

'Man means business,' the drummer said as the pianist reached into Magnani's case and took out some music.

'I have copies,' Magnani said.

'Don't need none. Say the key, name the tune, and hit it boy. We'll be there.'

And they were, three men who had played all night gave him the best backing he had ever had. He started with a standard, running carefully through the melody, too carefully, then moving around the scales in a trusted improvisation. He knew it was safe but he struggled to loosen up at this time of day. The strings felt leaden, the guitar cumbersome, as it always did when he was off colour. He sensed a lack of excitement behind him. This might be his only chance to impress, and he cursed to himself quietly: 'so be good.'

By the third number Magnani had shaken off the dross and his playing grew warmer, gaining a little confidence. Out front a few figures stood in the shadows, their presence betrayed by their cigarettes. He wondered who he was auditioning for but dared not look up.

He led the band into a quick version of 'Cherokee'. The music took him over; he departed from what everyone else played and put in his own ideas. Someone said 'Yeah man'; it was the boost he needed. They played with more urgency, Magnani forgot where he was and just played. He ran through rapid arpeggios and octaves which took him all round his guitar, showing all he had in the number. When it was over he did not have to play any more.

'Not bad, man,' the pianist said, 'for an ofay from I don't know where.'

Johnson reappeared. 'Hey man, that's praise. This guy here is from Kansas City, and from him that's praise, brother.'

'Thank you,' Magnani said to the three players.

Johnson tugged at his arm. 'Come talk. There's some people here.'

He led him to a back room that held two men, one black, one white.

'Did good out there,' the white man said. He stretched out a hand. 'I'm Joe Stein, I own this place. This here is Carlton Gaines, the pianist.'

Magnani had already recognised him from his record covers.

'Hello kid,' Gaines said. He was in his fifties, a large, greying man with a bear-like frame. His hands were huge, and hung like two shovels at his side but Magnani knew they could be exquisite.

'Frank,' Stein said, 'we asked you over because we think we might have something for you. Carlton is setting up a new quartet you could fill a spot in. I manage Carlton, as well as running this joint.'

'It'll be drums, bass, you and me,' Gaines said. 'I need someone who can comp good but do something more too, and I just heard you do that. You played fair. I'm what the critics call a mainstream artist, done well in that bag. But I'm changing, Frank, taking on new ideas. There'll be plenty for you to do.' He added the last sentence as a casual afterthought, and Magnani was not sure about the man.

'If you want the job you start here in three days, ninety dollars a week, no free drinks,' Stein said. 'I used to let you guys drink, but that came to more than you were drawing cash.'

Johnson laughed too loudly at this. 'Don't worry about the union, we'll fix up your card. It'll be a good move for you, Frank.'

Magnani could not believe his luck. Gaines was not his musical style, but he was known and respected. If he took the job he would be leaping over local players. It seemed as if the old soprano player in Paris had been right.

'All right, I accept,' Magnani said.

'I have something for you to sign right here,' Stein said. Magnani tried to read the contract through, but it was difficult with three sets of eyes staring. It looked a standard deal, tying him to Stein and Gaines for six months, with the option of another six if things worked out. It was not too long, and long enough. He signed where Stein pressed his finger.

'Good, man, good,' Johnson said.

'Coleford here will show you around, introduce you to people, Frank,' Stein said, 'he does that for me. He's on the payroll too.'

'Be over here at two tomorrow, we start work then,' Gaines said. 'You got two days to learn the arrangements. Don't be late.'

'I won't be.'

Johnson led him out again, fawning and pushing at the same time. Magnani tired of his imposed company.

'Whadya think of that Frank? You in, as easy as that, the man from nowhere.'

'I've been playing for fifteen years.'

'Sure, no offence. But you ain't been playing here, dig. And elsewhere don't count.'

Magnani shook off Johnson at the hotel, though he promised to return that evening. Back in his room, Magnani unpacked his sack. He straightened out his crumpled clothes as best as he could, but had nowhere to hang them. From the bottom of the sack he took his books, and made a short row of them on the floor against a wall, nine battered hardbacks. At one end he used a shoe for a bookend, at the other he leaned his red leather folder. It contained all the music he had gathered together, the 'book' that is essential to working professionals, standard material he was likely to need, plus his own musical ideas. Personal guitar tricks he kept in his head and his fingers. If anyone ever flattered him by imitation they would have to do it the hard way, and listen. At the back of the folder were his notes on Joseph Hadyn, sixty pages of research. Haydn was as far away as was musically possible from Magnani but played a big part in his life.

Magnani travelled light, even for a poor man. His wallet held less than a hundred dollars. The break with Gaines was opportune, and relieved the pressure. Few foreigners had made any impression here, Magnani could think of only Shearing, the pianist, from his own country. He allowed himself to hope he might be the next. In Britain jazz was played by determined, and sometimes talented people in smoky pubs in Soho or Surrey. It was a musical backwater, a second hand place of watered-down versions of the black masters.

Now he was in a world where jazz was a proletarian bar music as well as a study for the middle classes. It was the music of speakeasies, brothels and the clubs of gangsters and was the invention of the Negro; it came out of a troubled heritage. Whites were let in grudgingly, if they could play, and prove that they were not out to steal. Magnani doubted there could ever be a white Ellington or Parker, and was glad that he played the guitar. It was a more cosmopolitan instrument. There had been Reinhardt and Lang before him and the guitar players he would have to take on in the States were white, in the main.

Magnani was annoyed at his thoughts. Already he was thinking colour. In Paris, they saw and heard the music. Nothing more. Here there was an edge that might be a menace or threat, or just a stimulus. It was tangible. He felt it in the presence of Johnson: the more that man smiled the more he sensed it. And it had crackled in the hot air of the club.

Johnson knocked on Magnani's door at eight. It had been a short respite but he had caught up on some sleep.

'How you, Frank? Settling in nice?' Johnson's eyes strayed to the line of books and the wallet on top of them. 'Books huh?' He pointed a foot towards the wallet. 'You got much in that thing?'

'No, not much.'

'Well, if you're stuck Stein will advance you something. You safe, he reckons.'

'Safe?'

''Sure. You a white boy from over the water, and anybody can see you as clean as a whistle.'

Magnani did not know if he was being insulted or praised. Johnson laughed at his puzzlement. 'Clean, man. You're not a user. Dope, you know. Drugs.'

Magnani put the wallet in his pocket, wishing he had divided the money earlier.

'One good rule here, Frank,' Johnson said, 'watch your dough. You gonna meet a lot of people who will hit on you as soon as they see you. Famous people some of 'em. They junkies, man, and that's how things are with them. They'll rip the heart out of their best friend to get their next fix. Joe Stein says don't do dope, don't pawn your piece. It's good advice.' Johnson scratched his head. 'Hell, man, no-one ever takes it.' He laughed his thin, reedy laugh, like a piccolo being tickled.

'You said something about eating, and music, earlier?' Magnani said.

'That's right, I got a great little club lined up for you, the Village Vanguard. They have good players over there. First we'll swing over to Nina's.'

'Is she still open?'

'You kidding? Those places don't shut here — this is a city of the night.'

Johnson shuffled around the room, like a poor Fred Astaire. He had rhythm and style, but no class. Magnani smiled at his black and white shoes, but behind his hand. As they left Johnson caught Magnani's sleeve.

'Thing is, Frank, I'm a little short right now. You know how it is, things to do, people to pay. Could you loan me twenty, I'll pay it right back at the end of the week. Stein pays me then.'

Magnani felt he had no option but to give Johnson the money. The man was a fee that had to be met, for now.

They went out into the street, Johnson walking ahead, his tall, skinny frame bounding over the sidewalk. He was animated, linking his hands to his words in tight jerks, like an opera singer. Sometimes he seemed to be playing an invisible saxophone. Magnani was smaller, a little under medium size, stocky and square shouldered, built like a welterweight. His dark features and nose gave away his ancestry. The nose had a Roman kink in it, and curved in slightly at its tip, an aquiline profile that made his face appear thinner than it was. He was healthy and looked it. His complexion was good and his face marked only by a star shaped scar under his left eye which was noticeable when he smiled. For a jazzman in New York then he was unusual.

'Come on Frank,' Johnson said, 'here you gotta keep up.'

TWO

The rehearsals with Gaines went well enough, and Magnani satisfied his new employer without extending himself. He had thirty new numbers to learn, many of which he had never played before. And it was not easy to adjust to his American workload. Here they played five or six hours a night, very different from the short bursts he was used to. Musicianship was a test of stamina, but also a whirlwind existence into which Magnani entered with enthusiasm. Now there was just music, and he could lose himself in it.

'We start tomorrow, Frank,' Gaines said, 'should work out real good. You're fitting in well. Stein's isn't a great gig but we can take it easy there, get solid. Then we'll move upstate for a few weeks, I could use a little air. I like to work Christmas in Vermont, away from all the madness here.'

They were taking a break in rehearsal, talking about domestic arrangements while they were away. 'Are you married Mr Gaines?' Magnani used the formal address like the others.

'Not lately. Been a few wives, got me two boys, but I don't get to see them much. Families don't fit in with this life. How about you, Frank?'

'No, I've never married.'

'It shows. You ain't got the look. Take Bud on the bass. He breathes marriage, man. Look at him now, humped over that instrument. He's already dividing his dough, wondering how much he can sneak for himself, and thinking if he might get some spare in Vermont. He usually does.'

Gaines enjoyed his description of Filigree. 'Plays good though,' he continued, 'and I prefer my men to have female problems rather than dope problems. Dames are easier to deal with.'

It was the most they had spoken so far. Magnani hadn't noticed the 'look' in anyone before, but he acted wise. He was the youngest of the quartet, and wanted to learn. Bill Pearson was touching forty, no Max Roach but a good backstop, especially for Gaines. Bud Filigree could be a brilliant bass player but he lurched between moods and hardly acknowledged Magnani. He was a friend of Johnson's and they often disappeared together after rehearsal.

Magnani found himself in the company of Pearson, who was a soothing relief after Coleford Johnson. The drummer was slow-talking, when he talked at all, and tended to wave answers with his hands as a substitute for words. His dry humour appealed to

Magnani. Pearson was shorter but just as stocky as he, with light brown skin and a grey-tinged moustache that aged him prematurely. Unlike Filigree it was hard for him to maintain tidiness in his dress, let alone coolness. He was a mass of loose, dishevelled suits, and Magnani liked this.

The Carlton Gaines Quartet opened at Stein's on a Friday night. Word had got round and the club was full by ten o'clock. For twenty-four hours Magnani had sweated out his stage fright as though he was a raw youngster again, adding up in his mind what could go wrong. His pessimism gave disasters vivid treatment but his experience redressed the balance. Memories of Paris calmed him; Gaines was pleased with him; and he was about to play in New York. In this way he balanced on the tightrope that spanned his guts, first tilting into a chasm of blind panic, then tasting the expectancy of good music. The tension he needed to play well was created.

Gaines had written a few of the numbers, but most were established standards. Onstage, Magnani sat behind him, to the right of the drums and bass. Gaines had front-stage with his white piano, basking in the single spotlight and acknowledging the applause with a casual shrug that said he deserved it. But Magnani was not sorry to be in the pianist's shadow. He had managed to get his one suit pressed, his best shirt washed, and his shoes shined by the boy outside the club. It was the best he could do until he was paid. 'See me about the duds after,' Gaines told him just before they went on. Magnani could have done without this, but it was forgotten as soon as Gaines hit the first chord. He was a good pro who moved easily around the keys, in the expected style. Gaines was a copyist: there was some of Tatum, Teddy Wilson and Ellington, even a touch of Basie's swing, but not much of Gaines. Magnani heard a florid embellisher, who sought no new musical ground.

Gaines saw the quartet as three support musicians whose job it was to keep him flowing. Magnani played as smoothly as he could, establishing a good rapport with Filigree and Pearson. He pitched his guitar just above the lines of the bass and left all the space for Gaines. For one number Magnani played a counter melody to Gaines and a short solo break, but for the rest he kept to the chords, welding the rhythm section together with even comping. There was no sign of the new ideas Gaines had spoken about, and he was bored already. At times Pearson winked at him and Magnani thought this was a shared condolence, but he could not be sure. The crowd was polite and appreciative, there to see Gaines, more white than black. There was none of the electricity of Magnani's first night in the city; if he closed his eyes he might have been playing in Surrey. They played for an hour.

He drank with Pearson in the first interval. Gaines had joined Stein in the back room and Filigree had disappeared.

'It's going okay, Frank,' Pearson said.

'Huh huh.'

Pearson caught his mood. 'Don't expect too much from Carlton here. He's established his style, and he ain't gonna take no chances.'

'He said something about stretching out when I joined.'

'Yeah, well he says a lot of things. This is your first gig, man, so relax. There's people out there watching you, checking you out. Players. So settle in and be noticed.'

Johnson appeared, swivelling a bar stool around and draping himself over it, cat-like. Pearson glared at him.

'What you doing here?' the drummer asked.

'You nice as ever I see, brother Pearson.'

'Thought you'd be over at Birdland, peddling.'

'Hey, be cool man, Frank don't want to hear that stuff.' This stilled any further comment from Pearson.

'Great gig, Frank,' Johnson said, 'you doing real good.'

'Thanks.'

For once Johnson did not want to hang around. 'I'll catch you guys later,' he said, and disappeared into the crowd, undulating through the standing drinkers with his open smile.

'Stein sicked that mother onto you, huh?' Pearson said.

'He helped me settle in.'

'Like a snake helps a bird to lay eggs.'

'Come again?'

'Forget it. Just watch out for that guy, that's all. He's a bad dude.'

'In which way?'

'Look, there's a lot of stuff you got to find out —'

Gaines appearance shut Pearson up.

'Hello boys. Back on in two minutes.' He placed a jewelled hand on Magnani's shoulder. 'Stein is pleased, Frank.'

He glanced a little oddly at Pearson, then was surrounded by a group of well-wishers.

The second and third sets went just a smoothly. Towards the end Magnani was tempted to liven things up. Gaines nodded him a solo which he thought to extend, but he caught Pearson's warning frown and exercised restraint. They played out the night as safely as they had begun it and a pleased Gaines introduced 'the new Frank Magnani' to the crowd.

Stein emerged from his office as they packed up. He confirmed Gaines's satisfaction. 'A good night, Frank. Crowd liked it. Carlton needs a start like this, he's not been doing much lately.' He turned to the others. 'Smooth boys, real smooth. See you guys tomorrow night.'

Real smooth. Magnani had never wanted to be called that. He put his guitar away as solitary drinkers loitered at the bar, waiting to be thrown out. Pearson offered a last drink and Filigree left with a woman, a tall girl who locked arms with him. Magnani watched the swing of her hips and imagined her beneath her satin dress. Envy and loneliness stabbed at him.

Pearson smiled. 'I know what you're thinking, boy. Your thoughts got horns on 'em.'

Magnani laughed and swilled his drink around. There had been a lot of drink this first night and his head swam. He felt dog-tired. 'Is that Filigree's wife?'

'Don't be foolish.' They both laughed this time.

'Hits you, doesn't it?' Pearson said, pointing at Magnani's glass.

'I'm not used to playing so long.'

'I know, but these are regular hours here. Music is a commodity, son. You drink to jazz, dance to it, whore to it, do anything you want. Some even listen.'

Pearson downed his shot and wiped his mouth with the back of his hand. 'Stuff kills my gut. There were a few good players here tonight. We didn't exactly shake them up, a gig with Gaines is never like that, but we did all right.'

'How long have you been with him?'

'Ten years, on and off. We've had some ups and downs but he offers steady work, and that's rare in our business.'

'Didn't you want to do anything else?'

'Anything more, you mean. Damn right I did, but there's only so many chances, and I ain't getting any younger. Tell you what, Frank, give it a week or so to get your face known, then we'll go over to the Vanguard or the Door and you can sit in with some of the boys.'

'You mean after playing here?'

'Sure, what else time is there?'

'I'll need a week to work up to it.'

Pearson grinned and chinked his refilled glass. 'Here's mud in your eye, brother. I'll see you Frank, I gotta run now.'

Magnani was left with the barman and an ageing hooker, who eyed him hopefully. He studied the bottom of his glass until she went away, muttering to herself about 'white faggots'. He guessed what they were. Then the lights dimmed, and Stein's was an empty place with an exhausted air.

'Locking up now,' said the barman. He let Magnani out into the night and the guitarist walked the block back to his hotel, his case heavy in his hand. The fresh air scoured his lungs, and as he sucked it in he wondered why he was not bursting with content. He was caught in the anti-climax of a first night, and was experienced enough to know it. But he could not shake off the mood. The emptying streets echoed to it and he was relieved to gain the anonymity of his room. He resolved to find a better place, as soon as Gaines paid him. Somewhere warm.

Magnani defied his body to get up next morning, and was out of his room before the hotel stirred. It was not a morning place and the old man in the lobby looked at him in amazement.

'You sure are a foreigner, bud,' the clerk said, 'a musician up at this time. Weren't you playing last night?'

'Yes, my first gig.'

'Don't you English guys sleep?'

'Once or twice a month. That's all we need. It's because of what we eat.'

'That right? The grub, huh?'

To add to his confusion Magnani told the man he wasn't English. Let him sift through the peoples of the world in his head: it would be a change from comics.

The day was starting brightly and a pale sun had risen above the buildings opposite. Though the cold air mocked it the sun managed to cast the street in a kinder hue. Other walkers were well protected but Magnani shivered in his inadequate clothes. Already he had spent his first pay ten different ways in his head. He hoped he could afford a heavy coat.

He avoided Nina's, thinking Johnson might be there. He had not bothered Magnani for the last few days and he hoped it would stay that way. Instead he ate at a small café near Stein's. It was cheap and clean, Magnani's kind of place. A talkative Pole served him thick slices of ham topped with a mound of scrambled eggs. He was adapting to the size of the meals and had a greedy anticipation now. Each visit to the table was a novelty of new cooking and huge quantity. With a sagging gut he made his way along Broadway, checking out the clubs and feeling good in the crisp air. The disappointment of his first night with Gaines was forgotten as he explored his new world.

The city was a vibrant place of noise, smells and colour, quite different to his first impression. The mix of people astounded Magnani and he began to understand the strength of the American jazzman. The ones that rose to the top here travelled a very hard route. Professional adequacy in his own country had meant some sort of limelight, here that would barely get a player through the first door; competition was merciless and throats were cut and backs stabbed with abandon. Contemplating this Magnani recognised his achievement and took pleasure in it.

From a large poster, Alec Guiness looked down on him as he passed a cinema. It was strange to see a familiar face so much larger than life, and even in uniform the image comforted. Magnani hoped the film would do well. Guiness invited him to succeed in a foreign land. Was the American dream chafing him already? Hungry again, he stopped to buy his first hot dog, coating it with everything offered. Mustard spurted out over his cold lips and numb hands, and he loved it.

Magnani found his way to Central Park, the vast green heart of the city enclosed by miles of stone and glass. He felt it beat as he strolled. The last autumn colours of the trees matched the yellow tint of the sky. The peace there delighted him. A few people walked by, strangers, like him, perhaps, but the park was still, out of season and welcoming. It was the perfect antidote to the atmosphere of Stein's.

The cold nipped at his thoughts and it was time to go back. He found the hotel with some difficulty, unused to the numbering of streets. In the lobby the clerk was at his post, in his usual collapsed pose. His name was Thomas Oldswell, he told Magnani.

'Been out taking the air, huh kid?' Oldswell said. 'Heard you Limeys liked to do that sort of thing.'

Tobacco juice swilled against the stumps of Oldswell's teeth as he gargled and searched for his pail. He had not given the slightest thought to Magnani's nationality.

'About the room,' Magnani said.

Oldswell's brow lowered. 'Yeah? What about it?'

'It's not heated. That radiator in there hasn't worked for years.'

'Guess not.'

'Do you have another room?'

'Not for the same bucks. There's one on the top floor, cost you ten dollars more.'

'Is it warm?'

'Hell yes. Warmish. The hotel has a policy, see kid. In the winter we turn on the heat in the morning for two hours, and two hours at night. This ain't the Ritz.'

'No. What about the broken radiators?'

Oldswell shrugged. 'Get 'em fixed sometimes. As I said...'

'This ain't the Ritz. All right, I'll take it. Can I move up there now?'

'Sure. Here's the key.'

Magnani took it and turned to go.

'Kid, the ten bucks.'

He gave him the money. There was just change left in his pocket. As an afterthought Magnani asked who owned the hotel.

'Don't you know? You're working for him: Joe Stein. A lot of guys who work at his place stay here.'

'Not Coleford Johnson.'

'I don't know nothing about him.'

Magnani thought he knew a lot.

By the time Magnani had moved his few belongings up the extra flight of stairs the radiator in his new room was on. It worked, and its warmth, though meagre, was welcome. He stacked his books under it in homage. The chair and table he moved to the window and placed his notes and box of pens on the table in preparation for work. The window in this room opened, to a view of the rooftops opposite and uptown skyscrapers behind. It was an altogether better room, almost pleasant.

To celebrate his improved living quarters Magnani worked through some of the quartet numbers, placing the chair against the radiator and letting the heat seep through him. He played the arrangements by Gaines but had plenty of ideas for the guitar parts. From the street came the sound of people returning home from work, and a siren wailing. Always a siren wailed somewhere. He copied it on his guitar, bending the strings to harmonise with the sounds he heard. At times like this Magnani was aware his life was unusual, and was glad of it. He feared routine, and had run from it, yet he still worried that there might be no escape and that flight was futile.

By playing the guitar Magnani was preparing to write. If possible he warmed up his pen with music: to touch and finger something so familiar was an encouragement. On a good day like this he was uplifted, the master of one craft and daring to try another.

He didn't know when Franz Joseph Haydn had become an

obsession. At first the composer had been a leisurely interest, Haydn's sedate life a counterpoint to his own frenetic ways. As a young musician Magnani had traced classical music through its different periods, charting change. He had never wanted to play what he heard, it did not seem relevant to him, but when first in love with jazz he had determined that no-one should deride his music by showing up his ignorance of their own. In this way he came upon Haydn. Other jazzmen knew Ravel and Debussy better, composers not so far removed from them in time and style, but Magnani had gone back further to find his gem.

He had been digging at Haydn for years, reading what he could and listening to the music. It was preparation for a book. Haydn's life was pieced together, and in periods without work Magnani wrote up his notes. The composer's life became interlinked with his own and filled a gap in Magnani's often isolated existence. He could call few people friend. He had musical contacts, and occasional relationships with women whom he made sure meant little to him. There was a widening gap with his roots. His parents were alive but distant in place and environment. They lived in a narrow, jazz-less Welsh valley sunk with pits and locked in cruel work. Haydn had become a solid presence to hold on to. When Magnani's playing faltered Haydn was there, an accomplished life that did not disappoint.

Magnani planned to start his book in New York. It seemed appropriate, Haydn too had moved abroad to a land of opportunity. Perhaps he might make Haydn the platform for his own musical ideas: the slow development of genius might be an inspiration. After a year of deliberation he had decided to write in the first person. His mind raced with possibilities, and he was eager to get them all down. Heady with his own conceit Magnani sat at the table, filled his favourite pen and began to write.

I remember that day so well. I can hear the call of the hounds, a restless yapping echoed by the horns of their masters. And I feel the horse under me, and breathe in the fresh outdoors again. My tired lungs are enlivened by the memory and for a few moments I am no longer feeble. My thoughts are young...

I was glad to get away. Luigia had grown more difficult, and somewhat tiresome. Always she demands more, and always my guilt gives it to her. My wife Maria senses it and her tongue lashes over me; wherever I am in the house it finds me. Her words are harsh and honed by her long anger, and sometimes I retaliate, and there is yet more guilt.

The prince had a party down from Vienna and I was allowed to accompany them. I craved to be away from women, and God granted me my wish, foolish sinner that I am. I am vain enough to think He understands my frailties. Their excellencies wanted wild boar but we hunted the prince's noble stags.

It was a glorious day, on the edge of summer. The sky was wide and blue and the countryside over which we galloped was lush and yielding, and joyous to me. With the release of my spirit I heard music, it played all around me. I had sounds in my head that made me desperate with a fear that they might elude me, that I would not be able to find them again. But I usually do. Despite the many duties I have at the palace I am always able to write. Even now, as I urge my horse over a low hedge and my stomach churns I feel the call of an empty stave. What appetite God gives me.

We took a mature stag, with fine antlers. It pleased our guests and the prince was happy. The kills I never like; the hounds are devilish and fear is frozen in the eyes of the animal. So much fear in those limpid pools. But I never show my distaste. When I see such things I want to compose music which has hope and peace, and shows the good purpose in the world.

Magnani settled on this page after much rewriting and reading aloud. Under the table lay a dozen previous attempts. He was almost pleased. This was how he would do it, have Haydn looking back over his life, an old man in his dotage. He yawned, stretched his hands behind his head and looked out into the black night with pleasure. Then he thought of Stein's. It was a quarter to nine, barely enough time to get over there. In a panic he put the guitar into its case, threw on his coat and left, Oldswell laughing at his rapid exit. He was becoming a minor cabaret for the clerk, who would invent 'crazy Limey' stories when he got round to it.

Magnani walked quickly, brushing past people with the awkward case. One man told him to 'watch it, bud' and kicked at the case. Taking a corner too fast he skidded and fell, grazing his knees and smacking his right hand into the sidewalk. The guitar was better protected than Magnani. He got up feeling shaken and sick: Haydn had replaced his evening meal. It was a hard fall to take minutes before his second performance in America. He was beneath Alec Guiness again, but this time the face disapproved. There was disappointment in the eyes and Magnani's lack of professionalism was mocked. He walked the last hundred yards hurting, with wet patches soaking his trousers. A fine rain drifted into his face to calm him and crowd concentration into his head.

The doorman waved him in. 'You're late, Mr Magnani. Mr Gaines is waiting.'

He went straight to the stage and plugged his guitar into the amplifier. Pearson appeared at his side.

'Gaines ain't pleased, man. He phoned the hotel. Oldswell said you ran out of there like a man on fire. Christ, what have you been doing, Frank? You all wet.'

'I'm all right. I took a fall in the street, that's all.'

'You got a load on?'

Magnani looked at him blankly.

'You been drinking?'

'No, writing.'

'Huh?'

'Nothing. Don't worry.'

'Well let's get right on down to it brother, and give Gaines a chance to simmer down.'

There was no time to clean up. Gaines and Filigree filtered on to the stage and the quartet played. For a few numbers Magnani was leaden but he warmed up to play adequately, but without fire. Fortunately Gaines did not require anything more. His eyes drilled Magnani from time to time but he avoided them. Alongside, Filigree tittered as the patches on Magnani's trousers steamed. Magnani cursed himself for his stupidity.

Stein sent for him in the interval. Gaines was in the back room with the manager.

'Cut it pretty fine tonight, Frank,' Stein said.

'Yes, I know. Sorry about that.'

'What happened to you anyway? You been in a fight?' Gaines pointed to Magnani's hand, which had puffed up a little.

'No, I don't fight. Just a fall on the sidewalk.'

'That why you late?'

Magnani was glad of Pearson's warning. 'No, I left the hotel late. I was working on the arrangements and forgot the time. I want to do my best for the quartet.'

Gaines wore a suit of palest blue, and a tie to match. He weighed Magnani up, eyes probing for secrets.

'Thing is, Frank,' Gaines said, 'I run a tight ship. It didn't look good out there, you falling on to stage like a clown.'

'It won't happen again.'

'No. You go wash up before the next set.' Gaines turned to Stein.' 'Joe, can you give him an advance? I want him out of those duds.'

'Sure, Carlton. I'll get Coleford to take him over to the Lazurus brothers, get him something smart.'

Magnani felt like a slave being dressed by its owners, but he did as he was told. Later, he joined Pearson at the bar, where he plied his empty stomach with drink. He had been warned, and another day with Johnson was to be his punishment. He smiled at Pearson, and thought of Haydn.

THREE

Magnani was flush with his first wages, and excited by the prospect of a jam session which Pearson had arranged for the following Sunday.

'We'll go straight over, after Stein's,' the drummer said. 'Think you got the energy for it?'

'I'll have to, won't I?' Magnani answered.

He was adapting to the stringencies of the quartet and to life in New York. Since the shaky second performance he had behaved well, satisfying Gaines with his low profile and earnest will to please. Johnson had escorted him to a clothes store where he had chosen, with Johnson's approval, a suit, several shirts and a pair of shoes. He went for a grey, double-breasted affair which he thought matched the stain of his guitar. It was sharp yet quiet he felt, preening himself in the mirror. Johnson wanted him to get a fedora, but he baulked at this. Trying one he looked like a chunky Bogart, but without the menace. Hats were not his style, though he added a tie to his collection. It was silk, and the colour of morning sky.

Pete Lazurus opened an account for him. 'Yessir, Mr Magnani, always nice to get an English gentleman in here. Great cloth they use there. My brother went over to London one time, brought back some material. We cut some of our best suits from it. Style.' The tailor pressed together his hands, as if in prayer, and sighed. He looked Magnani over as he talked, and there was disappointment in his eyes.

Magnani left the Lazurus Brothers twenty dollars lighter, and signed to pay a similar amount each month, his first experience of paying later. An overcoat had proved beyond his credit worthiness. 'Get more gigs,' said Lazurus. 'Get famous.'

He wore the suit to the gig that night and played well before a sparse crowd. Now that Gaines had settled in audiences had dropped off. A small band of regulars was left, some of whom were there for the music. The rest were people who drifted in from the street, drawn by the club's sign and its promise of liquor and company.

Anticipation of the jam sharpened Magnani. Gaines gave him another solo, which he extended as long as he dared; he fought to rein in his imagination and dwell in the land of safety. At three he packed up quickly and left with Pearson. Monday was a day off for the quartet.

The Famous Door was closed when they arrived. Pearson knocked on the door and a hatch slotted open. A black face scanned them, smiled at Pearson and the door opened. Inside were twenty or so musicians, warming up with scales and booze. Their women, friends and hangers-on lolled at tables, showing signs of the six hours they had been out on the town. A brown-skinned girl with reddened hair smiled at Magnani, then sat on a man's lap.

His nerves tightened as Pearson introduced him to people. He knew some of the names, they were known by many. They greeted him in friendly fashion but there was an edge in the club. People tried hard to be casual but men were here to perform before their peers, to cut each other with skill if they could. They milled around the stage like boxers before a fight, words and drink their trainers. Magnani knew reputations had been forged on nights like these, and some extinguished forever.

Pearson nudged him. 'Don't look so tense, man, this ain't no war.'

'Are you sure?'

Pearson smiled. 'Sometimes, maybe. Set your stuff up over there, you the only guitarist tonight. You'll have the chance to lay down a lot of rhythm: it will be a chance for you to shine, brother.'

There were two or three each of trumpet, piano and sax, a few drummers and basses, a singer who had once been famous, and a vibraphone player, an instrument with which Magnani had never worked before. He sat in with Pearson and a bass player to form the first rhythm section. A few reed and brass players got up with them, flashed their horns, and the session was away.

Magnani was back in the atmosphere of his first New York night, but now he was a part of it. After the briefest of preliminaries the trumpet cut loose with a full-blooded attack, leaving the sax to answer if it could. The rhythm swung madly but Magnani locked himself into it and kept his playing tight. It was fast company but he revelled in it, nerves blown away by the first chorus.

The front line changed throughout the night. Sometimes they were a quintet, sometimes there were as many as ten pieces on stage. No-one flagged, though a few players retired bruised from the fray. Drink was consumed in huge amounts, sandwiches arrived, but always the music flowed. The Door seethed with it, a secret world cut off from that outside; nothing mattered but the music. Never had Magnani felt more a part of it, and he indulged himself to the hilt.

A point arrived when Magnani was left onstage with a bass player and the vibraphone man. The other musicians took a break to ply themselves with yet more drink, the sweat dripping from each brow might have been pure alcohol. They had an endless capacity for it, yet it did not seem to affect their playing. Now they leaned against the bar, or sat together, each a master of nonchalance. Magnani thought they had all played well, he had the new man's moderate criticism. He wanted all of it to be good, his own playing needed it.

Despite the apparent lack of interest in him he knew he was being given a chance. The stage had been cleared for him to show what he could do; they had left him exposed, without a drummer to lock on to. The vibes player was young, barely out of his teens, up from New Orleans to show himself off on his rare instrument. He was as sharply dressed as Johnson, wafer thin in a black suit, a matching tie a rigid knot around his neck. Magnani took to him, he liked his easy, serious air. And Pearson liked him; Magnani was learning that the drummer was a good judge

Magnani played the introduction to 'Lover Man', the old Billie Holliday ballad. The vibes man beat out a soft support on his keys and the bass player voiced complicated lines that felt their way to the heart of the song. Between them they gave Magnani the platform he needed. The Door grew quiet as he stretched out. He was heady with whiskey and the company but shut out everything other than the music and reached for all he had. He began with Holliday's phrasing but now arpeggiated his chords in the most innovative way he could, trying to achieve something smooth and round, but also fresh and his own. He sucked in confidence from the approbation of Pearson, from whom came the faintest whisper of 'play man, you've got 'em'.

And he did play. Music sprang to his fingers from his head. He controlled it but let it take him to high place. He dared to try things that had never before emerged, involving the vibes player in a complex call and response, playing difficult phrases and letting the keys answer and the bass sing out support. The ballad stretched out into everything Magnani could think of, ten minutes of his bared musical soul. At one point he saw Haydn in his mind's eye; he was solid and comforting, and approved of him. There was applause and a few shouts coming from the audience but Magnani was too lost in his sounds to think how rare this was for such a gathering and what a success he had made of the night.

Light was seeping into the sky when he got back to the hotel. For once Oldswell was absent and his Spartan room welcoming: any place would have been good enough for Magnani this morning. He surged with positive emotion, and was on top of his world. There had been handshakes and back slaps when he left the club. The Gaines quartet had been put into perspective although two weeks earlier he thought his place in it the zenith of his career. He took the guitar out of its case and propped it up in the corner so he would see it when he woke up. Magnani stayed in bed most of the day, trapping the room's two-hour heating under the bedclothes and sleeping a sleep of deep satisfaction.

Late afternoon he was roused by a knock at his door. He started into alertness and felt the cold as he opened the door in vest and shorts, the guitar forgotten. Johnson stood before him, grinning in a light blue outfit which did not suit him. The colour was too open. Magnani tried not to show his irritation.

'Caught you getting up, man,' said Johnson as he walked in. 'Heard you had moved to the third floor — you going up in the world.'

He extended his grin, the flash of his teeth was almost enough to illuminate the room. He flicked on a light and sat on the one chair. Magnani sat on the bed, anxious to be rid of Stein's man.

'Went well, huh?'

'What?'

'Last night.'

'Yes, the quartet was smooth.'

'Not the quartet man, the session down at the Door.'

'Oh that. Yes, it went okay.'

'Okay, the man says. The word is out brother, you hot. One hot honkey. The dudes there were impressed.'

Magnani feigned indifference, but enjoyed the news.

'Don't know about Carlton though,' Johnson said.

'What do you mean?'

'Well, you ain't been here too long, just off the boat you might say. Things is moving fast for you.'

Magnani shrugged.

'Can I give you a little advice, Frank. Gaines don't want another star in his outfit. The boys know that and they get along, cos the bucks are good and regular.'

Magnani wondered if Gaines had sent Johnson. It was hard to work out his smartest move with a head that throbbed to last night's music.

'All the guys jam.'

'Sure Frank, sure. I'm just saying to watch it with Gaines and Stein, they need the polite treatment.'

'Don't you work for Stein?'

'Yeah, but I kinda work for myself too.'

Magnani had no doubt of it.

'What are you doing today, Frank?'

'I've got a few things to do, some music I want to catch up on, letters to write.'

'I thought we might go out and grab a bite.'

'No thanks, Johnson.'

'Suit yourself, man.'

Johnson went over to the guitar and fiddled with its strings. Magnani winced but did not take the bait.

'Know how them boys keep going in those jam sessions, Frank?'

'The music.'

Johnson smiled. 'Sure the music — and these.' He opened a palm to show a cluster of coloured pills. 'These are uppers man, they keep you pumping on all four. You can reach high. You have 'em in England?'

'Some.'

'That right? Well, I can supply all you want, Frank. You made a hit last night, people will be asking for you now. You have to keep it up, do better. take some of these and you're a bull man, play all night, take two women home.' He laughed, as if seeing images in his head.

'No, I don't think so.'

Johnson was not surprised. 'You don't need 'em, huh?'

'That's right.'

'Don't tell me, you don't need nothing but the music. It gets you high enough, why do you want this shit, huh?'

'You've got it.'

Magnani was disturbed that Johnson knew the answer so well yet still came to him.

'That's all right, Frank,' Johnson said, 'I didn't think you should want something and not know where to get it. Now you know I'm your man.'

'I'll remember.'

'Good. Sure you won't come eat?'

'Some other time.'

'Okay, brother.'

Johnson twanged the guitar strings a last time, stretching them as far as they would go before releasing them. He left, laughing to himself. Magnani tried not to slam the door on him but could not help himself. He heard Johnson prancing down the stairs, still laughing. It was not a comforting sound. He checked over the guitar. Johnson had only touched it but Magnani wiped it down anyway. As he put it back in the case he saw the pile of pills, nestling in a pocket like diminutive eggs.

The quartet played out another week at Stein's, then left for the club in Vermont. They travelled in two cars, Pearson driving the second with Magnani as passenger. Gaines and Filigree were in the first, driven by Johnson, who worked at the country club every Christmas. This news soured the occasion for Magnani, who was relieved to be in a separate car. He had not told Pearson about the pills, which still lay in his guitar case.

Magnani thought a drive of three hundred miles a long one, especially in a station wagon piled with instruments and cases.

'Hell, this is nothing, Frank,' Pearson explained. 'When I started we used to trek all across the south and midwest, Kansas City to Florida, New Orleans up to 'Frisco one time. Never forget that desert man, it was hot as a burning sax. And things were pretty rough down there sometimes, best thing to be if you were black was a musician. No, a few hundred miles like this is a jaunt; pretty country, too.'

'I suppose so. I'm not used to the distances yet. What time will we reach this Country Shack?'

'Some time tonight, I guess. Say Frank, how big is England anyway?'

'Not big at all, at least not now I'm here.'

'Didn't you play in Scotland and all those other areas?'

Magnani smiled at his earnest driver. Like everyone he had met in America so far, Pearson's knowledge of geography was non-existent. Europe for him merged into one landmass of blurred newsreel images and names he had picked up in the cinema.

'No,' said Magnani. 'Jazz does not travel much in Britain.'

'Uh huh,' Pearson nodded sympathetically, like a cultured man hearing about some wild, infidel place.

Pearson was right about the countryside. They travelled on a day brightened by early morning frost and the palest of blue skies. It was too late for the display of Vermont's multi-coloured woods. Most of the trees had shed their leaves, and the fields lay fallow, but it still appealed to Magnani. It was his childhood films come to life. This was comfortable, tamed landscape, the nearest America could get to his own. The farms were clean and orderly, and looked new with their painted wood-framed houses and neatly fenced territories. He thought of the grey stone outposts of his own valley, sunk in drizzle and etched against twisting hills.

Each town had a trail of developments stretching from it to accommodate the rising urban population. If he lived in New York permanently he might want to come here too, to breathe fresh air and walk the uncluttered countryside. Until town merged with town.

Magnani watched and dozed as Pearson drove through the Green Mountains. Stein's place lay at their northern fringe, not many miles from Montpelier, the state capital.

'How long have you been coming up here?' Magnani asked.

'The years I've been with Gaines. It's his winter watering hole.'

'Well-heeled sort of place?'

'You bet. A lot of New York money comes up. We're going to a different world Frank, Stein's respectable side.'

'I'm surprised they want us.'

'Gaines is about the jazziest they get,' Pearson admitted. 'I don't think they could use Miles or Dizzie up here, cats like that. They too black — no offence.'

'Do you think its a question of colour?'

'Every time man, though they would reject the music no matter who played it. I don't blame people for it as much as some of the guys. Why should they want music you have to think about, and can't dance to? They're paying for it, after all. And some of the new stuff, I can't take to myself. I saw this guy a few months back, all he did was honk and squawk on his horn — that's not for me. I'm in the middle of the highway, Frank. I like music to have thoughts, but ones you can grasp without busting your brain, you follow?'

'Yes. It's not a bad philosophy.'

'What's yours.'

'About jazz? I haven't worked it out yet. I know what you mean, about that horn player, but part of me is moving towards those players. When I was in my hotel room I listened to some of the sounds outside and tried to recreate some of them on the guitar. You know, the sirens, shouts, screams. The loneliness. It all came out a little crazily, but I think it might be interesting to mix it up with the usual stuff. A lot of players are looking for something new.'

'Gaines ain't.'

Magnani sighed agreement and sank down into his seat.

They stopped once for food and reached their destination by nightfall. Stein's Country Shack did not live up to its name. It was an opulent building, set among tall trees and backing on to its own golf course. Magnani had never been anywhere like it. He viewed the uniformed porter who met them with amusement and some embarrassment. This was not the life he had envisaged on the boat. Films came into his head again. He half expected Astaire to dance out a greeting, or hear Crosby croon.

Pearson dug him in the ribs. 'Not like the city, eh? Wait til you see the rooms, they de-luxe, man. You live in velvet here, and pay for it in music.'

He handed a case to the white porter in a gold braided hat and whispered to Magnani.

'Shit, this ain't the south.'

'Will our stuff go down here?' Magnani wondered aloud.

'If we lighten it up some. They know Gaines here, remember.'

Magnani's spirit sank at this. The quartet's sets already bordered on the bland for his taste. Any further travel down that road and he would feel compromised, and still tied to his contract for another five months.

They checked into a place that reeked of money and poor taste. Stein mixed colonial style with the present in an effort to be traditional and modern, and ended up nowhere. The music room was long and flat, with an ample stage at one end and a wooden dance floor roped off with red cord. Large glass doors led onto a lawn.

'At least we won't have to play on each other's shoulders,' Magnani said, out of earshot of Gaines.

'Yeah, they can pack a lot of people in here,' Pearson said. 'There's nothing Stein likes more than to see a crowd with its wallet hanging out.'

'Will he be coming up?'

'Maybe. Sometimes he shows with a dame. It depends.'

Magnani shared a room with Pearson, a pairing that happened naturally. After that second night at Stein's the quartet had split into two halves. Nothing more had been said, but there was a tangible air of difference between each pair of men. Magnani was glad of Pearson's support, he had been in a minority of one too often.

Their room was sumptuous by Magnani's standards and he hated it at first glance, though he didn't spoil the drummer's pleasure. It had two new beds, thick pile carpets, furniture, and a television. It was the first time Magnani had shared a room with one. Pearson went straight to it and turned it on. Jack Benny appeared.

'Ain't this something, Frank? We got two weeks of comfort, livin' as high as hogs.' Pearson rolled his eyes and mimicked a Jim Crow drawl. It was seven days before Christmas and the end of Magnani's first month in America.

They rehearsed the next afternoon, relying on the New York set and a few numbers Gaines introduced. Magnani played what the pianist called a jazz arrangement of 'Tea for Two'. He wondered if he might be asked to jazz up carols. Outside the weather had closed in, the sky threatened snow and brooded darkly.

They played the arrangements watched by Johnson, who leaned against the bar with a drink. Magnani felt the man's eyes rake him from time to time, but did not credit him with a glance. He could not relax. It had often been like this, getting into a playing situation he needed, then quickly chafing against it. His head raced with ideas which tripped over his lifestyle and the need to earn a living. Today he played impersonally, secure in the knowledge that it would not worry Gaines. The man seemed quite pleased with Magnani: journeyman players who did not get big ideas were fine. Magnani thought more about his work on Haydn than the guitar in his hands. Despite his growing friendship with Pearson, sharing a room was a problem. He did not want the drummer to know about the project. Although he was not ashamed of it he worried that it would not make sense to another jazz musician.

The quartet worked that night. They played three one hour sets — a half night's work, Pearson called it. There was a sparse audience of office men on the make for a few hours before returning to their wives, a few students home for the vacation and some of Stein's friends. They sat at a front table that drank, and talked loudly. They were a sleek and well-groomed bunch, interested in each other and nothing else. No-one appeared much taken with the music, and Magnani could not blame them. The quartet was there to provide musical wallpaper, their job never to intrude on the awareness of the paying guest.

He was reminded of his first years as a musician, when jazz was firmly hidden behind a wall of necessity. For money he played popular songs in a popular style, infantile arrangements to prop up the tired musical hacks who littered the clubs in his home area. He hoped drunks in Vermont would not ask for the same songs, but feared they might. He felt a tinge of loneliness and distaste, an outsider in in this world of smooth drinks and smooth people.

Magnani played a wrong chord which jarred over Gaines' piano. The leader glared at him for an instant then the smile returned to his face and he reverted to his glazed entertainer look. No-one was listening, anyway. Magnani resolved to save as much money as he could here, to cut down on his drinking. It was all he had to pay for at the Country Shack. By working on Haydn as much as he could he hoped to minimise the musical poverty of the quartet.

He saw little of Johnson. Rooming with Pearson helped keep him away. Johnson shared with Filigree while Gaines had his own suite in another part of the club. Pearson was an easy room-mate. He was permanently unruffled, a calming influence. When Magnani was despondent about the set Pearson told him it was nothing to worry about, a short phase in his career; when he doubted his own playing Pearson offered soft praise.

As Christmas approached the audiences swelled. This made things easier for Magnani: the more noise on the floor the easier it was to hide. By now he knew the arrangements backwards and comped with a good tone, a smooth musical cog in the Gaines wheel. The Shack was a white club in a white world, musicians were the only blacks ever allowed to enter and Magnani was glad to be associated with them. Even Johnson's arrogance and shifty ways were acceptable here, the place deserved them.

Magnani developed a game. Early in the night he tried to spot the single people who might pair up. He had a nose for the lonely, and the desperate stood out with their conspicuously nervous movements as they tried to blend with the crowd. They wanted to belong and be noticed without sticking out. Men would approach women and dance with them. Sometimes a couple would stick together all night; sometimes the man would be banished to the fringe of the dance floor to dwell in a world of hungry looks. Once Magnani saw the roles reversed as a girl went up to a man in the shadows. She led him to the dance floor. Magnani gestured the action to Pearson with his eyes, who grinned and saluted with his sticks. The man danced but was ill at ease; what he had wanted so much had fallen into his grasp and he was confused. He talked too much and lost his chance. The girl went back to her friends, who giggled and lauded her with relieved and jealous looks. Magnani watched a blond girl with slim, unfashionable hips. She had a lissom walk and glided over the floor with sensual confidence. He wondered why she was alone.

They worked most of the night now, from nine until three to full houses. Many standards were covered, some weak and suffering from over-hasty arrangements. Magnani lived for the handful of good songs, saving his interest for them. The length of the sets still troubled him and it proved difficult to stay away from the bar. Four days before Christmas he sat at it, spending what he had hoped to save. By the early hours the alcohol drunk in each short break had accumulated into a load. A woman joined him, sitting at the next stool.

'They tell me you're from England,' she said to him.

It was the blonde of the previous night. Magnani tried to be cool but found he suffered the same agitation as the men he had watched from the stage.

'That's right,' he said. Her face was not far from his, a long face with a chiselled edge to it. The light blue eyes did not appear to blink much. Her teeth were slightly pointed and she licked them often with her tongue. It was the hard, attractive face of a predator, and he liked it.

'I like the music,' the face said, 'I've been here a few times.'

'Good.'

He placed her accent as north of New York, probably local. She made no attempt to buy a drink, so Magnani ordered one for her, a cocktail he had never heard of.

'They drink them in Cuba,' she said. 'It's wonderfully corrupt there.'

There was silence as she played with her drink. She pushed it around with its stick, glancing up to see if he was watching. He was.

'Do you live around here? Magnani asked, wincing at the lameness of the question.

'I'm up for the season. My parents live in Montpelier. I work in New York. I've never seen an English jazz man before. How did you get here, playing with Carlton Gaines?'

'I worked at it.'

He tried to hide his interest behind diffidence but he knew he wanted her.

'You don't say much. Is that English reserve?' the girl said.

Magnani shrugged. 'I'm not English,' he mouthed to himself.

'What?'

'I get tired. We play for a long time here.'

'I guess you do. And well. I like your guitar playing.'

'Thanks.'

'My name is Linda, Linda Pearson.'

'Our drummer is called Pearson.'

She laughed. 'I don't think we're related.'

Magnani joined her laugh and the path lay open.

'Are you bothered by the fact I came onto you — do you think I'm a working girl or something?'

Magnani rolled his eyes. 'Hardly. Not in the Country Shack, this palace of propriety.'

They laughed again. Magnani saw Johnson watching them. Spurred by this he made a blunt stab at what they wanted.

'Do you have a car?' he asked.

'Of course.'

'Will you be around when we finish?'

'Do you want me to be?'

He nodded.

'Okay, I'll be around.'

Magnani played the last set with vigour, and the better he played the more Pearson grinned.

'You on a promise, boy,' the drummer hissed between numbers. 'I'm gonna tell Carlton. He'll get you a girl every night if it does this to you playing.'

They ended with 'Body and Soul', a good number for three o'clock when the club was drained of most of its clientele. A few couples held each other in imitation of dance. Men sat with heads slumped on tables. The barmen drooped over their bar, cursing Christmas. Moody chords echoed in the room. At this hour the place turned in on itself, preparing to shut away its false soul for another night, and leaving people to linger in its empty shadows. The girl sat alone at a table to one side of the dance floor. She did not look at Magnani, nor he at her.

'Will you look after my guitar?' Magnani asked Pearson.

'Sure son, you gotta hop. Don't wake me up when you get back.' Pearson took him by the arm and edged him away from Gaines. 'Make sure you get back, huh? If you're not here in the morning you'll be on the man's bad side again.'

For Magnani's sake the girl drove wildly. She rushed her Buick around country bends, licking her teeth as the tyres squealed. To Magnani it was a huge car, with fins like a shark, white-walled tyres and red paint work. Secretly he took a firm grip on the side of his seat, a nervous non-driver.

'Speed is scary, huh?' she said. 'But fun.'

'As long as you can handle this thing.'

'No problem. It was a present from my parents. My twenty-first birthday. They like to give me things....'

'Where are we going?' He cut her off sharply, He wanted no families, no history, and none of her problems.

'There's a lake a few miles up ahead. I used to go there when I was a kid.'

She turned on the radio and a country fiddle filled the car with a square dance. 'Take your partners two by two...' a voice drawled. Magnani grimaced as she drummed on the wheel with her slender fingers.

'Good music, don't you think — my dad's favourite. Tell me guitarist, you know what a redneck is?'

'Tell me.'

'He's what runs this wonderful country of ours.' She was slurring her words.

Magnani stretched over a hand and ran it up her stockings. Not knowing if she welcomed it or was too drunk to care, he ran it up some more causing her to swerve into a side road. He saw the lake up ahead. It reflected a white moon and banks of clouds, and was fringed by pine trees. She stopped the car as the fiddler finished his tune. The silence was immediate and heavy, as though the blanket of night had been dropped over them. He could sense the movement of water, a silver gleam through the frosted side windows, a sluggish eddy against the shore.

She was breathing hard now, and Magnani was sure of himself. The long seat made it easy. She slid over to him and started to fight, wrestling, biting and licking like an alley cat.

'Am I the first girl you've fucked over here?' she asked.

It was an act, Magnani knew, but he was impressed. He wrestled back, joined in her games, and thirty minutes later told her she was. It seemed to mean something to Linda Pearson.

Drink had made them too cold. She snuggled against him and mewed a little, making noises of comfort as she played her tongue over his nipple. Magnani wanted to get back to the Shack but he trod carefully. Linda was not stable. He sensed unhappiness like a fire inside her. She seemed a little crazy, and capable of anything. If he prompted her to talk she would be off, giving him the whole deal on her family, trying to make her problems his. Then she would cry and feel dirty and say he had used her. And so he had. He stroked her head and smothered her mouth in his chest. When he sensed her falling asleep he chewed on her ear. 'Linda, we'd better be getting back.'

'Mmm...want to stay here.'

'It's freezing. Come on, drive back.' Against his better judgement he added, 'Come to the Shack tomorrow night, I'll play something for you.'

'Okay.'

They dressed, but it was too late to keep the cold out. Magnani shivered, and felt sick inside. As they drove, the moon came out. Back in the club car park Magnani quickly disentangled himself from her but could not escape the question.

'Frank, you do like me, don't you?'

It had not occurred to him.

'Yes, of course. It was a great night.'

He got out of the car and made his way to his room with the screech of the Buick in his ears. Pearson was still up.

'Pearson, it's nearly dawn. I thought you said not to wake you — you haven't even gone to bed.'

'Nah. I get like this sometimes, kinda strung out inside.' He held up a cigarette which Magnani shook his head at. He undressed quickly and threw himself into bed. Drifting into sleep he heard Pearson ask, 'Hey, who was that dame anyway? She looked a bit cuckoo to me.'

'She probably is.'

'She be around again?'

'I don't know.'

'Had me a bunch of white women once, went through a spell of 'em but I just couldn't get used to it in the morning. All that light flesh....'

Magnani slept and Pearson reminisced to the whiskey bottle.

The next morning Gaines called the quartet together, to plan what he called his Christmas show.

'Joe Stein will be coming up here, boys. Bringing some people with him, important people. They like to get away from their concerns in the city. Joe phoned me yesterday, asked if we could put on something special, you know, play all the seasonal stuff.'

Carols, Magnani thought, but could not believe it. Johnson lounged in his spot at the bar, smirking provocatively.

'You know,' Gaines continued, 'you can't expect those guys to know much about music — they don't, not even Stein. And they care even less, so we gotta liven it up some. I don't want the sets sagging.'

'How about rock and roll,' Magnani said, 'it's all the rage now.'

For a second Gaines thought he was serious. He considered the suggestion, then his face clouded.

'Look, Frank,' he said, 'don't get smart. I don't want that attitude. We have a living to earn and you're new to the band — and this country. You think those be-bop cats wouldn't play here, for this money. Shit boy, people do it, every time. For the dough, dig?' Gaines spelt out the last words, as if Magnani was a child.

'Some don't,' Magnani said.

'I don't give a coot's fuck what you think, boy, You play what I tell you to play. You been lording it with you Limey ways since I gave you a chance. You think I ain't got eyes and ears? You think you're too good for this outfit, think you got something special to offer, but you jumped at the chance to play with me — for the money and the ticket it gives. I've canned guys who can play your nuts off so get your head out of the clouds, 'cos there ain't no-one else up there.'

'Come on, Mr Gaines,' Pearson said, 'Frank didn't mean anything.'

'Shut up Pearson, and don't take his side. You should know better.'

Magnani hated the drummer's attempt at support. He reddened and felt his temper tug at him, holding himself in check with difficulty. It was not the time to take on Gaines, but the undercurrent of bad feeling had flowed into the open. Gaines subsided, surprised by Magnani's silence.

'Ain't you got nothing else to say Magnani?" he asked.

'I don't think I'm too good for the quartet.'

Gaines took this as a submission.

'All right then. Here are the new arrangements.' He pulled out sheets of music. 'Joe asked for this one specially' — he held up 'White Christmas'. 'We play these right up to New Year, then we go back to New York. There'll be two hundred bucks bonus for each of you. Money, boys, money.'

Gaines was friendly again; he played with his gold rings and led the quartet into practice.

To Magnani's relief Linda Pearson didn't show up that night. He was already depressed, by his trouble with Gaines, and the way the quartet was going. He had not come to America for this. He felt self-pity and hated himself for it. Usually music took him out of the mood. Playing the guitar was a trusted ritual, controlled by his own skill. He faded away after rehearsal and took the guitar back to his room, where he played through some of his most demanding arrangements. The music he made led his thoughts back to the eighteenth century and Haydn. He thumbed his notes and did not hear Pearson when he came in.

'What you got there, Frank?' the drummer asked.

Magnani shut the folder quickly. 'Oh music and stuff.'

Sure it's not love letters? You jumped like a jack rabbit.'

I'm a little edgy after that scene with Gaines.'

'Yeah, you skating on thin ice, bud. I know how you feel, but Gaines had one point — you need the money.'

'I feel like a hooker. Pearson do I come on as acting superior?'

The drummer's eyes creased in a smile. 'I'd call it different, You stand off from the guys. That don't bother me, I like a guy who keeps to himself, but in this business it don't win you no friends. You are a good musician and will get better, but it will always be a struggle to get the music to the people, man.'

'What do you mean?'

'It's like I told you a time ago. You can't make folks like what you do. If you try to push it down their throats they'll turn on you and kick you down. I've been there man and I've seen the best strung out because of it. You get special on your piece, years of ballbustin' woodshedding then no-one wants it. They can't see what you see, feel what you feel. No-one cares, and you hate them for it. But you need them, so then you hate yourself and you're in a circle. It brings you round and round. You do drugs and booze and it gets tighter. And you go out, like Bird and Fats Navarro and lots of others. The best...'

Pearson tailed off and lay on his bed with his hands folded behind his head.

'So what's the answer?' Magnani asked.

'Ain't one, brother. Luck, stamina, they play a part, but there ain't no answer. Perhaps we wouldn't do it if there was.'

'Now you're getting deep — for a drummer.'

Pearson cackled. 'You could try dying, if you go out on your way up it's always good business.'

'No thanks.'

'Remember what the man said, if there's no money in it, it can't be all bad.'

Pearson eyed the folder again, his curiosity not to be denied.

'You gonna tell me what's in there, Frank? Music be damned. Come on, I can't stand a secret.'

Magnani told the drummer. 'It's something I've been interested

- 46 -

in for a long time. Someone, I should say. I'm doing some work on Haydn, the composer.'

'I know who he is, the classical guy, from way back.'

'That's right.'

'You writing about him?'

'Trying to. I've been researching him for years.'

'Why, for Christsake? Ain't you got enough to do with *our* music?'

'I know he's a long way from what we play, but maybe that's what interests me.'

'I don't know about those classical cats. The ones around now think we are nothing; crude improvisers they call us. Hell, they can't play without them little dots. They have to be led by the hand, like dummies.'

'I know, and I agree. But that's no reason for us to be as stupid. Have you ever thought their blindness might come from fear? They might see us as a threat.'

'I doubt it. Anyway, why this guy?'

'He fascinates me. The way he went about things. Do you know he was an old man, really old for those days, before he made it?'

'Yeah?'

'I've learnt a lot about my own playing by studying him. It started when I got good on this thing' — he slapped the guitar — 'I wanted someone to relate to who was on another musical planet, someone I could never copy.'

'Hold on, Frank. Don't give it all to me. It's your thing. Hey, I remember. My Dad used to take me to free concerts sometimes. That Bach had a pretty good beat, you know. But that's as far as I go. Well, perhaps it's a good thing for you to do Frank, crazy too, maybe.... It gonna be a book?'

'Some day I'll knock it into one. I'm not thinking too far ahead yet.'

'I'll read it,' Pearson said, so earnestly they both sniggered like boys sharing a secret.

'I'll sign a copy for you — written by Frank Magnani, jazz guitarist.

Pearson closed his eyes. 'That'll be something, baby.'

FOUR

Magnani took Johnson's pills on New Year's Eve. It was the culmination of a week of wretchedness for him. It started the night before Christmas, when Linda Pearson showed up. He spotted her when the quartet was halfway through its first set. She bounced in, part of a group of young socialites and college boys, robotic with their new suits and uniform cropped heads. She stood in front of the bandstand, watching Magnani through slitted eyes. He half nodded to her and pretended to concentrate on the unchallenging music. Pearson enjoyed his discomfort and rolled a salute on the drums that Gaines did not notice. The Shack was full to bursting point with people determined to have a good time. Joe Stein sat in a corner and beamed at his custom, evaluating the booze it sank.

In the first break Magnani tried to slip backstage but Linda was too quick for him. She blocked his path and put a hand on his arm. He saw that she was quite drunk.

'Where you going, loverboy? Not trying to get away from me, are you, not after such a *great* night. Such a ball?'

She spat out the words angrily.

'Hello Linda. Happy Christmas.'

'You're petrified, aren't you?'

'What?'

He pulled her to the nearest thing to a quiet corner the club had. The dance floor seethed with hot couples dancing to old swing records, better music than the quartet was playing.

'I said you're scared,' Linda said, 'afraid of what I might do. You didn't want to see me again, did you?'

'Look, it's difficult when I'm working. Maybe afterwards...'.

'Screw you, Jack. I'm with a party. Jesus, you think you are something, don't you, having me that easy. Never thought I might be having you.'

He had not.

'You've had a lot to drink,' Magnani said.

'Little woman's drunk, don't know what she's doing.' Linda chanted this like a nursery rhyme. Johnson appeared, opulent in a cream suit. He grinned wide and took in the situation instantly.

'Hi, brother, what's happening?' He ignored Linda. 'Who's the chick, looks like a lulu to me.'

'Fuck off, Johnson.'

'My my, the man is touchy, full of Christmas cheer, right?'

'Hi,' Linda said, leaning on Johnson's arm.

'Hello yourself, sister.'

She tried to pour herself onto him, pushing her hips into his, looking at Magnani all the time.

'We got a hot number here, Frankie. What say we all go back to my room? We got twenty minutes.'

Linda's tongue worked around her teeth again. Johnson's nostrils narrowed, and he increased his grip on her.

'Do what you want,' Magnani said, and walked into the crowd. He tensed his shoulders for Linda to spring at him but nothing happened. She vanished with Johnson, and he felt relief, and just a flake of shame. His conceit was shaken somewhat as he thought of the girl's words. He joined Pearson on the corner of the largest bar and drank as the drummer chuckled at his face.

'I like Christmas, Frank,' Pearson said.

'Why's that?'

'It brings out the best in people, brother.' Pearson collapsed into laughter, but Magnani knew his best was not up to much. He saw the joke, but could not join in.

'What are we doing here Pearson?'

'You mean the Shack, or the great wide world?'

'The Shack, at this moment.'

'I know what I'm doing, playing for my living, for dough, dinero, lucre — and I'm drinking in a place that would slam the door in my black face, normally.'

'And that makes you feel good?'

'Don't make me feel bad. Loosen up Frank, you ain't got that many problems. Hell, you a beginner in them stakes.'

They played on until dawn, Linda did not show up again, and neither did Johnson. Magnani painted pictures of them in his head, and played his guitar.

While the Shack slept and the last drunk had been put out to sleep through his Christmas Day dinner Magnani went out into the morning, to rid himself of the fug of playing. To his irritation he found himself still fretting over the girl. His ego played with his jealousy. He knew it was crazy. Johnson would be her black sample, an experiment for the holiday, and potent boast for the office; it meant nothing to either of them. And it meant nothing to him.

Walking into the woods he knew there would be a reckoning with

Johnson one day. They were beginning to hate each other, for no good reason. Magnani thought it inevitable; things went like this sometimes. He put it out of his mind and enjoyed the pure air. It cut at his throat and he sucked it in greedily. He was in an enlarged Central Park, not a wild landscape, but it caught his thoughts and gave them a little peace. As he calmed Haydn came back to him, and the need to get ahead with his project.

Despite his unsuitable clothes Magnani walked for an hour, wading through the boot-high leaves of the woods. Creatures rustled away from him in the undergrowth. He heard them, but his city eyes saw nothing. Haydn loved country like this, made safe by the hand of man and invigorating to a degree that comforted. The open lands further west could disturb; Haydn the composer would have screamed at the loneliness there. Magnani heard the whistle of a train, a series of whoops that skipped through the wood. Pushing his way through the trees he watched an engine make its way across the valley, belching white smoke that mingled with the frost. Steam still ran here, not quite yet ousted by the efficient diesel. No doubt it carried late returners, home from cities to find Christmas joy, or misery, or nothing. They would be the poorer ones, not able to fly. Magnani was grateful Americans did not fuss so much over Christmas as his own people. Escaping it was easier here, and the loneliness it caused was less cutting.

The quartet sat down to dinner with Stein and a few others. Johnson was not around. In a detached way Magnani enjoyed the meal, it was the first time in ten years he had taken part in anything approaching ceremony. He sat at one end of a large table laden with food, flanked by Pearson and Filigree. They all ate too much from their stacked plates. For once Filigree talked, his tongue loosened by his spoilt stomach. He gave Magnani a brief account of his views on women and music — 'fuck 'em both, man' — and on the state of the world.

'That Sputnik thing,' Filigree said, 'that's the start, man.' He spattered out a little turkey as he talked.

'What?' Magnani asked.

'That thing the Ruskies sent up, they ahead of us man. In a few years they'll be dropping that nuclear shit on our heads. Don't you read no papers, boy. White America is crapping itself.'

'Why just white?' Pearson said. 'Are those bombs gonna miss us niggers?

Filigree ignored him. 'Retribution man, that's what it is. For what this country has done to the black man, and the red man, and any other colour that ain't pinky.'

'Do you think the Russians care?' Magnani asked.

'Sure. Some of the brothers in town told me about it. We ain't free man, anymore than back in them plantation days. Hell, you white and you ain't free either.' Filigree dropped his voice and grinned. 'You wouldn't be here in this crock of shit if you were. No, this "proud land" belongs to honky money, man.'

Filigree's eyes were pools of shifting brown liquid. Magnani had never been this close to him before. The bass player bobbed his head as he ate and talked, ignored by those at the other end of the table. Pearson winked at Magnani.

'Filigree gets like this sometimes,' Pearson whispered, 'he hangs out with some organisation, into political shit. And he's using a lot these days, dealing with Johnson.'

This explained the eyes.

'Doesn't Gaines know?' Magnani asked.

'Yeah, must do, but as long as the man can play he won't do nothing. And Filigree plays good.'

Magnani watched Filigree closely; after this, and noticed things that had always been there. The slight but continuous tremor in his hands, the food shaken as it was hoisted into his mouth, the feet constantly shuffling under the table, as if his mind was taking a walk. And the head nodding, almost imperceptibly, but it was there. Filigree nodding in tempo with another world.

They were back on stage that night, and every night until New Year's Eve. They played until their bodies burned with protest, and Magnani's head hammered with boredom. All work on Haydn was abandoned, there was just time for the quartet and sleep, the path to each oiled with drink.

At the end of one night Johnson told Magnani about Linda Pearson, picking a time when Magnani was drained to his limit.

'She was some bitch, man,' Johnson said, 'but I like them crazy like that. I had to slap her a few times in the car, she got kinda wild, if you know what I mean. Think she liked it some, being beat on by a nigger.' Johnson showed his immaculate white teeth, and Magnani wanted to smash them.

'Took me to a hotel,' Johnson continued, 'shit, it could never happen down south. I give it to her some more there, my Christmas present for a rich white bitch. Ain't nothing we didn't do, man, she made me miss my dinner.'

Johnson scratched his head and scanned Magnani for the effect of his words. 'Took off like a bat out of hell afterwards, going home to her daddy. She won't come back to the Shack, she got what she wanted, off both of us buddy.'

Magnani clenched his fists as an arm was put around him. Johnson beamed, but his fingers dug in like steel.

'See you brother, I got to find my man Filigree.'

The pills lay amongst his spare strings, scattered like sweets amongst the bits and pieces of his trade. Magnani was alone in the room, to give the guitar a check over before the New Years Eve gig, and to psyche himself up to get through the long night. He played through a few standards: 'My Funny Valentine' was picked out with the fattest chorus he could think of, to conjure the mellow emptiness around him. It echoed in his head, which he lay on the edge of the guitar. He felt the vibrations emanate from its hollow body, as if he was deaf. These pills will keep you going all night Johnson had said, and Magnani was so tired. A big part of him wanted to tell Gaines to shove the job, but valour lived in his imagination, and not in his actions.

Magnani took them quickly. He placed four on his palm, drew a glass of water from the hand basin and swallowed before he could change his mind. What worried him most was that the pills came from Johnson. But nothing happened. He went to work as tired as before with just a sensation of lightheadedness.

In the club it was as if Stein had taken some vast tool and with it pushed as many bodies as was possible inside his Shack. The dance floor was obliterated by a seething mass of sweating bodies, and the table area had been decreased to make more room for people to squash together and drink, if they could get near the bar. The quartet had been told to 'whip it up', there would be no breaks this night. Think of that dough, boys, Gaines had said.

The pills took effect steadily, without alarming Magnani. After an hour of playing, his senses had numbed to a minimum level. He coated himself in disinterest as he chopped his way through the numbers. He doubted that Gaines could hear over the hubbub of the crowd, and did not much care if he did. It was one way to sign off.

He noticed the cigarette smoke first. It was knotting together in front of him, forming wispy ladders that stretched upwards to an unseen ceiling. Chords were missed as the ladders mesmerised him. With difficulty he shook them off, and focused on the dancers again. The music came back. Magnani caught Pearson's questioning eye a few times and tried to smile a reassurance at him. He was not sure if he was successful, it was hard to be sure of anything.

Magnani watched his hands play as if they belonged to someone else, he was detached, floating somewhere inside his head, where everything was so red and light. He was aware that his body was bursting with energy but he did not feel a part of it.

Between numbers he turned up his amplifier. It bristled with sound and swamped the piano of Gaines. The smoke ladders came back and Magnani began to enjoy himself. He dug into his guitar and made the notes squeak. Faintly he heard Pearson shout, 'for Chrissake Frank,' and saw a few puzzled faces at the front of the stage. One man shrieked his approval and tried to dance with Magnani. He responded by playing the few rock and roll phrases he had picked up. He sent them crashing around the Shack, notes distorted by the overloading amplifier. Had the quartet stopped or had he imagined it? Gaines was tugging at him and his amplifier was silenced.

'You gone crazy, you fucking crazy honky.'

Gaines's face was yelling at him. He saw the man's eyes, bloodshot moons that he punched, sending his leader sprawling across the stage. Magnani was held by Stein's men and the guitar wrenched from him to thud down onto the floor. The dancing man was up on the stage, throwing wild punches in Magnani's defence. Others followed, and the Shack began to brawl. Magnani remembered trying to climb those ladders, before someone put out his lights.

Pearson's face loomed over his, Magnani focused on it through a headache that blinded him with its intensity.

'You really did it, man,' Pearson's grin was resigned, 'you fucked up good. You took Johnson's shit, didn't you, had to be that.'

'Get me some water,' Magnani gasped.

He wanted to drink an ocean. He gulped down a tumbler full, spilling some on his chest, and held it out again as Pearson pulled him into a sitting position.

'Do you remember what happened?' the drummer asked.

'Not much. Was there a fight?'

'I'd say. The whole fucking place was at it, best scrap I've ever seen, for white folks. Stein's out thousands, and we're out of a job.'

'What do you mean, there was no need for you to....'

'Gaines finished everything. He's gonna go to Hollywood, he says, write music for that television stuff.'

'How did I get back here?'

'I pulled you out of it. Just as well I did, Stein might have had you worked on some.' Pearson chuckled his throaty signature. 'Old Joe was busy hisself. He got socked by some football player, knocked his gold teeth clear out. I got us back here, locked the door and waited for it to cool down. The cops came and bust a few heads. They'll close the Shack down for a while, until Stein sweetens their 'gimme fund'. I saw Gaines an hour ago, keep you out of his sight, he said, and fuck off back to New York.'

'What about our bonus?'

Pearson's chuckle turned to booming laughter. 'You crazier than I thought boy. We'll be lucky if we ever work again.'

Magnani made a shaky attempt to stand, stumbling towards the window, which he opened. 'I've blown it for you Pearson, and for Filigree.'

'You surely have, but ain't nothing we can do about it now.' He shrugged. 'Bud can take care of hisself and what you said to me the other day, you were right. I was getting too set with Gaines, too safe. That ain't no good for a musician.'

'What now?'

'We'll go back to town. How much money you got?'

'Not much more than a hundred.'

'I got two. I might go back to Kansas, I can always work there —I think.'

'Do you think there's any chance of me working?'

'I don't know. You got Stein on your back, Gaines too. They got pull, but they got enemies also. Keep low for a time, work on that book of yours.'

'On a hundred dollars?'

'For a free spirit you sure worry about the stuff a lot. Come on, get washed up, I want to hit the highway, before any of Stein's mugs start thinking they owe us.'

As he washed Magnani wondered how Johnson had fared in the fracas.

They did not hit the highway; Magnani persuaded Pearson to take the smaller country roads. He thought it might be his last chance to see the country, for he had visions of heading back across the Atlantic with his guitar between his legs. His instrument had been wounded in the fight, the back split by a boot or a fist, but not enough to kill its sound. It would need to be fixed.

The first day of nineteen fifty-eight was icy and clear-skied. Magnani glanced up at it from time to time, considering Filigree's

Sputnik, but all he saw was a biplane flying low into the sun. They stopped at a roadside drugstore, where old men gathered around a stove and wasted time, watching every visitor, evaluating with chews, nods and winks. They sucked on hand-made pipes, one even whittled on a stick, the pile of shavings in front of him a testimony to his idleness. This was the America Magnani wanted to experience and believe in; it did not rush, and tried not to change.

The talk of the trip up was absent, each man sat with his thoughts of the uncertain future and the twists of life that led to it. They got to New York by late nightfall.

'Better not go back to Stein's hotel,' Pearson said, 'might not be too healthy.'

'It won't be any loss. Do you know anywhere, Pearson?'

'Yes. You can stay with me tonight. I got a place down in Harlem with a woman I see sometimes.'

'Your woman?'

'Her own, man, but we got an arrangement.'

Magnani knew that was as forthcoming as Pearson would be.

'I'll send someone over for your stuff,' Pearson said, 'do you owe Oldswell anything?'

'No, I'm up to date.'

Pearson drove into Harlem, new territory for Magnani. To be white and be in Harlem one had to be in the know, accepted in a way Magnani had never been even in his own country.

'Will it be allright, bringing me here?' he asked Pearson.

'If you are with me. You can hole up, get your act together, think what you gonna do. Tell you what you ain't gonna do, and that's take any more pills.'

'I have no need to, that was a reaction to what we were playing.'

'They all say something like that. Its 'cos they are tired, or can't play what they want to play, or it makes them play what they do want to play better, they say. Don't matter what reason, man, it hooks you , until you get the monkey sitting right up there on your back, tweaking your ears. You not a child, Frank, and I'm not preaching to you, but you know dope is the major fuck-up of players, black and white.'

They pulled alongside a wooden one storey building, divided into apartments, which reminded Magnani of pictures he had seen of the south, as if the huts of the cotton fields had been whisked to the heart of the city.

'Ain't much, are they, but they are run by blacks, ain't no asshole landlord breathing down your neck here. Come on in, Frank.'

Pearson turned a key in the lock and they entered a place of four rooms, comfortably furnished, and warm, the first warm room Magnani had experienced that was not a bar.

'Eileen is working, she's a hat check girl over at the Door.'

'Is she the one I saw you talking to at that jam?'

'Sure is. Ain't she a looker?'

'Yes.'

Pearson rummaged around and made some food, finding a half bottle of gin to wash it down.

'I don't usually drink this stuff,' Magnani said.

'Me neither, dames' drink I call it, but its all we got. Here's to us, Frank, long may we be stupid.'

Magnani slept under a rug on the settee. Vaguely he heard someone enter in the small hours, and smelt a woman's perfume, but he did not stir. He slept on, crowding out the thoughts of destruction that lurked on the fringes of his consciousness.

'Wake up, Frank, you been sleeping like a baby.'

Magnani focused his eyes on Pearson, who stood over him with a mug of coffee in his hand. Magnani reached out a hand for its wonderful steaming smell.

'Thanks Pearson. You're in the wrong profession, you should be someone's minder, a nurse or something.'

'Maybe. Frank, this is Eileen.' He ushered in a tall woman with dark brown skin who stood and put out a hand. 'Hello Frank, I saw you play at the Door, it was good.'

'Thank you.' He took her hand and pressed it briefly. Her eyes were bright and small, her face was delicate. It made her body seem longer than it was, her legs stretched on and on, with slim hips and shoulders and thin, delicate hands. There was a birdlike air about her. Pearson noted his appreciation and took it as a compliment for himself.

'Like I said, Frank, ain't she something, my Eileen?'

'I got to go, you guys,' Eileen said, 'I'm working afternoons this week. The boss thinks there will still be folk who want to drink, yet the place was drained dry over the season. Nice to have met you, Frank.'

She glided out of the room.

'Surprised, ain't you?' Pearson said.

Magnani was uncomfortable. 'No, of course not.'

'Sure you are, what's a dame like Eileen doing with an old tapper like me?' Pearson mocked a whisper in Magnani's ear. 'Cos I'm solid, dig, that's why. Women need that, after they've been around a bit. She calls me her father figure, can you beat that?' Pearson was bursting with pride, and Magnani concealed his jealousy.

Pearson called the apartment 'Buen Vista' to celebrate its back view of a canning factory, and Magnani spent three days there. He went uptown a few times and played the tourist, as much as his meagre supply of money would allow. He tagged onto the end of school parties going into museums, walked around Times Square and read the messages of its electric signs, and he visited Central Park again. Once he thought he saw Johnson on Fifty Second Street, but he was not sure and did not care. Magnani made no attempt to get work, leaving it to Pearson. He assumed they would work together now, and was content to place himself in the drummer's hands. It was easier.

On the second night in the apartment Magnani was left alone with Eileen. It was her night off and Pearson was out somewhere, checking the joints. There was an atmosphere of shyness in the room. Eileen was polite and friendly, but not confident with her white, foreign guest. She was keen to learn of other lands and Magnani gladly told her what her knew, making up what he did not know. He showed off, padding out his experiences with fantasy and self-importance, sensing Eileen's belief, which came from her natural naivety. It amazed him that Americans could be so streetwise, and yet maintain a childlike view of the Great Wide Yonder. He did not envy her insularity, here it was even more profound than that of his own island. It led to belligerent ignorance and for some the shrinking of the past self, but many people here were trying to forget sad histories in other countries. So perhaps they had good reason to develop in this way, clinging to the remoteness of a vast land and shutting out all others.

Eileen sat next to him, her hands in her lap. Magnani found her even more attractive without her night-club garb; she wore a simple black dress that merged into her skin. He imagined her supple body. He watched Eileen's reactions to his tales, moulded his words for effect and began to plan her seduction. Intuition told him it would be possible, perhaps not even difficult, he was more her age than Pearson, and father figures might not be much good in bed. Magnani had never doubted that he was, and kept guilt at bay by telling himself that he could not help it.

He told Eileen of Paris. It was the centre piece of his conversation, he dropped names of players he and never met and Eileen's awe grew.

'Gosh, Frank. Pearson never told me you knew those guys.'

Did no-one call Pearson by his first name?

'That's how I got here, meeting Americans in Paris.'

'Did you see that movie with Gene Kelly? I loved that.'

'Of course, great music — George Gershwin, you know. 'Porgy and Bess', that stuff.'

Eileen's face clouded. 'I don't really know much about music Frank, only what people tell me. Pearson takes me to see the bands. I like some of it, but I don't understand a lot.'

'Gershwin was one of your best composers; he's famous all over the world.'

'Oh, he was white, huh?'

'Yes.' Magnani resisted the temptation to apologise.

'That 'Porgy and Bess' was about black folks, wasn't it?'

'That's right.'

'I remember Pearson mentioning something about it once, said a white man didn't ought to do stuff like that.'

'Perhaps you are right.'

Magnani quickly got back to Paris again and Eileen's face resumed its radiance. Pearson came back as Magnani thought of pushing up closer to Eileen. The drummer was excited.

'We sitting in on a jam tonight, buddy. Some of the boys you played with at the Door just hit town. And I think I found you a place, a few blocks over, not Harlem. Who knows, there might be people tonight who can use us.'

Pearson was oblivious to the charged atmosphere he entered, but by her haste at absenting herself Magnani judged Eileen's complicity. He became Pearson's friend again.

Magnani re-entered jazz much fresher than he had left it, with his guitar polished and its back taped up. He wanted to display his talent to his peers, and needed their sanction of his distaste for the Gaines quartet. Pearson was eager for him to do well, and Magnani was heady with anticipation of the night.

'Give it all you got, Frank, like you did that first time. It could be a way back.' Pearson was becoming his father figure also. The man from Kansas needed to help people, Magnani judged. He was rare, and easily led; it was the reason he had tolerated the years with Gaines.

At the famous Door Magnani met the vibraphone player again. In three weeks the cool New Orleans boy had aged ten years. His eyes were glazed, his speech loose and softly enunciated, like his vibes.

'How you, my man,' he whispered to Magnani, lurching against him. His breath was sweet, with a tinge of peppermint to it.

'Hello,' Magnani said, 'are you playing tonight?'

'Sure thing, see you up there, brother.' And he was gone, dissolved in the growing number of players fussing over their instruments.

Pearson nudged Magnani. 'He's on his way.'

'Dope?'

'Of course. They can go that quickly, if they ain't got the constitution for it. That Kid is shooting up every night, he's already on the mainline to hell, man.'

'The change is incredible.'

'Like I said, some go like that. People like Bird could do a lot of shit, before it beat him, but Frank, do you know when they cut the man open they thought he was sixty-seven years old, and Bird wasn't forty.'

'Now you *are* preaching, Pearson.'

Pearson chuckled. 'That's what Eileen calls me, her preacher man. I'm gonna sit in for a few, get warmed up, then you can burn Frank.'

Magnani watched the action on the stage. It was fast and competitive but he did not feel a part of it. There was another guitarist in the Door, a West Coast man who played a smooth style of satin-like chords and pretty following notes. It was music too delicate for the ears present tonight, and the man left the stage quietly, followed by the vibes-player, who abruptly dropped his hammers onto the keys and walked off, waving a hand at those behind him.

Magnani played with Pearson, a bass, piano and a collection of assorted reed and horn players — almost a big band. He did not gell with the others. At first he thought it a hangover from Gaines that he comped without spirit; he was not called on to solo. In a break Pearson asked what was wrong.

'Nothing, I've just gone off the boil a little, that's all.'

'I thought you were so up for it.'

'So did I.'

'Give it another shot later, Frank.'

'I will.'

As he looked into Pearson's face he saw Eileen fade into view. The drummer moved towards some people he knew but Magnani stopped him with a hand. 'Pearson, you're drumming the best I've heard you tonight.'

'Why thank you Frank. I do feel kinda good, I'm always like it when I get back to Buen Vista. That girl makes me feel like a young buck again.'

Magnani did not burn. His second attempt raised barely a musical flicker; the more he tried to inject feel and style into his playing the more it eluded him. His fingers were leaden, his thoughts disrupted; the slender connection between man and instrument was missing. He was sure everyone noticed and by one o'clock he stopped playing and like the vibes player left the stage, stealing his shoulders against the mocking eyes of his fellows. Sympathy amongst musicians was an unknown commodity.

Magnani watched the others as he had watched that first night, on the outside again. To calm himself he drank steadily, small glasses of beer followed by two fingers of bourbon. He hardly noticed when Pearson took him home.

'I've packed up your axe buddy. Come on, you've got liquid legs tonight.' Pearson supported him out of the club, and carried his guitar.

'Did I make a fool of myself?' Magnani asked. 'I didn't play worth a shit.'

'No man, that's how it goes sometimes. Come on, hold onto me, or we'll both be in the street.'

The sky spun over his head. Neon light transfixed it; names, billboards, club signs merged into a crazy pattern of commerce. Magnani was in a world that sold every part of itself, and he did not know if he could compete, or if he wanted to compete. With the warmth of Pearson's body against him he was aware of a great coldness inside himself. Indecision gnawed at him. It made him question who he was, and what his motives were. Magnani had a fixation that he was not worthy of his talent, and he constantly proved it. He dived into shoddy actions and took a masochistic pleasure from the resulting angst. Usually other people were left to pick up the tab.

'I'm no good, Pearson,' Magnani said, 'no fucking good.' But it came out in an incoherent mumble that Pearson did not understand. Magnani would remember nothing more about the evening.

Pearson and Eileen helped him move the next day. His possessions were transported in the station wagon to a rooming house where a place had been secured. Magnani's first impression was good, his new lodgings had none of the bleakness of Stein's run-down hotel. People here stayed long term, attracted by its cheapness, and rare attempt to offer a fair deal. Two ageing spinsters from Carolina ran the house, the sisters McGraw, who had come 'from better things' Pearson explained. They greeted Magnani with genuine friendliness, arranging themselves on either side of him, and duplicating speech, each one an echo of the other.

'Mr. Pearson recommended you, Mr. Magnani. You are from England, aren't you? So nice to have a gentleman here. I'm Miss McGraw, and this is Miss McGraw.' She pointed to her sister, who nodded.

The misses McGraw were less than five feet tall; their voluminous skirts made them smaller still. Magnani imagined them swirling around atop a music box, or adorning some fancy cake. The room they led him to was clean and warm, its furnishings sufficient, with a writing desk in one corner. Magnani's eyes started at this sight.

'See the desk, Frank,' Pearson said, 'you can do your thing here.'

Eileen brought in some of his books. For an instant Magnani locked his eyes into hers, and a secret was established.

They left him to settle in. The move over had cleared his head but his performance at the Door still hurt. To console himself, Magnani arranged the room to his satisfaction. He piled the desk with his writing gear, inviting work with his stack of virgin paper. He lay his notes alongside, and arranged his pens in a pleasing geometry. Pearson had picked the place well, there was even a bookshelf on the wall, which he filled with his collection. Despite the few dollars left in his pocket Magnani gained a little security as he sat down in his new world.

FIVE

Early morning sleet had turned to a fine snow. It spattered the window-ledge outside Magnani's room, accumulating into piles at each corner. Magnani watched the storm build up and was glad not to be in Stein's hotel. It was his third day with the Misses McGraw and he had learnt to steel himself against their pink-powdered presence, to smile at their enquiries as to his prospects of work, and blunt their sharp nosiness with vague answers. He paid a little extra and ate his main meal with the other guests. There were three other male boarders; the sisters would not countenance women in their house. The McGraws made surrogate families of each crop of guests, mothering them if they were allowed, interfering often and generally being benevolent nuisances. One man, a fallen Southerner like themselves, had been rooming with them for many years.

Magnani stayed in his room as much as possible. He enjoyed the solitude. By feigning bookwork he was able to persuade the sisters not to knock his door every half hour. Most of the days he played the guitar quietly, with his back to the desk, and tracked the swirl of each fresh wave of snow. It had been like this since he had moved in, words would not flow, defying his inexperienced attempts to prise them from his head and onto the page. He could not establish a routine so he played the guitar, which was friendly in his hands but did not help.

Pearson phoned once and his message was conveyed by one sister, the first time Magnani had seen one not in tandem with the other. Emily McGraw circled around his room as she delivered her news, her eyes flitting to his desk and bed.

'Mr. Pearson says why don't you come over and have dinner tonight, Mr. Magnani.'

'Did he say anything about work?'

'No, he did not, but I am sure a young gentleman like yourself can find plenty of opportunity in this city.'

'I meant musical work, Miss McGraw.'

'Well music does not seem very constant to me, you should get something with a future to it, and a pension. Think of when you get old. You young people never do that, and it comes soon enough, believe me.'

'I'd rather not.'

She frowned, but changed to a smile to match Magnani's.

'You are joking with me.'

'Of course,' he lied.

'My father used to say the British have such a wit about them, he was over there in the first big war, you know.' Her eyes glazed with memories. 'He adored Oscar Wilde.'

'I don't think Oscar would like to be called British.'

But she was not listening; the sisters McGraw never listened, and it was a blessing. Contenting herself with a last sly glance towards his notes she rustled out of the room. Magnani wondered what she would make of his Haydn papers when she picked through them; she would undoubtedly do so when he was out. He thought of his gentleman status rising higher and took up the guitar again. He resolved to go over to Buen Vista.

Pearson was edgy all night, Magnani wondered if the drummer was aware of his intentions towards Eileen. They sat down to what Pearson called a Kansas City meal, chicken cooked in a fiery sauce with deposits of vegetables Magnani did not recognise heaped around the meat.

'This is soul food, brother,' Pearson said. 'Eileen fixed it up for us. Get into it.'

For once Pearson drank more than Magnani, whiskey and wine alternately, the wine to quench the thirst the sauce instilled, the whiskey to fuel it back up again.

'I haven't seen you drink like this before, Pearson,' Magnani said.

'Once in a while, man, I like to tie one on. Eileen can stand it, can't you baby.'

Eileen was quiet. She ate modestly and sipped very little wine. Sometimes her eyes flicked over to Magnani, but he did not know what he saw in them tonight.

It took Pearson some time to unload his unease. Eileen prompted him. 'Frank, Pearson's got something to tell you.'

'That's right, Frank. Thing is, I got a chance of work with James Ellery, the sax player. He's putting a sextet together to work on the West Coast, show those dudes how to play out there. If it goes okay it will be a long gig, three months maybe. Ellery says I could even go to Europe with him. You'd like that, huh Eileen?' He patted at her cheek with his hand, and stabbed at his empty plate with his fork.

'I didn't know what to do, Frank. I feel kinda guilty. We said we'd work together and all. I asked Ellery, but he don't need no guitar.'

'No, he wouldn't. Pearson, don't be stupid, we never actually said we'd stay together. It's impossible anyway. Take the gig, or I'll never talk to you again.'

'Are you sure? How will you do?'

'I'll get something. Anyway, there's always real work.'

The tension was broken. Pearson had a week's rehearsals, then would leave for San Francisco by train. Magnani fought down his envy, and thought of Eileen being alone.

Magnani's store of dollars had dwindled to twenty, barely enough to last another week. Without telling Pearson he visited the local union to scout out work, to be told the tale countless others had heard, that Jazz was on the slide, no-one wanted big bands small bands or even solo artists. In the bars rock and roll was taking over; it had volume and immediacy, and few people wanted to look beyond that for their drinking music. Jazz retained a loyal following, but it was tiny. To have a realistic chance of working, musical compromise was called for; some could do so, others not. His experience with Gaines told Magnani he was in the latter category.

On Magnani's desk lay his return ticket to Southampton, valid for six months, a condition of entry into the States. When he saw it he was tempted to use it. It would be an easy way out. He put it in the guitar case, put the guitar on top of it, and tried again to write. It was all in his head, years of research jogged around looking for an outlet. Images of Haydn and his world flashed up like the Times Square signs, but vanished again before he could use them, leaving him harried by frustration. When the music was good he could write, when not, all stopped.

He went out for a bottle of Bourbon, for which he had acquired a taste over his usual scotch. On his way back he saw Eileen on the opposite side of the street, and made a bee-line for her without thinking of the traffic. The screeching of car brakes, and the yell of a cab driver alerted her.

'Frank! You were almost run over.'

'Haven't got used to looking the other way yet. Where are you going?'

'I got some shopping to do, things to get for Pearson before he leaves. That man is hopeless with things like that.'

'Come back to my place, have a shot of this to keep out the cold. Look at our breath, we're like a pair of dragons.'

'You say some weird things, Frank. No, I don't think so, I haven't got much time. I'm working later.'

'Come on, just for a few minutes. You can spare that.' He was as casual as he could manage, and did not look at Eileen directly.

'Just a few minutes, then. I *am* cold.'

Almost reeling with triumph, Magnani guided her back to his lodgings, praying that the Misses McGraw would not see them. The spinsters were busy in the kitchen, and there was no-one else about when they entered.

'Come on in,' Magnani said, 'its a bit untidy.'

He took some papers off the settee and slapped its cushions. Eileen sat at one end of it, apprehension in her bones. Magnani poured two drinks and handed one to her.

'Jesus Frank, this is too much — its not afternoon yet.'

'Oh, allright.' He poured some of hers into his, and drank it down.

'Are you drinking a lot, Frank?'

'Not really. A little, it helps me with that.' He nodded towards the desk.

'How is it going?'

'Good. I'm getting lots done.'

'Pearson told me something about it. You're a talented man, he said, doing this stuff and playing good.'

Magnani waved away the compliment with his hands, but did not deny it.

'When is Pearson going?'

'In a few days. He said for you to come over before he does, and why haven't you shown up at his rehearsals?'

'I'd be in the way, and I'd want to play,' he admitted.

'Pearson says its harder for guitarists to get work.'

'Especially ones who have squashed the toes of Carlton Gaines.'

'I never liked him, he tried to come onto me once.'

'Really?'

'He was a lizard.'

Magnani saluted her with his glass, refilled with the same amount of drink. 'No chance of going with the drummer man?'

'No, we got to keep Buen Vista going. He wants me to go to Europe though, if that happens.'

'You must.'

'Will it be like you said, Frank?'

'Of course. Better. You'll have a great time.'

'Pearson says they treat you right there, don't see your colour.'

Magnani did not want to disappoint her. 'In Paris yes, all the guys say that.'

'I can't wait.'

Neither could Magnani. He watched every drop she drank, anticipating its effect, willing it on.

'How did you meet Pearson?' he asked.

'At the Door. I've worked over there for a few years, it just happened over a long time. Pearson was always around and I needed someone like him, I had bad times with guys. Musicians are fast company, you all got the glad eye.'

'And Pearson hasn't?'

'He says he's past all that.'

'Maybe. What would he think of you being here?'

'Nothing. He trusts me, you too.'

He's wrong, Magnani thought. He leaned over and kissed her, brushing her lips with his own, then moving back.

She held a hand up in defence but did not seem surprised.

'I'm not free, Frank, how could you try it?'

'Because I can't help it, and you wanted me to.'

'That's not true.'

He kissed her again. She dug her fingers into his hand and half-pushed him away. But for a few short seconds there was a charge between them, then she struggled out of his grasp.

'Cut it out Frank, it's wrong.'

With difficulty he stopped, and resumed his end of the settee, like an expectant fighter between rounds. 'Like I said, I can't help it.'

'I'd better go. I don't think I'd better see you again Frank, not alone.'

'Allright.'

She left. He watched her go through the window. Eileen picked her way over the light snow with delicacy. For Magnani sex oozed from her every motion, and he knew he was close to his goal. He took another drink, and the blank paper on the desk did not look so daunting. After several nervous circumferences of the room Magnani took to his work again, attempting another chapter. He thought to move Haydn's life back and forth in time, to make it cohesive by the strength of the man's own thoughts. The idea that he might be able to pull it off excited Magnani, he had the conceit needed to put himself in the mind of the great man and make him speak. The book had a hold on him now, and at the risk of splitting a career already shaken by America he put all other matters outside it. Magnani whisked Haydn forward some years, to London, and fame.

The boat creaks in G major, a low murmur of wood straining against water as the wind picks up. They tell me this channel is small, as seas go, but to me it is vast and grey. It surges past our vessel and I wonder that we can sail against it. Salomon points out the English Cliffs. To me they are welcoming, and glimmer white in the cold day. Salomon goes below. He is very sick, but I am not, to my amazement. I am a virgin traveller, and far from young, but it comes easily enough to me, I find. With the thought of London trepidation fills me, what that great city holds I cannot foresee, though Salomon has confidence, and his terms are exceedingly generous. The man strikes me as daring, and a gambler, perhaps I, Haydn, his gamble, will be successful in this new world, perhaps not. God will decide.

How rapidly things are changing, my once steady life is now a whirlpool of opportunity, and I must not drown in it. Liberty is heady, but dangerous; I will try to learn it well. It is comforting to have Salomon with me, he will ease my passage in a strange land; he speaks its tongue and I have not one word, and he has a confidence I find calming.

We spent Christmas day in Bonn, I met the precocious Beethoven boy there. Mozart tells me much of this one, and his young path will cross mine again, I feel. Dear Mozart, he counselled me against this trip, and I love him for his care, and despair at his haphazard life. He suffers from the misguided hands of others, and his own too, and knows poverty. I knew it once and its shadow is still upon me, I pray that he will know the providence I have found.

Our vessel leaps with the wind now, its sails billow with its force, and take me to a destiny I welcome.

Magnani wrestled with each word, ten pages were slimmed down to one, which he agonized over for the rest of the day. Was he making Haydn pompous? Could someone like Pearson ever relate to him? Did he want someone like Pearson to do so? His stomach rumbled a complaint at its treatment: the bourbon had left a queasy emptiness in it and he had missed the sisters' meal. On a whim he decided to go over to Nina's. He had not been there since his return to New York, and it would be a good antidote to the seclusion of his room.

Alec Guiness was still going strong at the cinema. The poster was weather beaten now, torn at the edges; it typified a city also battered by nature. Brown sludge topped with fresh snow was piled on the sidewalks. On the streets vehicles went carefully over iced-up surfaces and the temperature did not rise above freezing in the day. Walkers had a raw, wind-whipped look about them, and scudded from store to store, or taxi to office, in heavy clothing. Magnani was glad to make the steamy atmosphere of Nina's before his feet and hands lost all feeling.

Johnson was there. Magnani saw him at once and tried to circle his table, but was seen, and called over.

'Well it's the Limey axe player, still as smart as ever, I see.'

'Hello, Johnson.' He was with a girl of twelve or thirteen.

'This here is Elma. I'm her guardian, kinda.'

Magnani touched his hat to the girl and Johnson winked at him. She shrank from his attention and played with her ice-cream.

'Can you believe this, man,' Johnson said, 'her wanting this stuff in this weather? That's how you look, Magnani,' he pointed to the ice-cream, 'frozen. Hey, that was some fracas, huh, up at Stein's. You and Pearson vamoosed pretty quick. Ain't seen you since, have I?'

Magnani started to edge away. 'I've got to go, Johnson.'

'You just came in, buddy. You playing anywhere? Naw, you ain't, I'd know about it. Pearson's got something though, heard he's going out to the coast, get him some sun.'

'That's right, I might go out there myself.'

'The hell you say. Not to play geetar you won't. Gaines is there, dig, in film land.'

Magnani turned and left, fighting down Nina's wonderful smells.

He found a small Italian place not far away and settled for a pizza. It took two of his few remaining dollars but he enjoyed the peace of a restaurant waiting for the night. So far America had been a bustling experience; Magnani was beginning to understand its laden atmospheres and the effect it had on its people. It excited and charged, but its questions were unanswered; he had yet to meet anyone who knew where he was going. A drifting mass of poor people channelled their energies into exercises of survival that Magnani recognised, and was used to, but the race of the better off was more alien to him. He could not decide if it was more honest than his own, or more naked in its aggression and greed. Many of the people he watched seemed to have a barely maintained veil of sanity. They were shocked by a collision of cultures, a melting pot which remoulded them into images without any real identity. For Magnani New York society was transient, a shifting, conflicting concentration, which he liked.

Magnani did not venture out for the rest of the week. He finished a chapter of Haydn, and was satisfied with his start. The Misses McGraw asked him about future rent, and Magnani fobbed them off with a tale about funds arriving from England. By Saturday he had enough change left to get into the Famous Door and buy a few shots of their cheapest whiskey. Eileen was working, and a white combo played.

He did not so arrive until ten, it was easier to eke out his drinks that way. Eileen was at her counter but he made no move towards her. The situation called for the ultimate cool if he was to succeed. He settled onto a bar stool and watched the band blow. It was the first time he had seen more than one white player at a time here, and he was intrigued to judge if the gap in standard was as wide as was thought.

It was. The five musicians were very good, the baritone sax had a fine burr of tone, the antithesis of be-bop phrasing. This was the music of the east taken to Los Angeles, refined, anaesthetised, and re-imported. Each number was long, once a theme was stated the two saxes shifted through a series of moods, but never to the detriment of overall smoothness, and with no hint of urgency in the notes. This was ocean music, cool, fresh tone poetry that did not demand too much, very different to the earthy city wailing of be-bop. Pleasant was the word that came into Magnani's mind, the white man settling for second best, gaining control of instrumentation consummately, but not grasping at the very soul of the music. He wished there was more integration. The big bands had started the polarisation of colour: black and white rarely mixed. Billie Holiday worked with Artie Shaw for a while, but she grew tired of travelling in service elevators, hidden from hotel clientele. In the bands of Ellington and Basie there was not even a token white face. Even in the world of players trying so hard to be different, life was not so different. America's constitution still lay on the page, fine words never invested with action. Old prejudices were brought from old societies to flower afresh in the new world. In less than a century they had sent down unaltered roots which held fast. At least it appeared this way to Magnani as he drank sparingly, and watched Eileen.

In a break he waited until she was alone, then approached her.

'Hello Eileen. Is it safe to talk to you — plenty of people around?'

'Frank. Where did you come from?'

'The bar — where else? I've been here for an hour, checking out the band.'

'They're good, aren't they?'

'So so. They lack a little colour.'

Eileen did not react.

'Sorry about the other night,' Magnani went on. 'I was tired, and a bit lonely. The Misses McGraw would be shocked.'

'That's for sure, you being such a gentleman and all.'

'Did you tell Pearson?'

'Of course not. He left today. He was kinda sad you didn't come over to see him off.'

'After what happened?'

'That was nothing to do with him.'

'I hope he does well out there.'

'He will.'

Eileen took the hats of several newcomers. Magnani leant against her counter, to face the stage. The combo played a Gaines tune, out of his better, earlier ones.

'Christ, we weren't even allowed to play that.'

'What's that Frank?'

'Nothing. Feeling the need to play again, that's all.'

'Are you looking?'

'Yes. Well no, not as much as I could.'

'I know it's not what you want but they need a barman here next week. Benji has to go south to fix up some business. They'll be short.'

'I don't think they would want me.'

'They might, if I asked for you. An English guy would go down well here, with the accent and all. Your voice would sell booze.'

'Would you do that, ask them?'

'Sure.'

Magnani felt small and infantile. Eileen was brushing off his pass, diminishing it with apparent unconcern. For a moment he thought to abandon his designs on her, but he saw her body move beneath her clothes, and lust crushed the idea. Again he imagined consent in her eyes.

'What time do you finish tonight?' he asked.

'When the last guy leaves, when else?'

'Stupid question.' There was a silence between them. Magnani fingered the coin in his pocket and looked thoughtful.

'I'm not coming back with you, Frank.'

'No, of course not. I could walk you home though, perhaps have a drink on the way, in that little place down the street, it's always open.'

'Sam's bar? How much money do you have left?'

'None.'

She laughed. 'Frank, you are crazy.' He thought laughter a good ally, and added to hers with his own.

'So you want me to stand you?'

He shrugged.

'Go and listen to the music. I'll think about it.'

He did so, still feeling childish, but also confident. Eileen had not given him an outright refusal, and that was promising.

The crowd had mostly dwindled away when the combo played its last number, a soft blues that matched the bare club. The thread of its tune wound its way up to the high ceiling and lay there with the smoke and the echoes of the evening. Magnani's fingers itched for the fretboard, with the hand in his pocket he formed chords, until he noticed the barman looking at him strangely. Eileen joined him. She had on her coat and was ready to go.

'Just one, Frank, for the road.'

'You make me feel like Sinatra.' He hummed that singer's song and brought a softness to Eileen's face.

There was no let up in the weather. It had a stranglehold on the city, and they were at its heart. Eileen told him it would last another two months. They hurried to Sam's, where a few couples stretched out the night, and a pianola played.

'I was hoping that thing would be turned off,' Magnani muttered.

'And you a musician. People like sounds around them, especially at this time. They need the company.'

Eileen slipped money into his hand and sat at a table against the wall. As he stood at the bar and watched the tired Sam pour him a double shot of Jim Beam, Magnani tried to discipline himself. If he made another pass, and was spurned again, it would be the end of him. With the disintegration of the Gaines gig and his absolute poverty there would be nowhere else to go but back across the Atlantic. The danger of his planned action made it easier; self-denial had never figured much in Magnani's make up. Impulse had brought him to the edge of destruction several times in his short life. Then, as now, instinct, logic and, finally, experience told him of the folly of his actions, but he could never stand against them. Magnani was able to take the wrong corridors knowing that doors would shut behind him. Poets said this was a Celtic trait. If this was so, in Magnani it was compounded by a Latin potency that often shifted his feet from under him.

'What are you thinking, Frank, or shouldn't I ask?' Eileen said, as he rejoined her. He handed her a gin.

'What to do.'

'About that job in the club?'

'Yes,' he lied. 'Heard from Pearson?'

'He rang me in the club. I could hardly hear him but he said they had got there, and the town looked okay. A lot of hills, he said, but pretty.'

'I hope he does well.'

She is here with me, he thought, there must be a chance. His vanity burned. 'Eileen, about the other night. ..'

'Let's not talk about it Frank. Its over and done with.'

'No, it's not. It wasn't just talk, what I said. I can't get you out of my thoughts. I know it's lousy going behind Pearson's back, but that's how it is. How I am...'

He liked the sound of his words. He had a politician's silver tongue and loose conscience, and the ability to believe his own lies. He reached out a hand for Eileen's, it shrank in his but did not pull away.

'I should have done what I said, and not seen you again,' Eileen said, 'not without Pearson.'

'But you did.'

There was no-one else left in the bar except its owner, who looked at them with eyes that already slept.

'Come on, you people, ain't you got homes to go to?'

'Have we?' Magnani whispered. 'Let me come back to Buen Vista with you.'

'I couldn't do that to Pearson, can't you understand that? Not there.'

He knew he would never move her on that. A chance would have to be taken with the Misses McGraw.

'Come back with me then.'

'To the old ladies' place? You crazy?'

'Yes. I've got a key, they'll never be around at this hour.' Magnani pushed his knee against hers, the only contact possible with the round table between them but it was enough. He was close now.

'Eileen, I'm mad for you.'

It sounded ridiculous but she wanted to hear it. Her hand flexed in his. 'Come on, Sam wants to close up.'

The wind helped them along to the boarding house. New snow smothered their steps and they entered quietly, Magnani turning his key in the lock with great care. He was thankful that the sisters expected him to be out this late. In his room Eileen would not let him risk a light.

Guilt heightened Magnani's pleasure. It gave him a far greater buzz than Johnson's pills. He explored Eileen's body greedily, fumbling for her through her clothes. He was racist in his desire, fascinated by her colour. In his talk there had been one particle of truth: he was mad about Eileen, mad to sleep with her, to possess her. He undressed Eileen himself, he wanted to be in control and Eileen seemed content to play a submissive role.

She responded slowly. Her fear made her tense and wooden in his grasp until slowly she began to join him in his heat. She became salacious with an equal desire, wriggling from under him to straddle his body, the whites of her eyes catching the streetlights as she did so.

'Oh man,' she whispered, 'Oh man,' over and over until they were done.

Eileen smoked a cigarette, and within minutes of their climax there was a tension between them. Magnani knew she thought of Pearson and was ashamed. Perhaps she hated herself, but more likely she hated him. For Magnani it had been good, but no better than many others. Eileen was a target that had been achieved, now he thought of consequences. The immediate one was of getting her out quickly and secretly.

He ran his hand through her hair. 'What are you thinking?' he asked.

She did not answer.

'Was it all right?'

'Jesus, why do men always have to ask things like that?'

'We need reassurance.'

'You need to be told nice things, that's for sure.... babies.'

'What?'

'Yes, it was great, Frank. And wrong.'

'It had to happen Eileen, we both wanted it.'

'It did not have to happen. You .made it happen. You pushed like a bull, Frank.'

He was quite pleased with this image and knew it was wise to say no more.

'Pearson must never find out,' Eileen said. 'Promise me you'd never tell him Frank.'.

'Of course I won't. We'd better get you home, Eileen. It will be dawn soon, and the McGraws are up with it.'

They could not find a taxi at that time and the walk was long and wordless. Magnani left Eileen at the door of Buen Vista, and fought down the urge to ask her for a loan.

SIX

Magnani started work at the Famous Door on the following Tuesday, the club's quietest night. The manager, Quaid, told him to get used to the job quickly. Benji, the man Magnani was replacing would be back in six weeks; Magnani had until then to prove himself. There might be a permanent spot for him, Quaid said, there might not. He was a man who loved not to commit himself, believing it kept people on their toes.

There were two other bartenders at the Door. They were old and black and good at their job. John 'Boy' Broonzy and Tom Harrison had established a double act that was part of the club's ambience. Each patrolled his section of the bar with haughty insolence, trying to outdo the other in banter. Customers expected it. Magnani was there to provide what Quaid called a 'touch of Limey class'. He thought it a great joke. Broonzy and Harrison viewed him with suspicion but were not hostile, they knew he was not threat enough for that. It was not long before they picked up his accent and incorporated it into their bar show. They did not seem to care he was someone who had played at the Door a few weeks ago. Magnani was glad of that.

'They are both drunks,' Eileen told him, 'but never on the job. They got a way to limit themselves, don't ask me how.'

'They're not young', Magnani said.

'No, that's why they are careful. There's no other job they are ever going to have.'

After Saturday Eileen had made no attempt to contact Magnani and he thought it wise to be equally uncommunicative. He needed time to think and to worry, to consider his general state of dissatisfaction. Haydn was buried beneath it all and the puny chords that came from his guitar were bloodless, dying quickly under his fingers. He concocted several stories for Eileen, but dismissed them and decided to play it by ear.

With the promise of a job the Misses McGraw were persuaded to give him credit, but not without a lecture. They wandered from a potted history of southern chivalry to the perils of the motor vehicle, and Magnani did not listen to any of it.

He was slow to learn the prices of the rarer drinks but he served well enough, if somewhat perfunctorily. This was not a rare quality in New York barmen and no-one took it amiss. The first music he heard and viewed from his work station was a sextet, with a trombone player for a leader. A showman who harked back to the old schools of King Oliver, Armstrong and Bennie Moten. He had the easy smile of these men and their attitude towards entertainment, but just an echo of their talent. The man was an old friend of Quaid's and filled a lame week in the club's calendar. Magnani was relieved to start with old music and mediocrity. To serve whilst someone special played would have been galling. He would have to work up to that.

Magnani had a good sight of the stage. What was played there carried over the talk of the barflies. He served a few of the players he had jammed with but they showed no surprise at his new work. Even at this level musicians drifted into other jobs when engagements dried up. Magnani followed a worn path. He managed to get a small advance out of Quaid with which to placate the sisters McGraw and give him a little spending money. Eileen had vouched for him with Quaid.

In her break Eileen sat at the bar with Magnani. Business was slack and there were long gaps between serving. He gave her a small gin and waited for her to talk. She played with the drink for a while, whisking it around with a cocktail stick.

'I thought you would have called me before now,' Eileen said.

'Sorry. I had to arrange this stuff with Quaid. I knew I'd see you here.'

'Huh huh.'

'Everything okay?' There was a note of false optimism in Magnani's voice.

'Pearson phoned last night, he's started playing out there.'

'Are they going down well?'

Eileen was not listening. 'I feel so lousy,' she said, 'I had to listen to him tell me all the things we are going to do, about Europe and all.'

There was a man to be served, someone Magnani had seen at Stein's. He gave him a beer, and a bourbon chaser.

'Don't I know you, pal?' the man asked.

'No, I don't think so.'

'Sure, I got it. The guitarist, with Carlton Gaines.'

Magnani had to acknowledge it.

'Christ, you came down quick buddy. That was only a few weeks ago. What went wrong?'

He took his drinks to a table, not interested in an answer.

'Did you hear what I said,' Eileen continued. 'You got a way about you Frank, I don't know what it is exactly, but it gets people doing things for you. Like I did.'

A silver tongue and a loose conscience, Magnani thought.

'I don't know what to do,' Eileen said.

'In what way?'

'In what way? Jesus, you talk like a lawyer. In our way, Frank. I'm talking about us, you, me — and Pearson.'

'I don't want to spoil things for you and Pearson, so perhaps it would be better to forget it. He'll never know anything, not from me.'

'I don't know if I can do that. Pearson is a sweet guy, and it would be on my mind.'

'What do you want to do then?'.

Eileen finished her drink. 'I've got to get back.'

She returned to her counter and Magnani thought of taking her home when they finished. He had not known what to say to her. Quaid came up to the bar.

'Everything okay, Magnani?'

'Yes. Fine.'

'You ain't involved with that Eileen dame, are you? I don't allow none of that stuff, it makes for sloppy work.'

'No, it's nothing like that. Just talking about Pearson, that's all.'

'That's where I should be right now, in the sun, not here in this icebox, with an ulcer grabbing at my guts. There's folks need serving Magnani.'

The evening dragged to its tired close. The trombone player lost his ebullience as he went through his paces, he aged with the night and his lassitude infected the others. Magnani wondered if every night would be like this. The sextet entered a period of musical emptiness, greying, balding men who were corpulent or extremely thin. The words of Miss McGraw came into Magnani's head — get something with a pension plan. Like many musicians he laughed at security, but let fragments of worry cloud his mind when things we not going well. And he was not yet thirty. He did not want to end up like the men who performed before him now, boxed into a blind alley, and facing an uncertain future in their old age. Slyly sipping his beneath-the-bar bourbon Magnani doubted that any member of the sextet scoffed at security.

The Door packed up early, at two. There was no point keeping it open, for by then the sextet outnumbered the customers.

'I'll have to stop you an hour's pay,' Quaid said to Magnani.

'Of course.'

It was the final turn of the evening's miserable screw. Magnani stood at the exit to catch Eileen.

'Frank, I thought you'd gone.'

'No, I didn't want you walking home alone.'

'I've been doing it since I was a kid.' Frost caught her breath and turned it into small clouds.

'Cold, isn't it?' he said.

'It's bad this year. You came over in one of our coldest winters.'

'My timing was never good.' He offered her his arm. 'Night cap?'

'No, Frank. I said I had to think.'

But she walked with him, over packed snow which seeped into their feet and hastened their step.

'Perhaps I should give up the job,' Magnani said, 'it can't help.'

'You've just started. No, you'll be broke again.'

It was the answer Magnani wanted.

'All right I'll stay, but it won't be easy. I still feel the same way.' He could not help trying.

'I don't think you know what you feel,' Eileen said.

'What do you mean?'

'There's fear in you Frank, I can sense it. That's what made you make out with me like you did. I know lots of guys would have done the same, and most not thought any more about it. You have to worry. You worry and you still do it. I guess that is a kind of fear.'

'Oh.'

'You want me to go back with you tonight, don't you?'

His shoulders hunched but he did not reply.

'I've just realised something about you, Frank.'

'What?'

'You don't want to be left out of anything, do you. You act like you are cool on your own, but you are a boy. That's why Pearson took to you, he's a born father. And your talking, it makes you powerful somehow. I can't explain it, I haven't got the words like you do.'

You are explaining it very well, he thought. He abandoned his plans and walked silently with Eileen to Buen Vista. At the door he squeezed her lightly on the shoulder.

'Good night Eileen, I'll see you tomorrow.'

'No, its my rest day.'

His eyes searched hers for disappointment but there was none. She went in, leaving him on the fringe of a snowbound Harlem, facing another biting walk back to the rooming house. He heard noises from the canning factory, thumping, muffled sounds and the occasional clank of metal. Nothing human.

Magnani had drunk since his mid-teens and it increased when he became a full-time player. Drink was an easy ally, always available in places of work, consumed and offered by people who came to see him play. It took a strength he did not have to escape it. At the Famous Door he knew it was the wrong time to start, that he was in a state of flux, and his book and his music were creeping away from him. But he could not help himself. He started to drink heavily, accepting the drinks that customers sometimes offered instead of collecting the tips. When Quaid was not around he poured himself a quick shot from his bottle under the bar, copying Broonzy and Harrison. By the end of his first week his intake had doubled, and when he realised Quaid did not much care as long as the job was done he was further encouraged.

It was impossible not to think of Eileen. She was there, fingering hats and dispensing coats. Sometimes Magnani wanted to leap over his bar and take her away from the leering eyes and pawing hands, other times he knew she watched him, and would not look up. The second week at the Door tortured his musical pride. For two nights a trumpet played chaffed on his nerves with his brilliance and on Wednesday, when the horn player was blowing like Gabriel, Johnson appeared. Magnani turned from his bottles to the sound of clicking fingers.

'Hello Frank. I heard you was over here — serving. My my.'

'What can I get you Johnson?'

'No hello. Not very polite.'

Magnani rubbed a glass with his cloth and kept the agitation from his face, though he tightened his lips against his teeth. Johnson sat on a bar stool and swivelled it around to face the band. 'The man is hot tonight. I'll have a large rye, plenty of rocks.'

Magnani poured the drink and pushed it towards Johnson's back. He started to edge down the bar.

'Heard about Filigree?' Johnson said.

'What about him?'

'He ain't no more, man. Got hisself dead last night. He took some bad shit at his girlfriend's place. She's a mess.'

Johnson turned to face Magnani, to check for effect.

'So, you're working for Quaid. It don't pay much, do it, not for a music star like yourself.'

'He'll never know about his Sputnik theory,' Magnani muttered under his breath.

'What you say?'

'I said you don't seem very concerned about Filigree. I thought he was a friend of yours.'

'Just business man, just business. Filigree was okay, but he was a little bit crazy, you know. All that black power crap.'

Magnani knew what Johnson was doing but could not help chewing on the bait.

'And your business killed him.'

'Hey Frankie, you don't want to go talking like that.'

Magnani's hands were on the bar, his fingers gripped the underside of it and ached for the bottle. To drink from or use as a weapon. Over Johnson's shoulder he saw Eileen watching anxiously. Johnson's eyes clashed with his. They said come on you white motherfucker, don't let me get away with it. But Magnani moved away to serve another customer.

On stage the horn player muted his piece, and its low moan entered Magnani, gnawing his soul until he wanted to tear off his ears and smash Johnson down, to beg forgiveness from Pearson and Eileen and play good again. But he did nothing. Like always. Johnson left, nodding to the stage and slouching his shoulders with victory.

Eileen came to the bar when the club was quiet, and the musicians off stage.

What did that creep want?' she asked.

'Johnson? Nothing. He just came to needle me, and to gloat over Bud Filigree. He's dead, Eileen.'

'Oh no. What happened?'

'An overdose, Johnson said.'

'I can believe that. The man was using so much, for a long time. I'll phone Yvonne, she'll be bad.'

'He was somewhere else when he died.'

'They always are. She knew he fooled around, always had done.'

Magnani was still shaking from the experience of Johnson. Anger coursed through him, nourished by his shame. He felt very small, but did not show it.

'How are you Eileen?' Magnani asked, 'we haven't had much chance to talk this week.'

'I thought it better we didn't. You're dangerous, Frank.'

'Johnson doesn't think so.'

'What's with you and him? I could feel the air from the counter.'

'Hard to say. I never liked him from the first, and its gone downhill since then. He was the first man I talked to here, Stein sent him over to the hotel.'

'Jesus, what a start. Johnson is slime, Frank. He picks off people

like a vulture. Guys like him force a habit on you then feed off it —
he did that with Filigree.'

'I know.'

'Is that why you hate him? Because you do hate him. I can see it
in your eyes when you talk about him.'

'Maybe.'

Magnani compared himself to Johnson and hoped he was more
different than he felt. Perhaps he was a vulture too, but of emotions.
Either way people got hurt. He tried to put Johnson out of his mind
and concentrate on Eileen. She was easier with him, the drugseller's
appearance had bonded them together once again and the death of
Filigree gave them a need for company. Hope stirred in his heart
once more, moments after he had castigated himself.

Magnani worked on the need and turned it into sex. He spent
what was left of the night and the following morning with Eileen at
Buen Vista, in Pearson's bed. It had been easier than he had
expected, either Eileen had forgotten her earlier words or gave in to
to his persistence. Magnani accepted the situation, as he had always
done. He left the aftermath of recrimination for later.

As the room lightened he smoked a cigarette and fought his mild
hangover. Eileen was still asleep. She hugged the sheets as if trying
to immerse herself in them. Although the room was warm she still
burrowed down, leaving only her hair visible, Magnani brushed it
lightly, sifting through the black sheen with his hand. He decided
not to wake her and left before midday, placing a note of apology
signed with his usual inked guitar under the pillow. It excused his
absence with the need to work on his book, and his playing. He
intended to do neither.

'Been out early today, Mr. Magnani?' Miss McGraw asked. She
had caught him coming in. There was an air of aggression in her
hands-on-hips stance, faintly ludicrous in the old lady. Her eyes
raked his dishevelled barman's outfit, loosely covered by his coat.
Even Miss McGraw knew he had been out all night.

'No, Miss McGraw,' he answered, 'I didn't get back last night.'

Her eyebrows arched and the pink of her powder deepened.
Magnani had flashes of honesty come upon him and did not see the
point in lying this time, though prudence told him he should.

'We really can't have this sort of thing, Mr. Magnani. We expected so much more of you. With the use of the 'we' she was joined
by the other Miss McGraw. Reinforcements. She chipped in on cue.

'My sister is right, it is not becoming in an establishment like ours.
Not becoming at all.'

'Not respectable,' said the other.

Magnani spread his hands and smiled, and felt devilish.

'Ladies, I am sorry if I have disappointed you, but you must not set such heights for me. I am not English, you see.'

They gasped with perfect timing, recoiled and flashed indignant eyes.

'Not English?'

'No, I'm afraid not. I'm Welsh. You know, the land of song, coal mines.' He thought for a moment, 'Ivor Novello, Dylan Thomas?'

'That drunken poet?'

'The very one. We are a bad lot, on the whole — quite un-English.'

There was a short period of bluster from the spinsters, then they went into a conference of murmurs and huddled talk. Action decided on they stepped forward. Magnani still had not shut the front door.

'We are sorry Mr Magnani, but we will have to ask you to leave.'

Magnani had not quite expected this. He thought of charming them but his mood was strange, and he did not want to bother with subterfuge of any kind.

'When do you want me to go?' he asked.

It was their turn to be surprised at his immediate acceptance of his sentence. Magnani went closer to them and hardened his voice.

'Tell you what, sisters, how's about giving me one more week?'

He winked at the elder sister, who shrank away from him. 'I need that long to recover,' he said, 'I had a hell of a fuck last night.'

He thought their gasps might develop into screams but the McGraws melted away from him to disappear into their kitchen in a flurry of silk. Magnani whistled his way to his room and sank onto the bed. He had tried to sound like Humphrey Bogart but the old ladies had not picked it up. Bogart was probably another beyond their pale. It had been a puerile show and he was glad it was not thirty years ago and further south, when the McGraws might have called someone with a bullwhip.

Magnani stretched out with his hands behind his head, and eyed the pile of paper on his desk, willing it to fill itself with words. He knew he was making Haydn the vehicle of his own dreams, investing him with pure thoughts in an attempt to scrub clean his own tawdry soul. His motives were all wrong.

Later that day a note was slipped under his door asking him to vacate the room within two days. It was written on a piece of paper with pink flowers and rabbits in the corners. Magnani was not able to work until night fell. Then the sisters retired and their house was still, the quiet that comes with loneliness and backwaters, with the closeting of dreams until they crumble to dust. Magnani had no plans for the future but was glad to be going.

He stopped off at Nina's for his dinner. He entered the diner hesitantly, apprehensive that Johnson might be there. Magnani had never lost the sense of unease about him since Vermont. But there was no sign of him so he sat and ate quickly, slipped into the club before the first customer. He thought to talk to Eileen and tell her about his eviction but she was not there.

Magnani served through the night with the others in a Door without live music. There was a break in bookings so the club reverted to being just another drinking joint. Eileen did not show up and her place was taken by a new girl. He asked about this and was met with the usual bored disinterest by his fellow barmen.

'Maybe she sick, man,' Harrison offered, as a sop to Magnani's dour mood. He resolved to go over to Buen Vista when he got off.

Magnani did not get to Eileen until much later, and by then his life had been turned by ten minutes of madness. Not much before twelve Johnson appeared. He made a point of being served by Harrison at the other end of the bar though he glanced at Magnani, and twirled his hands in a gesture of dismissal. Magnani ignored him, and got on with the business of attending to the habitual drunks and the few visitors who came seeking music and quickly fled the dead club. Later, when he turned in Johnson's direction, the man had gone. He asked Harrison about him.

'The man's not right tonight,' Harrison said. 'He's been cut loose from Stein.'

'Fired?'

'Yeah. Johnson, he's a boy who'll push too hard. Each and every time. Stein got fed up with his deals and pitched him out. He's back on the street permanent now.'

'Did he say anything to you about me?'

'Nah. Why should he? What you care about Johnson anyway?'

'I don't care anything about him.'

Harrison saw a spark of interest in the conversation.

'I watched you guys. When you meet it like two cats stuffed in a sack, you eyes each other up with your hackles raised.' He chuckled. 'Next it'll be all fur and claws.' The chuckle turned into a deep burr that rattled down in his lower throat.

Magnani went back to his part of the bar. It would have been easier to have someone behind the bar he could communicate with. Harrison was given to cynical observation, and Broonzy specialised in brooding, bottle-fed silences. Magnani was a soft target for them.

Johnson was waiting for his when he left the club. 'Hey Frankie, come over here.'

It was raining softly, there had been a rise in the temperature and the wind had dropped. Johnson's face was backlit by a streetlight. It was moonlike, and his eyes were craters. Malice glittered in them the sleekness had been stripped from him. Carefully, Magnani crossed over to him.

'What do you want, Johnson?'

'I got something for you, man.' Johnson tapped his pocket.

'Haven't you learnt, I'm not interested.'

Johnson giggled, like a young girl being tickled. Magnani was close enough to see his pupils were enlarged black pools that reflected back the light. Johnson tugged at his arm.

'Frank, I want to help you, don't be hostile, man. Forget how I was before. You can play good, I dig that. Walk a little way with me.'

Magnani began to edge away but Johnson applied the hook.

'I got a message from Eileen. Didn't you wonder where she was?'

Magnani was being led into the alley that flanked the club.

'She wrote it down for you, where is it now?'

Johnson made a play of fumbling in his coat. They were out of range of the streets — and only Johnson s eyes were visible in the dark. Every instinct told Magnani to get away but he was unable to, Johnson was pulling on a chord that made him stay. Two cats in a sack.

It was so obvious that Johnson meant to harm him that Magnani was not surprised when-the knife appeared. He felt it rake his face and sink into his shoulder before he managed to get a hold on Johnson's arm. A hot flush of pain cut through him, increasing the strength of his grip. If he relinquished it he feared himself dead. Johnson swore in his ear and kicked out. He bit Magnani on the back of the neck, but Magnani hung on. They tumbled over, rolling amongst packing boxes and pools of water. Incredibly, Magnani tried to reason with Johnson as they fought.

'This is stupid,' he gasped, 'you don't know what you're doing.'

Johnson answered with an incoherence of threats and curses. For a moment the knife was free, it cut at Magnani's hands as he blocked its passage to his body. He managed to grab Johnson's arm and they rolled some more, until Magnani was on top, and smashing Johnson's head into the ground with his forearm. He did not know how many times he did it, but he realised Johnson was inert. There was silence and no more resistance.

For some time Magnani did not dare to move. He lay on Johnson like an exhausted lover, bleeding heavily from his hands and shoulder. He felt warmth seep beneath his coat as he raised himself, pushing with his hands. As he did so Johnson's breath escaped. If hell smelt Magnani knew it would smell like this. He was sure the man was dead. He lurched from the alley, still holding the knife in his right hand. Somehow in the struggle it had passed between them, a token of their enmity. He folded it and dropped it into a bin, and began the walk to Buen Vista, spilling his blood as he went. It made splashes on the wet stone but was washed away by the rain.

Getting to Buen Vista was a half-remembered blur of pain that racked him with each stumble. He shrank against walls when people passed him by, desperately wanting help but praying they would take him for a drunk. The indifference of the New York streets helped. In his own land he would have been investigated. Here they let bloodied bodies be. It seemed an age before the door opened to his knocks. Pearson stood before him, Pearson who was in California, in a white shirt that dazzled Magnani. He saw the grin of welcome turn to concern as he fell inside.

A black man bent over Magnani, probing him with his hands. There was pain but not the searing kind he had experienced when he walked. This was dulled, and called faintly to his brain from parts of his body he could not identify. Pearson came into his vision.

'How you doing, man? We was worried. This here is Doc Lawrence, he's fixed you up, Frank.'

'You were cut up pretty bad,' the doctor said. 'I had to stitch you up here, and here.' He pointed to Magnani's shoulder, and face. Instinctively he tried to touch the spots but his hand was held.

'Take it easy son, you'll bust the stitches.'

The attempt to move filled him with nausea. The doctor read his thoughts.

'It will leave a scar here, but a small one. Like this.' He traced a crescent on his own cheek. Your back will be pretty colourful for a while but I don't reckon many people will get to see that. Don't get up for a few days. I'll be back then to take the stitches out. I've given you a few shots so you'll feel woozy. Pearson here has the medication for you.'

Pearson saw the doctor out as Magnani scanned the room. Each turn of his head brought a wave of sickness. Eileen was not there, and he was in her bed again. Pearson came back.

'Don't worry about Lawrence, he's cool. Fixes up the guys when they in trouble. He ain't exactly a doctor no more, they took his licence away from him. I think he started using his own dope.'

Pearson saw the worry crease Magnani's brow and smiled. 'He's all right, rest easy now.'

Magnani lay back but was afraid to close his eyes. He found he could talk but his words were thickened by whatever he had been given.

'Do you want to tell me what happened?' Pearson asked. 'Is anybody going to come here looking for you?'

'The police, maybe.'

'What you done, Frank?'

'I've killed Johnson.'

'You serious?'

'Have I ever been anything else?'

'How? Where? Jesus Christ, what happened?'

'A fight. He was waiting for me outside the club. He got me into an alleyway and pulled a knife. I came out on top somehow. I left him there.'

Pearson whistled. 'You lucky to be alive, boy. Johnson is good with that knife. You sure he's dead?'

'He must be. I cracked his head on the ground enough times. He must be.'

Whilst Magnani slept Pearson went over to the club to scout around, but there was no sign of Johnson in the alley and no police activity. He stopped in at Nina's and knew by its atmosphere that no clubland killing had been reported. Very casually he asked about Johnson but no-one had seen him. He collected Eileen, who had been visiting Filigree's widow overnight, and told her the news. She was shaken and clung to his arm. Pearson was chided for leaving Magnani and urged back to Buen Vista. At one point Eileen pushed him along. He loved her when she was like this, when he was needed. And he admired her concern for his friend.

For some time they sat by Magnani as he slept in their bed. He moaned occasionally, and indistinct words came from him. Eileen was sure she heard her name and held her breath, but Magnani did not elaborate and Pearson thought nothing of it.

'Will he be allright?' Eileen asked.

'The doc said so. Said he'd be feverish some, but he gave him a shot for that.' Pearson shook his head. 'Shit, I never thought Frank would get himself into a street fight.'

'He can't have killed Johnson, can he?'

'Nah. I can't see anyone hauling Johnson away and keeping it quiet. Why should they? No, I think the man got hisself up and hightailed it out of that alley. Probably had a head as hard as his heart. But that's not good, Eileen.'

'Why? I don't want Frank to be a killer.'

'I know, but it means that it isn't over. Johnson will come for him again, you can count on that. He won't let it rest, he's one bad nigger.'

'What is Frank going to do?'

'He'll have to get out of town, or the country even. He ain't American, don't forget and that complicates things some. With that accent of his he stands out like a dick on parade.'

'Don't talk that way Pearson.'

'Sorry babe, I'm kind of fired up. I like Magnani, like him a lot. He's different, kinda. You like him too, don't you?'

'Yes, I like him.'

Magnani woke up. He saw Pearson's encouraging smile and Eileen's worried face. As his head cleared he realised the predicament he had heaped on her, he had brought trouble literally to her door. Eileen was a mask of stifled emotion and for a moment he wished Johnson had killed him. Then he felt the warmth of the bed and the reassuring tug of his stitches and changed his mind.

'Is the word out, about Johnson? he asked.

'Ain't nothing to be out,' Pearson said. 'You didn't kill that mother, Frank. He's upped and gone, I checked out that alley.'

'I was sure he was dead. His head...'

'No such luck. Man needed killing though.'

'Pearson!'

'Yeah, all right, babe. I know you don't like me talking like that. But you don't have to worry about no murder rap, Frank.'

It was not relief that Magnani felt, more a surge of ease, as if the hook which had settled in his gut had been loosed. Pearson's next words pulled it taut again very quickly.

'It's not over with Johnson, Frank.'

'What do you mean?'

'He'll do his best to kill you. Has to now. His kind always has to. He'll be around the streets, telling it his way. And you are white, he'll use that. It won't be safe for you here in Harlem, or anywhere else in town. You'll have to check out, go home maybe.'

'Yes, that would be best, Frank,' Eileen said.

'No, I don't want to do that, not go back anyway. I've done nothing wrong, and if I go now that's it as far as playing here in concerned.'

Magnani could hardly believe his own words. In the aftermath of the fight, his treatment and the returning sting of the wounds, he found he could talk bravely, and was not sure if he was acting.

Pearson scratched his head. 'Well, if your mind is made up on that, best get out of New York for a while. See how the dust settles. Maybe Johnson will get sunk by some other dude, or choke on his own dope. He's sliding down now that Stein has cut him loose.'

Eileen nodded.

'Go south,' Pearson said, 'I got a few contacts in New Orleans and Florida — Miami would be best, quieter there for a jazz man.'

It came to Magnani that he knew very little about America. It was a series of visual references gleaned from Hollywood films, and a thin vein of knowledge learnt from a few books.

'You mean I should play down there?' Magnani asked.

'Hell no, you'd be too easy to spot. No, you'll have to do something else, a job where you can hide away. When we know where you are, Eileen will write you if it's safe to come back. Think you can do this, Frank?'

'We'll soon see, won't we?'

'I still think you should go home Frank,' Eileen said. She barely concealed her agitation.

'No, my mind is made up. I came here to do something in music,' Magnani said.

'And that book, man, don't forget that.'

Pearson beamed at him and gave Eileen a squeeze. The more the implications of his cheating made inroads into him the more Magnani liked Pearson. The drummer had in abundance qualities he desired in himself. He was the first man he could call friend without unease, yet this friendship might soon be arrested, if not ended, if the truth came out.

They left him to sleep and rest. Eileen went to the Door to work and Pearson stayed at Buen Vista. He brought Magnani food and a bottle of beer. Eileen's absence made it easier.

'Pearson, I haven't thought to ask you, with all that's happened. What are you doing here, you should be in California.'

'Gig fell through, man. Too many junkies in that outfit. They was shooting up every chance they got. I came back on the Greyhound, without my drums, can you believe that? Lenny, the alto player, is bringing them in the station wagon. I lent it to him, but I can trust him — I think.'

'I'm sorry about that.

'Forget it. Another day, another gig, another dollar. And I got quite a few of them.' He fanned bills in Magnani's face. 'Feel the cooling breeze of money, Frank. They paid good see, while it lasted. I can stake you to go down south.'

'No, I've got money.'

'Like shit.

'I can get it.'

'How?

'The guitar. I can pawn it.'

'Pawn your axe! You crazy?'

'You said I could never play down there. What's the point of it wasting away here?'

'The point is you don't know when you will be back. You can't take a chance on that. If the guitar goes where you gonna get another like it? They cost.'

'There's always guitars.'

'I seen you with that thing. It's part of you, Frank. I seen you polish it and fawn over it like it was a dame.'

Better, Magnani thought. 'I can't travel with it,' he said.

'Then leave it here with us, I'll be your pawnbroker. Give you the same money as Mo down the street. Pay me back when you want it back.'

Magnani knew it was hopeless to argue with the drummer. He acquiesced but made plans to pawn it anyway. That night Pearson went over to the sisters McGraw and brought Magnani's possessions to Buen Vista.

'I told those old buzzards you had gone back to England. Said you got religion and didn't need no guitar no more.'

'Did they believe you?'

'I don't know. One of them said that music was one of the arms of the devil, but whether they believed me or not they sure as hell will tell everyone what I said. It ought to cool your trail some Frank, make it harder for Johnson.'

'Any news of him?'

'Nah. He's dropped into a sewer somewhere.'

Magnani was able to get up later. He moved gingerly from bed to sofa, the stitches tensing with each step. The room swam a little but he was glad to be out of the bed. As the shock of the fight wore off, tension replaced it. It thrived in Buen Vista. Eileen had the night off so the three of them sat together, Pearson the garrulous cuckold, Eileen silenced by guilt and Magnani trying to act normally. Pearson's natural honesty was a badge of which the man was not aware and it coloured Magnani's thinking. The drummer was determined to see no ill in his friend. Magnani could not understand how his seduction of Eileen brought him closer to Pearson but it did. When Eileen retired early Magnani found himself talking about his past, something he had never done. It was as if a show of openness on his part could lessen his guilt.

He described the Welsh valleys to Pearson. It was hard for the man from Kansas to grasp the idea of almost permanent wetness. He came from a land of brown prairie, where dust lined the backs of farmers' throats. Pearson knew extremes of heat and cold but Magnani's valley, crowded with industry and people, and perpetually green-black,could not be visualised. Poverty could. Both men had experienced it, it permeated their past and gave them a common ground. Because of it they held similar views on how their societies should change.

Pearson drank liberally but Magnani was not allowed any. The drummer grew maudlin.

'Yeah, well Frank, perhaps things are changing slowly, like you say, but I can't change the colour of this.' He tapped his cheek.

'You don't want to change it.'

'No, not now. There was times though, when I was younger. You'd see some of the boys go into them stores, buy stuff to de-curl their hair, lighten their skins. After a few weeks they looked like black ghosts. I understood it though. Seems we had the worst of both worlds, poor and black, black and poor. Jazz was the only escape for someone like me. Tell me some more about that Welfare State of yours — you got to be kidding me, ain't you?'

Magnani had to wait three days until he could leave Buen Vista. Pearson did not want him to show himself on the streets, despite the disappearance of Johnson.

Mo's Pawn Shop was half a block away. Magnani had often passed it, wondered at the complexity of its goods. Establishments like it were a fundamental part of a jazz musician's life, his place of barter. Hopes were left in abeyance there, or abandoned to die by people on the slide, to collect dust until they were bought by the next wave of aspirants.

He peered through the window, cupping his hands against the wire grill. He saw that many players had been here before him. Lines of brass instruments hung from hooks in the ceiling, out of reach of the inquisitive young. They lorded it over the shelves of watches and assorted bric-a-brac. There were racks of faded suits and clothes from other generations. Magnani scanned the street both ways, like a man about to do something wrong, and quickly entered Mo's moribund world.

He was met by the smell of profitable decay. Mo was at his station behind the counter. His eyes dwelt on Magnani for a few seconds and rather longer on the guitar case. People did not much interest him, unless there came a time when they too could be pawned. By the insignia on the case he had already priced the guitar within, before Magnani said a word or showed it to him.

Mo adjusted his beret, tilted it for business and bade Magnani good day.

'Hello young man. Come to leave that with me?'

'It depends...'

'On how much I'll allow.'

'It's a good instrument.'

'Sure, let's have a look at it.' Mo's sleeves were rolled up and his eyes were keen in his grey head.

He was quite fond of jazz players, they were such good customers, and so few ever came back. He had established a trade in instruments that rivalled music stores. By necessity he kept up with the music, though he hated its modern cacophony — so impossible to understand, so unlike the waltzes of the old country, so like the hard streets of the new.

'You play be-bop?' he asked Magnani.

'Sometimes. I play all sorts.' The last thing Magnani wanted to do was talk music.

'You are English, I see. Been hurt too.' Mo looked at him more closely and thought to ask something, but did not. 'I hear be-bop is out,' he continued, 'it doesn't seem long ago they were saying it would never catch on. Then it was the thing, now its over. This is one fast country. Musicians like you deserve more recognition —' Mo was now into his musical spiel — 'Jazz is the classical music of this century, America's music.'

Not knowing Mo, Magnani was softened by his words and took two hundred dollars for the guitar, a hundred less than Mo would have paid. The pawnbroker wrote him out a ticket and took the guitar to a backroom. He carried it like a prize. Magnani stuffed the notes into his pocket before they could soil his hands. As he left the store he tried to keep his mind as blank as possible, but it was hopeless, the sense of loss was too great. His career was aborted and might be fractured forever. He had to fight the urge to rush back to the shop and plead with Mo for the return of the guitar. At least there was the book, he tried to buoy himself up with this thought. Paper and pens were cheap, and he could write anywhere, without the long chain of circumstance that music needed. Buen Vista was still empty when he got back.

Magnani's stitches were taken out the next day. A sweating Doc Lawrence fumbled at them and was in a hurry to leave, anxious not to be seen in daylight. Pearson drove him back to the heart of Harlem in the station wagon he had regained that morning. Magnani lay on the sofa until he heard the motor fade, then got up and dressed. In the bedroom he had vacated Eileen slept off her night shift. He looked in on her and wondered if he was seeing her for the last time. She slept in her usual position, sunk in bedclothes with just her hair showing. He mouthed goodbye.

He left Pearson fifty dollars for the doctor and took the Greyhound for Miami late afternoon, a trip that would take almost three days. He carried his sailor's sack and felt the same raw cold of his arrival. His right hand was free of the weight it had held for the last eight years. In the sack were the Haydn notes and one book, a volume of Walt Whitman he thought suitable for the journey. The rest he left at Buen Vista to lessen his load, and perhaps encourage faint hope of a return.

By the middle of the night they were already through Philadelphia and into the heartland of Pennsylvania. The irony of a night passage through a land Magnani longed to see was not lost on him as he huddled in the back seat of a full bus. Even in the middle of a cruel winter people wanted to move in America. It was a country with a shifting populace, people looking for roots and finding none; its myths were founded on it.

Magnani glanced at faces as haunted as his own. Others were expectant and waiting for journey's end, a few were as blank as the seats they sat on. He tried to sleep, leaning his head against the rain-splashed window. But it was cold and it caught the drone of the engine. Magnani fingered the knife marks in his cheek and wondered where he was going.

SEVEN

The bus made good progress, churning out a steady fifty miles an hour on the unclogged roads. Magnani dozed fitfully. In between snatches of sleep he remembered the lights of heavy industry, large plant spewing out flame and smoke into the night as the bus cut through their world. He knew this was the America most like his own country. His people had migrated to the coal mines and iron works of Pennsylvania. He scanned roadsigns for any names that hinted at the presence of his countrymen but saw mainly Anglo-Saxon ones, with a smattering of other European influence. Harrisburg sounded promising, but they did not pass through it.

Magnani missed the guitar. It should be at his side on the spare seat, his familiar companion, a reminder that if all else failed he had it with him. Now he felt naked without it, and each steelworks or belching foundry incited further pessimism. He hated their despoiling of the valleys of his own land, and knew their filthy hold on communities. Here they appeared even more dominant, for they were stranger, more vast and threatening. The bus stopped in a place that was a maze of twisted steel, its air heavy with heat and grime and thundering noise. It had a feel of inevitable control. Things would always be produced here and men would always serve; machinery had taken over. He wiped clear a piece of window and watched the night shift of a foundry stumble out into the dawn, slightly dazed by their labour and the cold air. A man walked past the bus, his tread leaden, his eyes glazed with fatigue. He looked at the passengers as if they were creatures from another world, and turned up his collar in disgust. It had never occurred to Magnani that work in such places might be anything other than awful, or that men might even see value in it.

They were on the outskirts of Washington before he gained full alertness. He could not get excited about the capital for his would be the briefest of glimpses. There would be just time to breakfast in the bus depot. His attempt at solitary travel might consist of shabby stopping points and dank washrooms, used by travellers as furtive as himself, all sharing the same miserable cold. And Magnani was more a fugitive than most, his travel was a flight, and might have no end. Someone muttered about the White House 'being over there' but Magnani did not bother to look. Washington was cloaked in fog and he was glad of it. He wanted to pass through the north with as much memory as possible blotted out.

People left the bus at the Washington depot, new travellers boarded. The vehicle filled up and the seat next to Magnani was claimed, by a young man who stood looking at Magnani's coat until he realised that this was the last seat available. Reluctantly he removed the coat and hunched closer against the window. His new companion grinned and started talking, as Magnani knew he would. He was just out of boyhood with a rock and roll quiff in his hair and he smelled of grease and cheap aftershave. His name was Arthur Malloy and he was on his way to Nashville, to get married. Magnani wondered at this for a moment and managed to parry loquaciousness with nods, shrugs and the occasional grunt. Malloy did not care at all and they endured each other until Richmond, where Malloy disembarked for another route. He was going to take a train, he said, and ride across Tennessee like Casey Jones. It was the only thing Magnani remembered of his constant talking.

Railroads. Magnani thought how little he had seen of them in America, yet they were at the heart all his ideas of the country, symbol of growth and movement, and domination. The bus had skirted tracks from time to time, and diesel trains stood waiting at factory sidings, but he had not seen more. There was a longer stop in Richmond and the weather grew milder in Virginia. Magnani ate lunch and read a newspaper. At the bottom of one page he saw an advertisement for a railroad company. It showed the sketch of a steam train, the type he knew from Hollywood westerns, a large funnelled engine with a huge cowcatcher on the front. It intrigued him with its hint at the past, a past Magnani once thought of as romantic and noble but now doubted its existence at all. He asked about the company at the lunch counter.

'Yip,' an old man told him, 'still running 'em old puffers. Not many lines left now, the diesels have taken over, but they still go to Lynchburg, Roanoke and into the Blue Ridge area.'

The names meant little to Magnani but the news excited him. He could not believe·this new land could retain such throwbacks to another age. It would be an extravagant waste of his bus ticket but he decided there and then to throw it away, and ride the steam train.

The Penn Flyer chugged rather than flew. Its progress was a smoky forty miles an hour at best, half this on gradients. Magnani loved it. He sat in an open carriage with old people and children, conscious that he was a stranger but not feeling so much on the run. The train was on its way to the ominous sounding town of Lynchburg. New

York was a long way from here, more so in ideology than distance. As he had in Vermont, Magnani marvelled at the changes America could encompass in its regions.

He smelt poverty. It was something he could always pick out, no matter how unfamiliar the land. The train made many stops at small stations where people lounged aimlessly. Magnani recognised the same workless look as his own valley. Groups of old men scanned the train for what or who it might bring. The clear light showed up their scrawny turkey-like necks and thin frames clothed in denim dungarees. He knew most of them must have worked the trains, they had a look of permanent attachment, unable or unwilling to leave the place of their labours. Some had faded railroad hats, which they wore high on their heads. There were hamlets of shacks that might have been derelict were it not for the trails of chimney smoke. He was heading south, but these people were white — white and poor. Magnani was not prepared for this but it made him feel closer to the place. As a small boy stood in front of him and dared him for his name Magnani thought how strange the initial impact of America had been, how linked by language to his own country and divided by almost everything else. On hearing his name the boy told him he 'talked stoopid' and ran back to his mother, scowling at Magnani from behind her legs. Casual thoughts of working in this region went through his head though most of the smaller towns looked patently not in need of the little he could offer. He sensed a gentler pace to life here. There was no rush. He hoped this trait would increase the further south he went. Being carried by a relic of a quickly passing age confirmed the feeling. Not yet thirty, Magnani took pleasure in the past. It could be judged, twisted to conform to his viewpoint, worried over, grieved and longed for. Whatever stance one took it was always safe, always behind one.

In this mood Magnani was given to going over the forty or so years of his chosen music, tracking its sources back as far as the African brought to the plantations of America from West Africa. When his thoughts were positive he saw the intricate threads of jazz's existence, how whole peoples were mapped out by it, how each decade was signposted by musical changes, how it made some people happy and interested in it, and hence interested in themselves. How it provided an escape for a tiny percentage of the downtrodden and gave them a secret code to live by. Jazz was a metaphor for any sharp part of life, and the blues was its rawer brother — the first feelers of sound that hit people in the fields and the streets. Each emotion it produced could be found anywhere, in the factories Magnani had watched with fearful eyes, in the closeness of the valley he had come from, anywhere. Music was his chosen path in life, he had fought to stay on it and even if he strayed now he doubted he would find another road.

When Magnani's mood was bad he despaired. Creativity turned inwards became self-mockery and hopelessness. To walk a thin line between these opposing forces was the lot of all artists, 'the whisper and the shout' some called it. The best side was never more than a whisper to Magnani but it could be enough; it propelled him to the next stage of playing.

The abandonment of the bus and discovery of the train put Magnani in his best frame of mind since that first New York jam session. After a short doze he rummaged in his sack for the Haydn notes. This act increased the attention of his fellow passengers. They did not know which was more alien, the person or his strange act with pen and paper.

Lynchburg came and went. Magnani saw little of the place from the station, and forgot his foreboding about it. He was going to Roanoke for no other reason than liked its name. The train was hauling him into the Blue Ridge mountains. It climbed stoutly through wooded hills, and skirted the slopes of deep-sided valleys. Each wooden town was stopped at, the train had a duty to them all. Magnani could not get used to the way settlements appeared alongside the tracks, especially when night fell. Once they stopped at a place where he could look up a main street at the shuttered stores and deserted boarded sidewalks. There was no stone platform to divide track from town here, the train wheeled itself in, a trusted part of the community. From Joe's Eats came a yellow light which only served to enhance the town's state of abandonment. Magnani watched a dog select a favourite post to piss against and did not wonder there were few people about. Where could they go, what could they do? The dog sprayed the wood with one squirt and pawed its way back inside Joe's. Magnani began to wonder how many countries America might hold within its borders. Like New York it was cut up into racial and physical territories.

The first Negro family he saw in the south got on the train. They sat at the end of the carriage and stared at the floor, parents and three children concentrating on a patch of wood in a collective trance. As the pulled out of this unknown town the lights from the diner caught the man's face, etching it with lines. Bud Filigree's dreams of power for his people came to Magnani's mind, but they seemed a long way from here, hot thoughts that might ferment in white cities but not in the poor breaking grounds he was travelling through.

It was past midnight when Magnani stepped down from the train at Roanoke. He was loathe to say goodbye to the Flyer but his ticket ended here. He took a last look at the steaming engine and left the station. This was the largest town he had been in since Lynchburg but like the others it might have been empty. A few passengers melted away from him on their way to known destinations. A woman was picked up in a farmer's truck which roared off into the darkness, with no back lights visible. Magnani was envious. He put up the collar of his coat and slung his sack over his shoulder, wishing he had packed his Lazurus Brothers suit, rather than worn it. The trousers flapped as he walked, he must have looked like a city slicker, sloping back to the family home to cause trouble, and be looked after.

Arriving in Roanoke in the quiet hours of a winter's night served Magnani well, in the bustle of a morning he might never have met Wilbur Kaine. The old man was sitting in a car parked outside the one diner Magnani found open. It was a car almost as old as its occupant, a monster of chrome and steel that might have ferried gangsters in the Twenties. Like the train it was out of place. Magnani stopped by it, and looked into the diner and its emptiness.

'Nothing like a Virginian town at this time of night, eh? You can breathe the lonesomeness, don't you think?'

The voice was soft, with a burr to it that put Magnani in mind of a smooth malt. It was a moment before he realised the words were addressed to him. He looked into the car to see a small man return his gaze, a thin shouldered figure with a panama hat on its head and a tobacco-stained moustache on its upper lip. The man looked like a creation of Faulkner or Tennessee Williams, the token liberal in the twisted backwaters town. Magnani was wary and did not answer at first.

'Just off the Flyer, are you?'

Magnani was looked up and down. 'Don't much look like a fella from round these parts.'

Magnani wondered if the man could be the police but surely he was too ancient. 'Just travelling through,' he said.

'Would have thought you would have stayed on the train in that case.'

Magnani shrugged and went into the diner. He sat at its counter and ordered coffee from a woman aged before her time. Unlike the man in the car she served him without interest, hardly looking up as she poured her tepid liquid. Magnani heard a car door open and shut and braced himself for company. The old man took the stool next to him, looking even smaller now. His light suit was good quality, but faded and bulging with over-filled pockets. Around his neck was a string tie which suited his colonial appearance.

'Where you heading?' the old man asked.

'I'm not sure.'

'I'm on my way south, to Tampa, Florida — that's a long way.'

He drank from the same coffee-pot, smacking each draught against his lips. Magnani felt eyes drilling him again.

'Don't want to talk eh? Can't blame you. You probably think I'm a dadblasted old fool but I like talking to folks. No point travelling otherwise. Learnt most of what I know about people from talking. You are not American, are you son? I caught something in your voice out there.'

'No. I'm British.'

'Thought so. You're a rare creature in these parts.' The old man framed a question with his mouth but did not ask it.

'I've been up to Roanoke to see a few people — family business, you know. It's Tampa I live now. I run an institution down there. I suppose you'd call it that.'

The man looked as if he should be well into retirement. Now the questions had stopped Magnani relaxed, and talked a little easier.

'What type of institution?' he asked.

'One for Mongoloid kids.'

The old man sucked on his coffee again; it sounded as if he had slurped all his life. He reached into a pocket for a thin cigar case. Magnani refused the one offered to him.

'I don't like that name,' Kaine said, 'conjures up images of Genghis Khan and the like, but its what they are known as so I use it — saves time. I'm Wilbur A. Kaine, by the way.'

Magnani took the hand offered and shook it, surprised at the strength in the old bones.

'Magnani, Frank Magnani,' he said.

'Italian name, eh? Yes, you got some in you, I can see. Good meeting you, Frank.'

Magnani stilled the complaints of his stomach with a piece of stale pie and tried to count the rest of the change inside his pocket without Kaine noticing. There was precious little of it left and soon he would be paying for his profligacy with the train ticket.

'Broke, huh?' Kaine's eyes twinkled.

'No. I'm all right.'

'Hmm. A broke Britisher in the depths of Virginny on a cold February night — in a city boy's suit yet.' Kaine smiled at the look or Magnani's face. 'Just kidding, Frank. Could you use a lift? I hate travelling alone. I like to talk. I guess you have realised that. If you are travelling through you must be going my way.'

The offer was a chance to eke out his money but Magnani held back. Kaine did not press him. He finished a second cup of coffee and left, tapping a goodbye on Magnani's shoulder as he got up.

'Good luck with your journey son. I hope you find what you are looking for. When I was your age it took me some time to realise what that was.'

Magnani waited until he heard the motor start up before joining him. He left more coins than were necessary on the counter in his haste to catch Kaine but need not have hurried. The old man had the passenger door open for him.

'Thought you might have a change of heart. Glad you did. Get in Frank, I want to drive through the night. Don't need much sleep at my age — you can get some though.'

Magnani was still going south, with a talkative old man he knew nothing about. Since stepping off the Southampton quay he had managed to turn every aim he had on its head, and his guitar lay fallow in a pawn shop. He slept fitfully, driven and, in a way, protected by a man more than twice his age.

Virginia was a bridge state between north and south; it liked to dub itself the home of civilised America. When Magnani woke he saw the truer south of North Carolina.

'I filled her up while you slept,' Kaine told him. 'We've covered a lot of ground — not bad for two old wrecks.' He tapped himself and the dashboard of the car. Magnani rubbed his eyes and stretched on the long seat. He wondered how old Kaine was. The man might be seventy, certainly too old to be running an institution. It was hard to tell from his face which had been weathered by the sun from an early age, the criss-crossing of lines meant little. Almost hidden in these crevices Kaine's blue eyes sparkled. They showed no sign of fatigue from driving, or from life.

Kaine was a fountain of talk but he did not bore his passenger. As they headed into the heart of the south Kaine offered a precis of his life. He was Doctor Kaine, a psychiatrist and Yale graduate, a product of the Old Dominion as he liked to call Virginia. His family could be traced back to Jamestown and 1603, from the first Americans of English stock. He was a bachelor 'long confirmed', a democrat with liberal leanings, the latter becoming evident as Kaine commented on the country they passed through.

'We'll stop in Atlanta, Georgia, capital of the heart of darkness.'

'What?'

'Conrad. Haven't you read him? I took you for a reader.'

'I am.'

'Right. Remember that guy Kurtz? Reminds me of Georgia somehow. This here,' Kaine took one hand from the wheel and spread it around laconically, 'this here is a tinderbox, Frank. It hasn't stopped smoking since the Civil War. The blacks won't be denied much longer.'

'I haven't had much time to follow the politics here,' Magnani said. 'It is a confusing system for an outsider.'

'Hell, not just for an outsider. American politics thrives on mess, I guess. I was over in England once, in the war, the first big one. I liked the parties you had there, it was easier for a man to choose. Here it is more of a game, and definitely a business.'

'I think it's that everywhere.'

'Hah, what do we have here? A young cynic?'

Kaine laughed, a dry rasp that rose over the car's engine.

'You are the age for it, I guess. Not too young, not too old.'

Kaine seemed as if he was talking to himself at this point.

'Doubt always comes after hope,' he muttered. 'Sometimes hope comes again, like a fresh tide.'

Magnani saw that Kaine might appear an opinionated old buffer but he liked his host.

They reached Atlanta by mid evening. Kaine had stopped once for two hours to sleep under his hat and let the engine cool. The weather grew steadily milder, until it was clement and almost spring-like. Sometimes Kaine kept to the highways, other times he took the car on what he called 'scenic routes', offering Magnani a commentary on each region they reached. Magnani received America through the viewpoint of Wilbur A. Kaine.

In Atlanta Magnani offered to pay for some of expenses of the journey but Kaine shooed him away.

'The gas I would have to buy anyway,' he said, 'but you can buy the food here if you must.'

Kaine drove through the outskirts. Pillared houses spread from the roadside, some of them achieving mansion status.

'This is the money end of town,' Kaine said, 'only poor folk you'll see here are the ones serving the rich folk.' He nodded at a white suited butler who stood in a doorway, his face lost in shadow.

'Waiting for his master's voice,' he said.

The feel and spirit of Magnani's surroundings was changing. The climate and hustle of the north was gone. Virginia had prepared him in part for this but the languid, timeless air of Atlanta still surprised him. He imagined its heavy inactivity in summer, the exotic heart of a great power which had ripened in another age, and still clung to it. Kaine divined his thoughts.

'Not like New York, eh? I like to call Atlanta the rotten core of the States. Not exactly fair on the place but I've never lost the sense of frustration I felt when I first came down here. When they lost their slaves a lot of the southern whites curled up and hibernated. They still sit around discussing the old battles, as if they were there, for Christsake. Living off Bull Run. They reject the future because they can't find a place in it, and their jealousy of the north maintains their hatred. Sort of a warped kind of life.'

'You don't sound optimistic,' Magnani said.

'Hard to be son. But there is a slice of folks down here who would change things, if they ever get a chance. Change is a very dangerous thing down here.'

'I met black people in New York who were very radical.'

'Did you now? That's why they are in New York. Wouldn't last long down here. The Klan is still powerful, and no-one is really interested in stopping them. Hell, half the police force is in it.'

'I read in the northern papers that there has been some attempt to integrate black students into high schools.'

'Some. Perhaps that might start things moving. Trouble is the south has not got much the north wants, or needs. Its good for providing men in times of war but otherwise it's an embarrassment, I guess. Not what America wants to show to the world.'

'I was surprised how poor parts of America are.'

'Sure. Poverty is the rock we were built on. Our system demands it. Wealth only trickles down so far, or it would not stay wealth. Roosevelt's New Deal stuff before the war tried to address the problem but that was never going to work.' Kaine's eyes flashed as he laughed. 'Hell Frank, it was un-American. Nowadays its bad if you had ever been a part of it — makes you a dangerous Red.'

They had another five hundred miles travel to reach Tampa. Entering Florida from the north presented a strange perspective to Magnani. He had expected a softening of the harsher qualities of Georgia but was greeted by a land almost bare of human imprint. Timber covered most of it, and they passed vast farms with few outbuildings.

'Small places are being swallowed up,' Kaine said. 'They got these huge growing factories now.'

He waved a dismissive hand at the landscape. 'They ship in migrant labour, blacks and Mexicans, to do the seasonal work, then they ship 'em out again, before they put down roots. They got it down to a fine art. Were you expecting beaches and everglades? That stuff is down south.'

'How about Tampa?'

'Halfway between the two. Not much there, not for an exciting young man like yourself.'

Magnani was not sure if he was being made fun of.

'Tampa Bay is the kind of place they'll be developing for tourists and suchlike. Its already started in places. Folks will be coming to us to die, its perfect for that.'

Even Kaine had to sleep that night. They pulled into a truckers' stop and slept in the car. Kaine made no mention of getting a room, which eased Magnani's worry about money. Fortunately the car held two sleeping men easily. Magnani slept in the back with his sack for a pillow and was quite comfortable. In the morning he used some spare change to share a washroom with grizzled truck drivers. As he showered he was eyed suspiciously by tattooed bodies. Someone whistled at him but he was left alone. After breakfast they set out on the final leg.

Throughout the journey the realisation grew in Magnani that he would be staying with Kaine in Tampa. Nothing was said directly but as Kaine's wing enveloped him Magnani felt the need to make some offer, perhaps a commitment to work at the old man's home. He knew that a subtle manipulation was in play but he did not care. He had no ideas of his own and nowhere to go. The road was full of chance encounters, perhaps this one with Kaine would prove useful.

The weather had warmed to a pleasant balm by the time they reached Tampa. Magnani sat in his shirt sleeves but Kaine had not changed any of his clothing. 'I don't feel the sun until June,' he explained. He waited until they were entering the grounds of the Kaine Institution before formally asking Magnani if he wanted a job.

'We could use someone,' he said. 'I can't pay much but there'll be a room for you, and the food is plentiful — and sometimes edible.'

'What would I do?'

'Things that needed doing. Are you handy, can you fix things?'

'Do I look it?'

'No, I guess not. John Carr, the man who does those things here, is getting kind of old.'

He wondered whether Kaine meant older than himself.

Magnani was intrigued by Kaine's set up. He imagined left-behind children cared for by geriatrics, but his first sight of the home was positive. It was larger than he expected, a two storey colonial-style house newly painted white. Two columns guarded the entrance, and low outbuildings added to the breadth of the house. They were ill-conceived and detracted from the gracious lines of the main building. Bougainvillaea grew on walls, as if to compensate for their ugly blackness. They would make a good show in spring.

It was mid-afternoon on the fifth day of Magnani's journey and he was glad it had come to an end, even if he did not know what kind of end. Kaine halted the car on the gravel drive between neatly trimmed lawns. It sighed and settled itself, at home.

'Well, she's done it again. A round trip of a few thousand miles without complaint. Be the last time, though. Welcome to my world, Frank.'

'I still don't know what I'm supposed to do here,' Magnani said.

'You could help out with the kids,' Kaine replied. 'We need young blood here. I still have ideas, but it gets harder to see them through. Here comes John Carr.'

Carr was not older than Kaine, though he was in his early sixties. He came down the front steps in a white coat as fresh as the paintwork, wearing a tie as black as he was. Magnani thought of the servant they had seen in Atlanta, and felt uncomfortable. Carr smiled at Kaine and arched his eyebrows at Magnani in a silent question.

'This is Frank Magnani, John. He's from England, a ship that passed by in my night, you might say. He's going to be working with us.'

Carr's eyebrows arched even higher as he took Kaine's bag from the car and preceded them inside.

The house smelled of cleanliness. Magnani stood on a polished wood floor and drew in the atmosphere which was quiet and undisturbed, the opposite to what he had expected. A large wall clock ticked by the door, a sonorous rhythm that suited the place. A desk stood opposite the entrance with a flight of stairs to one side. At the desk sat a woman, of similar age to Kaine. So far the institution was a more a home for the aged than a place for children.

'It's quiet,' Magnani said to Kaine. He noticed the marvellous acoustics of the room and felt a sudden ache for his guitar, a stab of recent memory which he had kept at bay in the car.

'Yes, it is,' Kaine answered. 'The kids are in another part. Come and meet Miss Muldaur.'

Magnani knew it had to be 'Miss'. In a way she reminded him of the sisters McGraw, sharing a similar air of faded gentility but the resemblance ended there. Miss Muldaur had a firm handshake and a steady gaze. It was open and friendly; it expected the best of people and promised to match it.

'This is Frank Magnani, Helen,' Kaine said. 'Picked him up on the road but he's no bum — he's English.'

Kaine laughed at what he presumed was a joke but Helen looked puzzled.

'She never can understand my humour. Frank, this is Helen Muldaur, been with me thirty years.'

'Thirty-one, Wilbur,'

'Still counting, eh?'

'Will you be working with us, Mr Magnani?'

'Of course he will,' Kaine answered. 'And call him Frank. Helen really runs this place,' he explained to Magnani, 'she keeps the wheels of finance turning, and papers over my failures of organisation. She's the only person who really knows what's going on around here.'

Kaine ushered him past the desk and up the stairs, his energy undiminished by the drive.

'We've got a room up here you can use,' Kaine said. 'It'll be a little dusty but Carr will fix it up for you. Quick he ain't, but he's thorough.'

They stopped at the top of the stairs and Magnani looked down at the expanse of wooden floor. It gave off a mahogany sheen that comforted the eye.

'Makes you feel like Rhett Butler, don't it?'

'Something like that.'

'Well, ain't no slaves here. John Carr likes to wear a white coat, but its his idea. He's got as equal a say as the rest of us.'

Magnani was curious at Kaine's increasingly colloquial speech. He was not used to 'ain't' from a doctor and dared a question. 'Why do you talk so unlike a professional man, Mr Kaine?'

'Call me Wilbur, the surname makes me feel too Biblical. The kind of places I first worked in rubbed off on me. I spent ten years unlearning Yale. I'm a working stiff and I talk like one. An affectation, I have to admit, but one that's taken me over, especially when I get back to this place. You think there's something wrong with it?'

'No, not at all. You are very different from a British doctor, that's all.'

'Good. Besides, I ain't got much of a chest to stuff my shirt with.'

Kaine showed Magnani to a large room half way down a corridor. Through its window Magnani saw the distant blue slash of coastline, with sails dotted on it.

'Sailboats,' Kaine said. 'You get a lot of them in the bay now. As I said in the car, times are changing here.'

'For the better?'

Kaine shrugged. 'Depends on your point of view.'

He sat down on the edge of the bed and Magnani saw age tug at him for the first time.

'Mine's not bursting with hope, Frank. We might as well have lost the last war, I reckon — we've been on the retreat ever since. This Cold War mentality, paranoid conformity, sterile values — "hey, he must be a good guy, look at his house" — the death of any sort of individuality. That's not my way. I still dream enough to think its not truly the American way, but I don't know.'

'Are you bitter?'

'Too old for that. But the fifties sure have been a disappointment. The decade of blankness, I call it. You see Frank, this country took a fall in 1929, the only time belief in the god of money was shaken to the core. That might have done some good, for people saw how like paper money really is., how it can vanish in the wind. The Roosevelt years were kind of hopeful but then the war came and the money came back and the men who controlled it came back and this time there was no way they were going to let go their hold. War was great for them. Our boys died in droves overseas while some people over here grafted like hell to produce defective material for them.'

Kaine's eyes were alive with emotion. Magnani was taken aback at the old man's ability to animate himself so quickly. He wished he knew more about America; to plead ignorance now would be insulting to Kaine.

Kaine got up from the bed, took him by the arm and wheeled him around the room.

'Do you know Frank, when the administration got round to doing something about that, those guys just had their wrists slapped. And now they hold sway, and always will I guess. Hence the glorious fifties. What must you think of me, Frank? I welcome you to my institution with a rail against my own land.'

'That's all right. It's a national trait in my country.'

'It's not like that here. If the wrong person heard me talking like this I'd be closed down. Rest up now Frank, come down to the desk at six — we have dinner then.'

Magnani rested but did not sleep. Kaine's bleak pronouncement on his country echoed on his own recent past. He agonized over his dislocation from his trade. His hold on any firm direction in his life was threadlike. He was twenty-eight years old, a worldly, immature man. The nightmares of his childhood haunted him but they wore adult clothing now and adapted to the passage of his life. Snakes still came through walls which talked about him, crowds of strangers still jeered at him in a public place, he was still a very small man in his dreams. Now he saw some of himself in Kaine, a man who was left out, perhaps by his politics, personality; or choice. So far music had protected Magnani, given his survival an edge, but now the guitar was gone, and he was alone.

The bed was comfortable,without the usual staleness of disuse. Despite not sleeping Magnani enjoyed it. He attacked it with his elbows until it enveloped him. Outside the light was fading to a soft yellow and it was time to go down to meet his fellow diners.

It was a sedate meal. Magnani shared a table with Kaine and his two assistants, Joyce Mendel and D.Bell. The latter's first name was never used, she would always be D.Bell, her initial merging into one name. It was how she wanted it. John Carr's wife Lena had cooked the food and he served it, again making Magnani feel uncomfortable. Lena helped with the children and was with them now, allowing the women an undisturbed meal.

They sat at one end of a table big enough for twenty. Magnani's presence instilled silence in the room. Whether there was disapproval of his being there Magnani was not sure, but he knew the group's equilibrium was disturbed. Kaine ran a quiet ship that had been unchanged for years.

Magnani ate some very good chicken, trying not to betray his hunger by bolting it down. D. Bell eyed him occasionally. She was a small woman of indeterminate age, perhaps fifty, possibly sixty. She had her hair cropped short as a boy's, which emphasised the thinness of her face. She looked like a bird about to flit. He thought her an unlikely person to work in Kaine's home but knew she could never be more unlikely than himself.

Magnani hoped Kaine would clarify his role, give him a firm base to work on. He looked across the table at the old man who smiled back at him. The garrulous driver of the journey down was changed, Kaine was pensive, and more like Magnani's idea of a doctor and principal. There was an air of lassitude in the room, and Magnani guessed it was a refuge for more than the children. The faces of Carr and the women yielded little. He wondered whether Kaine had gathered him up knowing that he was a bruised fruit, a man falling without direction, to be swept up like flotsam in Kaine's beach-combing sack. Then he wondered why.

'Is the food good?' Kaine asked him, breaking a silence of several minutes.

'Yes, fine.'

'Lena's a good cook, the kids love her pies and biscuits.'

'As do you, Wilbur.'

This was Joyce Mendel speaking. She was the youngest of the three, brighter and more cheerful than D. Bell. There was an air of faded glamour about her, like an old movie queen. She wore her hair long and over her shoulders, and there was a touch of make-up on her face. Magnani thought the table might break into conversation but there was a collective sigh and silence resumed. It became so heavy that Magnani took care not to break it by chinking his plate with his cutlery. No-one asked what he was doing in America or where he was from exactly. Either these people exercised the heights of discretion or they were too cut off from life to be interested.

When Magnani got back to his room he found it cleaned and the bed linen changed. He assumed Carr had done it whilst they ate. He slept for ten hours and dreamed of his first days in America, when hope was high. In the dream he played brilliantly on a silver stage and was warmed by applause, but the mood was violently fractured by a jump cut to Johnson and the smashing of his head against the ground. Magnani woke to a fine day with the bitter taste of realisation that he was far from music. He drew open the drapes and looked down on his new world.

There was a knock on the door and Carr stuck his head inside. 'Breakfast will be at eight-thirty, Mr. Magnani,' he intoned. His speech as flat as a plain, with just an edge of mockery in it, in the manner of true butlers. It would be hard to ever divine Carr's thoughts but he made Magnani feel like the charity case he was, which he had been for Pearson.

Kaine was more animated at breakfast, but the rest of his staff were absent.

'Things start moving around here at seven, Frank,' he said, 'especially when the sun shines. And the sun usually shines. It brings people out early, like plants. D. Bell and Joyce get the kids washed, dressed and fed, that's the first hurdle of their day.'

Kaine filled Magnani's cup with coffee. 'Do I make them sound like cattle? I don't mean to, but you have to have a good routine to survive. Some of our 'children' are forty years old and need constant watching. Ever been around Mongols, Frank?'

'There was one in my home village, a boy. He seemed happy enough, and impervious to the taunts most of us offered him. His parents never got over the shame of him.'

'No, that's the saddest thing. But they kept him?'

'Yes, I don't think anyone ever questioned that they should.'

'They can be happy souls, when things are going their way. But there's all types, like any other people. Folks seem to think the mentally retarded are like leaves off the same big cabbage. Its not like that at all. They show as wide a range of traits and emotions as our so called normal populace.'

'How many do you have here?'

'Sixteen. We haven't took anyone on for three years now, so they are all settled in, as much as they can ever be.'

'And their families?'

'Some come to see them, some don't. Some are dead. None of the kids are ever taken back. But they pay well for our services, enough for us to survive.' Kaine poured his third cup of coffee. He had a dependency on it. 'I liked to think we offered a chance at a dignified life here, somewhere where the kids could try to be people and not lumps to ridicule.'

'Why do you use the past tense?'

'Did I? Didn't mean to. That's what the Kaine Institution should be, Frank, but for our patrons we are a place where people can be hidden, secrets kept, and guilt exchanged perhaps. I did have schemes to return them into communities once but it proved so difficult. And I am much older now.'

'What am I to do today?'

'Joyce will be across for you in a while. She'll introduce you to our flock. See how you take to them, how they take to you. Try not to patronise them. Its easy to do but they'll sense it. They have an innate ability to detect bullshit, even if they don't know what it is. Some, like Wesley, our oldest, will annoy you greatly at times. He's sly and can be kind of ornery, he can be a puncher too. And Patricia, she's our Siren. She has an engaging little habit of lifting up her dress to strangers — she has been know to take a pee on the lawn in times of stress. You'll know pretty soon if you can live with them.'

Kaine was again the man Magnani had first met, the tiredness peeled from him to reveal another layer of sceptical energy.

'There are rewards,' he continued. 'They can ooze with love, and that comes straight from the heart when they give it. They have not the means to contain it, or condition it, or spoil it. They don't know how to use it at all so they just give it. And it has kept me going down all these years. Joyce too. Here is the girl. He's all yours, Joyce. Take him to the day house and let him loose.'

As he walked with Joyce Magnani thought how lax Kaine was. There had not been even the most cursory questioning of his past or his character. His suitability to work in a place like this had not been examined. He was in Tampa on the hunch of an eccentric old man.

They crossed a lawn to one of the outbuildings. Magnani heard noise coming from it, a garbled hubbub of humanity that increased as he neared its source.

'Don't be fooled by the atmosphere you have found here so far Frank,' Joyce said, 'you are about to enter the front line.'

She ushered him into a large room where D. Bell stood facing ten of Kaine's charges. They were engaging in exercises, or at least D. Bell was. She raised and lowered her arms, animating her meagre frame into a semblance of rhythm. A girl Magnani knew must be Patricia copied her rather well, the rest were a shambles of unsuccessful effort. Patricia increased her motions when she saw Magnani. She gyrated her hips and swirled up her dress, and a thin sliver of saliva ran down her chin. He was instantly the centre of attention, D. Bell ignored as the children crowded around him. A boy with a huge moon of a face tapped Magnani on the arm. His smile was disarming; it cracked his face and displayed an array of ruined teeth, which looked at odds with the slavering mouth and the moist, lost eyes.

'This is Tony,' Joyce said, nodding to the discomforted D. Bell. 'Children, this is Mr. Frank Magnani.' She spelt out his name as if he was a foreign country.

'We always call them children, Frank,' she said in an aside. 'It's easier that way.'

Although hard to gauge the ages, Magnani saw that no child was under fifteen years. Patricia sidled up to him. She talked quite clearly.

'I like you,'she murmured. 'You are nice.'

She made a grab at his genitals which he just avoided. Magnani stumbled into the arms of the amused Tony. Patricia's act caused an outbreak of giggling and a gasp from the reddened face of D. Bell.

'Patricia, will you stop that.'

'It's all right,' Magnani said. 'No harm done.'

'That's not the point.'

'They don't see many new faces,' Joyce explained, leading him to the far end of the room. D. Bell continued with the exercise, which was now hopeless. Heads swivelled in Magnani's direction, and a fresh wave of giggles followed each subsiding one.

'Is this a usual kind of day?' Magnani asked.

'Yes. D. Bell takes them through a work out, then we have a crafts' hour. We go out from time to time. We have a deal with a cinema downtown, and a few other places. A high school donated us their old bus a few years ago.'

'But what do they actually do all day?'

'Live here.' Joyce sounded glum. 'If you have any ideas Frank, we'd be glad to hear them.'

'I don't think it is my place...'

'Sure it is. You work here now, don't you? We have no caste system, say what you like when you'd like to. Wilbur, he had a lot of ideas when I first came here. Treat them as individuals, he said, find out what each one wants out of life. We tried, but it became somewhat blurred as time went on. And he has so much administration to do nowadays. Ideas rarely get out of his office.'

Joyce left him with D. Bell and the group. Making sure he knew where Patricia was at all times he tried to talk to some of them. Tony took it on himself to do the introductions. He gripped Magnani's arm with considerable strength as he marched him around.

'This is John, this is Emilio, this is Frank, same as you. Frank is very stupid.'

At first it was hard for Magnani to decipher Tony's speech. It came in wet spurts, accompanied by sprays of spit and effort. When he waited for an answer Tony's mouth sagged, revealing teeth to contrast the perfection of Patricia's. Yellow stumps twisted over their neighbours to form a reptilian-like wall, a row of dereliction which might have made Tony appear fierce but only added to his vulnerability. Magnani let him be in charge, an instinct that worked. He was the buffer between newcomer and in-mate and he smoothed a way for Magnani. D. Bell was amazed and not pleased as Magnani answered questions he had never been asked by the staff. He felt like an early explorer trying to describe the Old World. If the children had the vaguest grasp of life outside the institution they showed little evidence of it. None of them thought further than downtown Tampa but they were eager receptacles for stories. Magnani was aware of the flapping ears of D. Bell and determined not to weave fantasies.

He lunched with Kaine that day. The old man was keen to ascertain his initial reaction to the children.

'How did you find them? he asked. 'I hear Patricia got a little fresh.'

'I was flattered.'

Kaine laughed. 'She tries it with anything in trousers. Frightens the wits out of the delivery men. D. Bell tells me you were having no trouble talking with them.'

'No, I don't suppose I did. Tony chaperoned me.'

'Uh huh. He's your man from now on. He'll be harder to shake off than a polecat with its teeth in your arm.' Kaine laughed again, spluttering coffee on to the tablecloth. This seemed to be a place where everyone was careless with their mouths.

It took Magnani a week to settle into Kaine's world. In this time he saw the two sides of the children for which Kaine had tried to prepare him. After his first session when his charges were peevish, cross and in a few cases malevolent he thought less of D. Bell's harsh silences. He had never felt more tired at the end of his day: he had learned quickly to be a minder, alert for signs of danger, or of a fracas, to signs that a child might be inadvertently about to harm himself.

The children usually split into two groups. D. Bell took charge of Tony's group, Joyce handled the older ones. Sometimes they merged and Kaine would be present. His was a calming presence; Patricia never tried to grab at his crotch. The old man was loved as a distant and kind personage, his tired smile anticipated and enjoyed. Kaine was the same whether he doled out approbation or rebuke; his manner told even the most remote child that things would always be all right.

In the days he watched the children Magnani formed a loose plan to use music as a bridge to them. He noticed they liked to listen to sounds in groups and thought a less random noise than D. Bell's hand claps might be stimulating. She had the habit of bringing her hands together to gain attention or order. It never failed, though Magnani wondered if her success might owe more to the implied threat of her actions. As if to counter Joyce's friendliness Bell withdrew into herself whenever Magnani tried to speak to her, though she offered a few words of explanation when Kaine was present.

Music was all Magnani really knew, and it made sense to use it. The sense of loss for his pawned guitar was always with him, and he missed playing it before sleeping. He decided to ask Kaine to get him a guitar instead of wages.

On the Saturday afternoon of his first week all the children went to the cinema in Tampa, an afternoon matinee which few townspeople attended. D. Bell drove them in the institution bus, an orange, pre-war vehicle that rode high on its thin wheels, which put Magnani in mind of the Joads heading out for their brave, false new world. Magnani and Joyce went also. It was a three person job, Kaine said, when all the children went out.

Next to the Bijou Theatre was a record and music store which had cardboard figures of rock and roll stars in its window. Strapped to them were colourful, cheap guitars. Magnani helped the women shepherd in their flock, they were placed in the back row of the Bijou by anxious staff who inwardly cursed their employer for allowing such a visit. Tony was last in. He trailed ice-cream behind letting it fall from his hand into a snail-like line of goo. Patricia insisted on sitting next to Magnani and most of the film passed him by, such was his preoccupation with fending off her hands. She enjoyed herself.

The film was a recent western in which John Wayne made safer the west, and punished the Indians. He searched for ten long years, and the children searched with him. They screeched when the Indians attacked, some clumsily hiding under seats. They cheered at the cavalry charges, and cried when they sensed sadness. It was not much different to Magnani's own childhood viewing. At one point he turned sideways to see a row of Asiatic faces, wide-eyed, with full lips hanging down like fleshy pendulums. In their hands popcorn was forgotten as they gazed up at the large moving images of colour before them. D. Bell's cigarette smoke curled up into the projector's beam and was turned to silver. Magnani thought back to his own early illicit smoking, when he puffed up small clouds into the air of his local flea pit, waiting for the main feature to roll. Sometimes being sick before it came. Now he was with simpler children, who could never grow up, and who he found were beginning to affect him. Openness was a quality from which he had long been removed, if he had ever experienced it at all. As he saw it displayed by the children his own tawdry existence of the last ten years was put into perspective. Not the music, that had been magnificent at the best times and always worth it at the worst. But the rest. The endless wasting of time, the getting through grey days in anticipation of playing, being alone, or with too many people. If he could take in experience like Tony or Patricia and give it back selflessly, there might be another chance for him.

The prospect of the children hearing his type of music excited Magnani. It would be his first innocent audience. He left the Bijou in as high spirits as the rest, D. Bell excepted. Tony charged the girls with an imaginary sabre until stopped by one of Bell's most scornful stares. He sidled up to Magnani and locked an arm in his, demonstrating his special relationship. They were watched out by two usherettes until they were all back on the bus. Magnani glanced back to see eyes of incomprehension, revulsion, and superiority, a seemingly inevitable but hateful mix. He knew the look. In a small way his own trade had given him a taste of it. Now he had an inkling of what it would be like to be completely beyond the pale.

At dinner that night Joyce spoke of the trip. It was a success, she said. Other visits had not been so calm. Once Tony had responded to the taunts of teenage boys by running at them and knocking one down. They had almost lost the Saturday concession. D. Bell winced and sucked on her cheroot as Joyce praised everyone.

'And Frank here,' Joyce said, 'he's a real hit. Kids took to him right away.'

'That's good,' Kaine said. 'Want to tell us about your first week, Frank?'

He did not expect his views to be sought so publicly.

'It's very new for me,' he answered, 'but I think I can get used to it.'

'But can you get used to them?'

'I've had no problems so far. No real problems.'

'Not yet,' said D. Bell.

'Yes,' said Kaine, 'you've had a pretty smooth week. Won't always be like it, of course. Any ideas you want to throw into the pot, Frank? Do you have any skills we might use here?'

Magnani thought he saw a sly gleam in Kaine's eyes. He often had the idea the old man knew all about him, even though it could not be possible.

'I've done a little guitar playing in the past. I thought I might be able to get something musical going here. The children seem to enjoy sounds, they like the radio.'

'Guitar eh? Interesting. You don't have one though.'

'No. It was cumbersome to travel around with.'

'Uh huh. Joyce, can we get a guitar?'

'Depends. How much are they, Frank?'

'They're all prices. They don't have to be expensive. There are a few cheap ones in that store next to the Bijou.'

'Helen told me we have a little left over from the Christmas donations, Wilbur,' Joyce said.

Kaine waved a hand. 'Okay, get your guitar. Liven the place up a little.'

Kaine asked Magnani to take a stroll with him round the grounds as Joyce and D. Bell went about what he called the 'bedding down duties'. He took Magnani's arm lightly and breathed in the smoke of his cigar.

'The only time I enjoy it,' he said, 'is after the evening meal.

He knocked a tip of ash into the grass.

'Filthy habit for filthy times,' he murmured.

Magnani wondered if he was about to receive another homily on the state of the Union. He found Kaine interesting, and was in tune with the views he had heard so far but tonight he craved a lighter mode of thought. He missed the banter of other musicians, although the granting of his request for a guitar pleased him. Before turning in he would write to Pearson. He was learning to turn in early. It was a new experience to take to a bed before midnight, or even three in the morning. At first getting up not much after dawn had been unbearable and he was shot through with tiredness by midday. But it was becoming easier and he could see a time when the process might even be natural.

They made a circuit of the grounds.

'So that's what you do, eh' Kaine said, 'play the guitar?

'Yes, mainly.'

'Make a living at that?'

'I have done.'

'You're a jazzman, aren't you?'

'How did you know?'

'Your age, character, that suit you wore in Roanoke.'

Kaine flicked the stump of his cigar onto the gravel path. 'I hope D. Bell didn't see me do that.' The old man chuckled. 'I get stir crazy here sometimes. I feel the need to break the rules — my rules. This is the height of my delinquency. You one of those modern players, Frank?'

'Partly. I like it all. That's not fashionable at the moment, not for my generation, but I can't see the sense in being any other way. If it's good, it's good.'

'That's a good philosophy. I don't keep up with it much now, but when I was your age I saw them all. All the New Orleans stuff in the twenties, and the big bands after that. I went to Kansas City in the Prohibition days. That place took no notice of the law, hell they drank more than before. I saw the best. Waller, Lester Young, the Count swinging his butt off, Ben Webster — he breathed into the sax like it was a woman. Those guys had soul, they crooned with their instruments, sang with them. And Basie, he was always there. I still hear him now on the radio.'

Kaine broadened his southern accent. 'They was jumpin' honey.'

Magnani hoped Kaine would elaborate. He had not heard many first hand tales of the early jazz days. His be-bop generation were unwilling to acknowledge much of it, as if afraid it might devalue their modern credibility. Magnani was comfortable with Kaine the knowledgeable lay man.

'There was a drummer I knew in New York,' Magnani said, 'he came from Kansas.'

'That so? How long were you in our great city for?'

'Not long.'

They stopped by the dormitories, on a warm night moistened by light rain. Magnani smelled plants readying themselves for spring. The bougainvillaeas gave off a musky scent, like giant geraniums. It was pungent and comforting, speaking of hot lands and slow lifestyles. The children slept in separate dormitories. An adjoining door between boys and girls was locked each night. 'Sex is not the privilege of whole minds,' Kaine pronounced.

He looked Magnani in the face. 'Frank, you on the wrong side of the law? Are you running from something?'

The question had come at last.

'No to the first question,' Magnani answered.

'I wondered. You were travelling real light, and without your guitar. I know enough about musicians to know they don't readily abandon their pieces. I'm not a prober, man's past is his own I reckon. But I had to ask, for the sake of this place.'

'I'm surprised you didn't earlier. And I could be lying.'

'You could. What about the running part?'

'I had some problems in New York. I came over to further my playing career.'

'On your own?'

'Yes. It was the only way I could get in. I had a few contacts. I played for a time, things looked promising but ended quickly. There was some trouble there, a fight. I thought I'd killed a man. It's a long story. After that I thought it best to get away.' He was amazed at how readily he told his story to Kaine.

'Will this affect my working here?' Magnani asked.

'I don't see why it should. I decided on you on the drive down. Nothing has happened to make me change my mind. Go into town on Monday, pick up that guitar. Who knows, you might find another use for your talent.'

'What makes you think I have any?'

'Because you're not a fool. And only a fool would go to New York without it. Besides, I can sense something driving you. You're taut with it Frank, but you can't get at it yet. Life's gotten in the way.'

Kaine chuckled at the surprise on Magnani's face. 'Don't worry son, I can't read minds though they paid me to do just that once. I talk as much bullshit as the next man, but I do sense things sometimes. What you just told me fits in with what I see in you.'

A wail came from the boys' dormitory, a thin keening carried to them by the wind.

'That's Tony,' Kaine said, 'gets like that some nights. Doesn't remember in the morning.'

'What's bothering him?'

'We don't know. He's crying for something in his past perhaps. We haven't seen his father for five years now — but he sends regular checks. I've never been able to stop Tony doing it. One of my many failures.'

'Doesn't he keep the others awake?'

'Not any more. They are immune to it by now. They sleep the sleep of angels.'

They walked back to the main house and Kaine left him. The old man's room was on the other side, a declaration of private territory with which Magnani empathised. He went to his own room and wrote to Pearson, with a small paragraph for Eileen. He tried to make it warm and formal but his guilt left him unable to write more than a series of bare facts. He told Pearson where he was and that he would be staying for a time. He excused his disappearance and 'hoped they understood'. The fate of the guitar was revealed and Pearson asked to watch over it.

Magnani tried all the cheap guitars in the Tampa store, finally choosing a pre-war acoustic model, a type used by early bluesmen. He recognised it from photographs. It had a brittle tone but considerable volume, ideal for solo playing. It wasn't easy to come to terms with and very different to his jazz guitar. He ran through some chord passages, playing simple things less the attention of the store owner be attracted. The few weeks in which he had not played seemed an age, and his fingers had already slowed. They moved reluctantly over the fretboard. He settled on the richest chords he knew and strummed them gently, until he was satisfied the guitar would suffice. It cost twenty-five dollars, to the disgust of D. Bell, who had driven him in.

'Can't you find something cheaper?' she asked. 'There are some cheaper.'

'They're not playable. This one is tough enough.'

D. Bell sighed and scowled at the same time, something she had perfected down the years. She handed over the money to the storekeeper and marched out to her orange bus leaving Magnani to trail after her. He begged a plastic case to keep it in.

'Hope its worth it,' Bell said.

'I think it will be.'

'Have to watch it won't get busted. Don't let the kids get at it.'

'No, I won't, Miss Bell.'

As her fingers tapped on the steering wheel Magnani recognised the mutual straining of nerve ends. The rhythm of Bell's fingers highlighted it in an irritating way. Magnani tightened his grip on the guitar and hoped he could make something of this chapter of his life.

EIGHT

Magnani spent a morning adjusting the new guitar. He found a secluded spot in the institution grounds and played there until his finger-tips were sore and his wrists aching. There was much he could not attempt on his humble acquisition. Its taut action and shoddy manufacture precluded any playing of subtlety, at least subtlety of the fingers. This guitar needed a brisk percussive approach to get the best out of it, a technique which had never been Magnani's forte. His was a busy, delicate style which he would have to modify. His new instrument needed to be bashed. Magnani gave himself a crash course in this.

Magnani kept to the old blues tunes he had picked up, with a smattering of traditional folk songs. There was much of America's past in his playing. He picked out bass dominated twelve bar blues that had been forged in the work-fields of the Mississippi Delta country, and the deep south-eastern states, or Texas. Magnani had never looked down on this poorer cousin of jazz as so many jazzmen did, white and black. He loved its intricacy of rhythm and deceptive simplicity, the childlike lyrics that stated repeatedly a simple theme but really talked of other, darker things, of a world which could not be penetrated by any but the bluesmen themselves. Certainly not by any white man. As he played it occurred to Magnani that he knew far more about the music of this country than his own.

It was only the complaint of his hands that stopped Magnani. For hours he had been lost in music; he was grateful to know he still could be. He cast a sheepish look around but no-one watched, his indulgent morning had been a private one. He joined the others for the midday meal after secreting the guitar under his bed. Throughout his career he had found this the safest place.

'Well, Frank,' Kaine said, 'I hope you made good use of your morning off. I saw you walking past my window with the guitar.'

'Yes. I've gotten a little used to the beast now.'

'What are you going to do with it?' D. Bell asked bluntly.

'As I've said I'm hoping to —'

'They'll want to take it from you, it'll cause fights. It will be no good at all.' She was in a particularly sour mood.

'We can't be sure of that,' Joyce said, 'at least Frank is trying something. An innovation here might help. The days might be shorter.'

Is that what they are trying to do here, Magnani wondered. Trying to shorten their days, their lives perhaps? D. Bell almost succeeded in taking the shine off his idea but he withstood her pessimism. In a way he found her useful; Bell was a fount of negativity that he could chafe against to diminish his own. And his modest achievements as a musician did not seem so futile in here.

Magnani used the guitar that afternoon. He was allotted a small group consisting of Tony, Patricia, Wesley and two of the youngest children. He had not seem much of Wesley so far. They used a small room in the main house, close to Kaine's office. Magnani wanted to get the children away from their usual outbuildings and had coaxed Kaine into making the room available. It had good views across the lawn and down to the coast where the sea met the sky in a gentle merging of blues. At first the children were more interested in their new environment, especially Wesley, who looked out of the window and gnawed his fingers. He nibbled and sucked at them like a rodent, an action so long formed it was incessant and unnoticed. Magnani was struck by the unwavering stare on Wesley's face, the still eyes at odds with the working mouth.

With difficulty Magnani arranged them in a semi-circle around him. Tony helped him arrange, and almost punched Wesley when he refused to move. At least Patricia was quiet, as she had got used to Magnani her interest in him had lessened, Even so he kept a careful eye on her hands.

It was not a good start. The guitar stuck in the already disintegrating plastic case. The strings resonated as Magnani extricated it. Alert to the noise Tony waited for his friend to do something remarkable. The others just waited. It was a long moment. Magnani was nervous, a private stagefright came on him as he saw the row of expectant faces. And he felt part charlatan: what was he doing with this guitar, could the children really give a damn, and was it himself he was trying to save?

He played a few American folk songs he thought might have registered in the childrens' minds at some stage. Mouths sagged, apart from Wesley's, which still had fingers in it.

'These are famous songs,' Magnani mumbled, 'I'll play the melody first, then the rhythm. That's the part you can clap your hands to. He put the guitar down and clapped out a simple beat. 'You can do this, it's fun.'

Tony immediately copied him. Magnani had to play against Tony's clapping, which was enthusiastic, but hopeless. Patricia and the others joined in, a desultory slapping of hands that forced Magnani to change the rhythm to accommodate them. When he did so they changed, and so it went on, a musical chase around simple tunes. They were grinning now, letting saliva run down their chins. At one point Magnani thought Wesley might take his fingers out of his mouth. He stopped chewing them but could not quite bring himself to join the others. By this time they were making a fine, unco-ordinated noise, Magnani belting out twelve bar blues, the children adding their accompaniment. Tony tried to pull Wesley's hands from his mouth and was promptly punched. The others joined in, forming a jostling melée as Magnani tried to protect the guitar and maintain order. This was how Kaine found them.

The old man stepped into the room carefully.

'What's going on here? Seems more like football than music.' Kaine separated Tony and Wesley. His presence quashed any further fighting, and severely embarrassed Magnani. D. Bell came in to help herd the children out. She had an 'I told you so' gloat on her face.

'Well Frank, you certainly made a start,' Kaine said.

'It was going well until the fight.'

Kaine laughed. 'Don't worry. You reached them — what's a little fracas from time to time?'

'So it's all right for me to continue?'

'Yes, of course. And there'll be other disturbances. They are excited by you, you're a novelty at the moment, and that's not a bad thing. The children lead long lives here. I've got to go now, to see a lady who says she wants to help us. Probably some powdery old dame who's had a rush of conscience and wants to spend some of her old man's money to soothe it.'

Kaine smiled his encouraging, but slightly servile smile. 'How's this, Frank? It's my "we are proud but need the money smile".'

'It's fine, Wilbur.'

As usual Kaine had boosted Magnani's confidence. He was not sure he wanted to be a 'novelty' but at least he had made a start.

By the end of the week Magnani had introduced the guitar to all the children. Kaine was right, they were just like other people. Some delighted in the music, some were mildly interested, a few were not touched by it at all. A group of eight children evolved around Magnani's sessions, with the remote Wesley on its fringe. Magnani managed to stop Tony antagonising Wesley, and he was allowed to suck his fingers. As they advanced to singing songs Magnani hoped he might suck them in time.

Tony was the first to hum along, if a spitty, low-throated gurgle could be called a hum. The more alert began to learn some of the tunes. They liked folk songs with a percussive ring and mellow sentiments. After much effort Magnani's group of eight managed to mouth the tunes in some semblance of order. Wesley sucked. They sounded like young children with premature baritone voices scattered amongst them. Kaine and Joyce were impressed. Kaine even called Helen Muldaur from her desk one morning, to hear the 'concert'. She clasped her hands to her breast and pronounced herself captivated.

Magnani was pleased. It was a mutual therapy, and he benefited with the children. He was less dominated by self and enjoyed this most basic music in a way he had never done before; the innocence of his participating audience made it pure and intense. The group performed for Kaine and the ladies, after two weeks practice. They attempted Woody Guthrie s 'This Land is Your Land', Shenandoah' — Helen Muldaur's favourite — and 'Tom Brown's Body', the last song floundering to a halt in a confusion of noise. It did not matter. The staff heaped praise on the children and they responded. D. Bell managed to banish her scowl for a while and Magnani realised, with some shock, his pride in the children. Kaine took him to one side.

'Hell Frank, they could be making records soon, eh?' He winked. 'Woody Guthrie — I met him once. Curious fella. Full of hate and good sense, a little spit of a man.' Kaine measured five feet high with his hand. 'Is he still alive, I wonder? I haven't heard of him in a long while.'

'I don't know.'

'Well, its not the land for Woody now anyway. That song is played in all the schools, did you know that? A great irony. He had a sign on his guitar that said 'this machine kills fascists', can you believe that?'

Magnani shrugged. He was too full of the children's triumph to think of much else.

That weekend Magnani went into Tampa on his own. He had not received a reply from Pearson yet and was feeling the need for his own kind of music. His work with the group had revitalised his appetite.

'You'll find little of it around here,' Kaine told him, but the old man mentioned a downtown club that had live music — saloon songs, blues and God knows what else, Kaine offered. Magnani strode out into the Saturday night with the ten dollars Kaine had thrust into his hand.

There might still be snow on the New York streets but it was mild in Tampa. Magnani wore a jacket with an open shirt and felt overdressed. His fedora had not left his bedroom, Kaine's description of him in Roanoke had put paid to that image. He found the bar Kaine had mentioned. A smattering of people drank to the backdrop a small combo, and the singing of a lady whose small voice was at odds with her considerable weight. She ran through few Billie Holliday tunes and Magnani wished she had not. She smothered 'God Bless the Child, and made 'Lover Man boring. Not that the customers cared. They drank with their backs to the stage, talking loudly, and intent on their partners. It was a place Magnani had been in many times.

For the heat that would come later a twin-bladed fan limbered up overhead. It pushed stale air from one spot to another and pulsed as listlessly as the music. A Cuban served Magnani then sat back on his stool in the corner of the bar, picking at his slick moustache. Behind him were posters of his island and Mexico, and one of a Spanish bullfighter with sword raised and blood-red cape swirling. It was the liveliest scene in the place but Magnani did not mind. He had not expected much and to hear music played by adults, even to this standard, was a change. No-one talked to him, and he talked to no-one. He got back to the institute before midnight, with change in his pocket after the taxi ride. He was not living the life of a jazzman in this place, and he did not mind that either.

On Monday morning Carr brought Magnani his awaited letter. Pearson wrote in his large script:

Hi Frank. Glad to hear from you. You gave us quite a shock taking off like that. Eileen was kinda upset, but I can understand it. Man gets crowded sometimes. Eileen thought Johnson might have hit on you again but I told her you'd make out okay. Listen, about your axe, don't worry. I've fixed it. I redeemed it for you — yeah I know, I didn't have the ticket or nothing, but I know Mo, and there's always ways. I convinced him you were never coming back, gone home over the water, I said. And when I started drumming them greenbacks on his counter it was easy man. We got it under the bed back at Buen Vista. You said that's the best place for it. You can pay me back later. So, you in an institution, huh? Sounds kinda freaky brother, but maybe a good place to hole up. Hang loose Frank, and write if you are on the move again.
                                                              Pearson and Eileen.
P.S. I got a gig at the Door — resident drummer in the house band. Pays regular and good.

Eileen had added her name in print half the size of Pearson's writing. There was one cross under her name. Magnani was no longer surprised by Pearson's generosity of spirit, and now he found he was no longer shamed by it. Not long ago there would have been a question in his mind that he would ever pay Pearson back, now there was none. With faltering steps he was learning to give something of himself to Kaine's children. It was a growing process, and completely new, but Magnani was aware that he needed it. And it was good to know the guitar was not in Mo's wasteland.

At breakfast, with perfect timing, Kaine offered Magnani wages.

'I appreciate that you haven't asked for anything, Frank,' Kaine said, 'you had every right to. Helen is on a regular salary, and the Carrs, the rest of us are part of the fixtures and fittings. We draw money from our fund when we need it, if there's anything there. But I can offer you an intermittent salary, if you can live with that.'

Kaine passed a tan envelope to Magnani. 'Here's fifty dollars, courtesy of Mrs Delamare, our latest sponsor. She's paid for the next round of repairs here, and the resuscitation of that old warhorse of a bus of ours. Is this all right?'

Kaine had waited until Joyce and D. Bell had left the table.

'Yes. I need to pay someone back in New York. I can start now.'

'Good.'

'Don't you get any official help here at all?'

'Not really. Odd bits and pieces. Some of the local high schools give us old pieces of equipment from time to time. It might be better if we were in a northern state. But we are not an official place, Frank., I started it up. As far as the federal authorities are concerned we could be a home for loopy old dears, or retired colonels still fighting a war somewhere. America is awash with homes for the odd.

Magnani wrote a short letter to Pearson and put twenty dollars in it. It was another step towards rehabilitation. His musical classes were now an established part of routine. Three mornings a week he played for the children, trying out every style of music, and noting which had the most effect. A few years before, Magnani had adapted pieces of Haydn for the guitar. They had never quite worked on the instrument but he played them anyway. It was the rhythmic folk and blues songs which went down best — they were the most 'clappable.' Magnani's feet were kept on the ground by the realistic appraisal of his charges. Not for them the intricacies of modern jazz, or the calm of Haydn. They favoured the direct punch at their heart-strings and feet. Gradually this caused Magnani to question his own musical ethos. He asked himself why he had chosen a music which had never been accessible to a general public. Elitism worried him but he had still followed that road. To think himself different had been a comfort in the last ten years, and in low moments of conceited despair he had thought himself better. And the conscience that led to creative tension he had thought enough until now. His growing relationship with the children showed up the folly of thinking so. His playing for them had shown him what had been lacking in his own music. Warmth. There had been emotion in his playing, linked to technical expertise, but the earthy tenderness of primitive music like Guthrie's had never been there. And it was missing in most of his generation of jazzmen. It had become a feared, misunderstood quality. 'Cool' had replaced it, intensity of playing had taken its place until players believed this was warmth. Magnani wondered if he could ever infuse his playing with this quality. He knew he would have to feel it first.

When he had the energy Magnani began practising before sleeping. His scope was limited by the guitar. Its classical styling denied him the upper reaches of the fretboard, but he overcame the frustration and began to make a poor tool work for him. His finger speed and wrist strength returned — even the shortest lay-off for a professional could quickly slow the hands. Magnani took pleasure in going through his book of standards, and cutting out his hard won embellishments. He simplified his style in a search for its essence, a core on which he could rebuild. He enjoyed his playing. It was shed of the need to impress and conform, and reach goals other people set. And it did not have to earn money. Magnani knew again what it was like to play for pleasure, like an amateur.

Late evening, when the night had stilled to a low murmur of sound the guitar was at its best. Magnani sat with his bathroom door open to enhance the acoustics of the bedroom. The guitar was vibrant with tone, a full ringing sound which filled the space around him. Once he heard footsteps in the corridor stop outside his door, and wondered who it was who listened.

Wesley Martin Gibbon was the child Magnani most wanted to reach, for he was the most inaccessible. Wesley was in his thirties, a long-time resident. Ever since the fight at his first music session Magnani had thought about Wesley. He sensed the need in him to belong, to reach out for the little that Tony and the others had. But his way was blocked. Whenever D. Bell told him that Wesley's sullenness was incurable Magnani strengthened his determination to gain at least a foothold of a rapport with him. He decided a session alone with him might help, away from the jealousy of Tony, and the general mayhem of the group. Magnani put it to Kaine one day.

'Wesley will be a tough nut to crack,' Kaine said. 'Been here more than twenty years. His father was a senator — not for long though. He got involved in some money scam or other. A Republican.'

'Has Wesley always been so remote?'

'Always. He knew he was being dumped here, more than some of the other kids. And when we increased our numbers he got worse. I tried various things with him to bring him out, but I didn't have much success. If you push him too much he'll come out punching like a good welterweight. You've found that out, Frank.'

Kaine rubbed his nose and considered a cigar, then thought better of it. 'Besides,' he continued, 'when faced with someone like Wesley I ask myself what right I have to probe and change. There's a lot out there in these fields — mental health generally — who are hell bent on pushing their latest theories. Run electrical charges through their heads, might spark something off, stuff like that. And people like Wesley are the ready fodder. A long time ago I asked myself a question, am I doing this for them, or myself? And you've got to ask yourself the same question Frank. Is the music for you or them? We're all looking for some kind of therapy, it will be the next growth industry, mark my words.'

'What answer did you come up with?'

'Its all right if the carer benefits from the caring, for then it's a sharing thing. And it has to be that, or it's sterile at best, a sham at worst.'

Kaine's question was not expected, but Magnani had already asked it of himself. He was not sure how much his selfishness had diminished here. Some, he was sure of that, but when the time came would he leave rejuvenated, with a safe distance between his new self and old guilts? The children a fond memory but someone else's concern? And would he have used them? They were questions he could not yet answer.

'Go ahead,' Kaine said. 'I'll arrange for you to have some time with Wesley. There's a room in the right wing you can use. We've got a buzzer in it which you might need. Wesley is powerful you know.'

Magnani knew.

His solo session was on a Thursday, a day without sunlight, when thunder pounded the bay area and a fierce storm gripped Tampa. As Magnani watched arcs of lightning vein the sky Kaine pronounced the storm to be mild.

'This is hurricane country,' he said, 'after a few of them these things are just enthusiastic gusts of wind. We always have 'em around this time.'

It was hurricane enough for Magnani, the wind able to make the window glass flex in defence, and there was a constant rushing of the trees and shrubs in the grounds, as if the sea had advanced two miles. He hoped the weather was not a foreshadowing of his one-to-one with Wesley.

With difficulty Magnani managed to get Wesley to come with him to the allotted room. 'We'll play some music,' he told him, as Wesley loped along besides him, his hands swinging by his side. Although it was cruel to think it there was a distinctly simian air to the man-child. His large, mis-shaped head and open working mouth was almost a caricature of the others. 'His lifespan will be the shortest,' Kaine had told him earlier, 'with that head of his and the pressure on his chest he's a prey to every infection going. He has had sinus problems for years, when he hits forty the bad stuff will come. The havoc an extra chromosome makes.' But as Magnani walked he was conscious more of the repressed power in Wesley, and how easily he could smash the guitar in those ham-like hands.

They sat on two hard chairs opposite each other, Wesley sitting sideways on his, suspicion adding dimension to his fine sullenness. On a whim Magnani offered him the guitar, bracing himself to have it thrown back at him. Wesley recoiled, and might have thought what Magnani feared. But he did nothing for some moments, then reached out a hand and touched the guitar, his fingers hesitant, as if expecting a bite. They were moist from their resting place in Wesley's mouth and left sticky marks on the surface of the guitar. Wesley put the guitar flat on his lap, and stroked it. He rubbed the strings and tapped the body, but lightly. He strained to keep his clumsy force under control. His face lowered to the sound hole and looked into it. He blew and the strings resonated faintly. He pulled his face back with surprise, but his sullen look was muted, and his eyes no longer glazed with hostility as he held the guitar. At first Magnani did not know what to do. He had not expected a response so quickly, if ever. Coming out of his wonderment Wesley saw him in the corner of his eye. He grabbed the guitar firmly, holding it to him like a baby. Magnani feared trouble.

'It's all right Wesley. You can keep it if you want. I thought you might like me to play it for you, that's all. Do you want me to play it for you?'

There was a long moment's hesitation before Wesley answered, 'nnnn...nnnnn.' It was his most used sound, a clenched-teeth moan that sufficed for most situations. Magnani took it as an affirmation. He gambled his hand and Wesley passed him the guitar.

Magnani played some of the most tuneful folk songs, with attractive refrains and choruses. He kept the pace even and the tone sweet. After three songs Wesley began to rock back and forth on his chair, making it squeak on the wooden floor. At first his movement was at odds with his face, which maintained its sombreness, but, as Magnani relaxed himself and played well Wesley's look changed to one of enjoyment; lines of pleasure replaced his sullen set. It was a good moment.

Magnani played for an hour and Wesley did not want him to stop. After a selection of institution favourites he played a few of his own jazz tunes. They did not disturb Wesley. His mouth was open and drooling, he hugged himself and almost smiled, but his face did not yet know how to do this. Magnani would have given much to know what he was thinking, and what the music was doing to him. He felt his musicianship, and the time he had spent on it, vindicated by this audience of one. Behind the half-open doorway Kaine stood and listened for a while, Magnani's accomplice in his secret triumph.

It was time to join the others. Wesley's eyes followed Magnani's every movement as he put the guitar back in its case. Despite the low quality of the plastic case he had made a ritual of putting the guitar away. It signified a formal end to the music making and stilled any demands for more.

'Did you like the music Wesley?'

'Nnnn. Nnnnn. Nice.'

The last word struggled out triumphantly. Wesley offered to carry the guitar and Magnani let him do so, praying they would not meet Tony on the way back to the communal room. They did not, and were there before Joyce's group returned. Magnani put the guitar on a shelf and watched as the children came in. Wesley watched too, from his usual defensive corner. But it was not the same clenched fist stance he displayed. Magnani tried not to read too much into it, to invest more in the power of music than it could ever justify. He had met too many people who were genuinely oblivious to it. But there was change in Wesley.

It was rest time, the half hour before dinner when the children sat around and thought of food. As he shut the door behind him Magnani saw Wesley edge up to Patricia and wondered what he had started.

A gradual success was achieved with Wesley. The sad elder statesman of the group had built up a wall which would take a long time to dismantle but chinks were appearing in it daily. Four days after his session with Magnani, Wesley joined in a game, shuffling after a softball and trying to scoop it up in his great hands. Tony sensed the change in the make up of the group and the threat to his role in it. He clung to Magnani all the more, watching for any signs of affection towards Wesley. Magnani trod a careful path, and the peace was kept, more or less.

Magnani had been at the institution for several months, a time when worry had dimmed and hope renewed. He now knew Tampa was a crossroads for him, and saw the wisdom of trying to shape a firm road from it but he backed off the examination of his life he thought necessary. Such a basic accomplishment had always eluded him, so his life had drifted with his talent instead of being mapped by it. Too often he had been shaped by the whims of other people.

There were more visits to the cinema, and, when the weather warmed sufficiently, to the beach. Even Kaine came on this one, following the orange bus in his car. The day was quite hot, a prelude to the sticky summer that would follow. It was shirt sticking weather, and the only wind was a mockery of freshness. D. Bell started the bus to a backdrop of clear sky with a fringe of fine cloud at its edges. The children piled onboard armed with the accoutrements of their outing — bats, balls, nets, hats that never stayed on heads.

'Was a disaster last time,' D. Bell said drily, as she gunned life into the engine. 'Said they'd ban us from the beach, bringing a bunch of geeks onto it.'

'Oh now it wasn't that bad,' Joyce answered, 'and besides, that was a Saturday. It will be quiet today.'

She whispered to Magnani. 'Wilbur won't let us go on a weekend. Patricia kept taking her costume off whenever boys came near and there was trouble between Wesley and some high school people. The children were irritable that day.'

Magnani smiled at the scene Joyce depicted. High school kids with hair razored into their skulls hanging around Patricia, making derogatory jokes around, and hoping to glimpse her considerable tits. He looked out of the back window of the bus to see Kaine following. He was panama-hatted, as in Roanoke, and hunched over the steering wheel like a man behind it for the first time.

D. Bell drove to a quiet section of coast a few miles from the institution. There was a flat expanse of coarse sand, dotted with odd groups of people, spreading out like plants under the strengthening sun. With D. Bell leading, and Kaine trailing at the rear, Joyce and Magnani flanked the group. They moved in a muddle towards the centre of the beach.

'We won't go too near the sea,' Bell said, 'they'll want to go in it.'

Magnani surpressed an answer to this.

The temperature hauled itself up to the mid seventies with a moderate humidity.

'This is nothing,' Kaine said, 'come July and August it's steam time — no air, baking wet heat, you want another shower as soon as you come out of one. Florida cries out for the air conditioner.'

'Wilbur dreams of having those things at the institution, but they are too expensive,' Joyce said.

'Another ten years and they'll be everywhere,' Kaine said. 'You see them now, ugly, droning machines stuck out of house windows, fooling people they are living somewhere else. That's progress, I suppose.'

'He'd love it really,' Joyce muttered.

She wore a floral dress that looked from another age. Cautiously she drew it up to her knees, her white legs inviting the sun. D. Bell wore her usual trousers, and prowled the beach with her nervous stride, looking for misdemeanours.

'She seems more down than usual,' Magnani said to Kaine.

'It's the onset of spring.'

'What?'

'Spring. Gets folks all kinds of ways. If you have much to look forward to you are renewed and those dreams that fail every year can be believed again. If there's nothing, that gets heightened too, I guess. It becomes a big nothing, a crushing nothing, and time does not pass easily.' Kaine tilted his hat over his face. 'Life gets hard to spend then. D. Bell is in this category, poor woman.'

Magnani would have liked to ask why but Tony jostled him, landing by his side in a shower of sand.

'Come play,' he said, tugging Magnani up.

They played a game which incorporated many sports. Baseball turned into football, then basketball. At one point Magnani built wickets and tried to introduce cricket to the Florida beach, but it proved too alien. Wesley joined in and was one of the group. It took two hours to exhaust them, an hour less for the staff. Kaine watched all from his rattan beach chair, an avuncular, cigar smoking presence. A few people approached them but turned away when they saw the children.

They ate the food the Carrs had prepared for them in the afternoon.

'This is the earliest we have had an outing like this, Frank,' Kaine said. 'You have revitalised us.'

'I've played the guitar, that's about all I've done.'

'Don't diminish it. You've drawn Wesley out. We could not do that. You offer a dimension oldsters like myself cannot.'

Joyce took the children for ice-cream, their final treat of the day. Magnani watched them straggle up the beach. Tony running ahead, so that he could be seen as leader: the rest a slouch of clumsy humanity. Magnani felt a great fondness for them.

'Why did you describe Bell as a poor woman?' Magnani asked Kaine, now that they were alone.

Kaine crinkled up his eyes to the sun and pulled the panama further down over his face until only his mouth was visible. 'She has a history, as do we all. But that's her business. I know about it because it led her to us here. That's as much as I should say.'

'All right.' But Magnani still wondered.

They were back, flopping down like camels onto the sand, with ice-cream dripping from their cones. Tony proclaimed his difference in the form of an ice lolly. It was shaped like a skyrocket and he attempted to fly it on its stick until it broke off and hit the beach. He sat crying at its fate, prevented by D. Bell from eating the melting remnants in the sand.

It was time to head back. The children were exhausted into peace and most slept on their bus seats. A few stared out of the windows with weary eyes, saying goodbye to a world they were not part of. There was a sense of calm in everyone. Even D. Bell had lost the grimace Magnani had thought permanent. He saw her face as Kaine overtook the bus. Magnani was travelling back in his car.

'The kids love me doing this,' Kaine said. He beamed at the children and waved an arm, causing the car to swerve across the road. The old man chuckled and punched Magnani's arm. 'Good day, eh? I kind of feel spring in myself. I can feel the residue of sap stirring in these old bones — they're straightening out again.'

Magnani agreed, and advised a firmer hold on the wheel.

Music was not a magic wand that could be waved at will. Its usefulness to the children varied with their moods, and there were relapses with Wesley. But it helped, the bridge to the main group, and then to Wesley. After a few weeks Tony began to forget his jealousy and accept the situation. Wesley was no longer alone. The institution funds ran to another visit to the music store, to buy cheap sets of bongos, triangles, and other pieces of percussion. Slowly, Magnani was forming his first big band.

They had two full sessions a week now. On good days Magnani was able to get his rhythm section into a semblance of order: they thumped in time. Sometimes there were lurches into other time signatures, sometimes they crashed to a staggered halt. Always, when the group got into its stride, Magnani's guitar was swamped and forgotten, which was how it should be, he told himself.

Time passed quickened with activity. Magnani received another letter from Pearson in May. He was drumming in his native Kansas City, and Eileen was with him.

If we like it here we might even get rid of Buen Vista, he wrote, *New York is good for work but it gets too much for this small town boy. Eileen wants a change too, too many goons trying to paw her at the club. We haven't heard so I guess you are still at that place — it ain't no asylum is it, boy? Hey, Kansas City is nearer to you than New York, perhaps we can meet up. And how's that book going, you must know all about that Haydn dude now. Eileen got one of his records. Its kinda quaint, it relaxed me, though I don't know if he swings, man! Write us soon.*

Magnani had been planning to ask for a weekend off, but he wasn't ready to meet up with Pearson and Eileen. Especially Eileen. He was unsure if he could blot out his experience with her and see her as Pearson's partner. Re-reading the letter Magnani realised how settled he had become in his short time with Kaine. In a quarter of a year he had learned to belong somewhere.

His Haydn notes had lain untouched in a drawer in his bedroom. A few times he thought to restart, but each time excuses had been found. Spurred by Pearson he got the papers out and fingered a few of his pens, going through his ritual of preparation. It was early Sunday evening. By midnight he had brought himself up to date with what he had written. He still liked it and began to work out his next section. Haydn's first spell in London. It took him days of false starts to shake off the rust and come up with anything he could bear. Writing sessions had to be snatched between his duties with the children and he left his table strewn with semi-orderly chaos. Carr looked through it, Magnani knew that, and possibly others also, but he no longer minded. His over-riding need for secrecy had diminished with his integration into Kaine's world. After a week Magnani added a few more pages to the thin pile he already had.

London is so vast. Before experiencing it I thought Vienna a metropolis, the centre of my world. I see now we are on the edge of life. London is a great core of humanity. It is difficult to work, such is the noise in the streets, but I feel alive, so alive when most are withered before my age. There is so much to see and do here. And so much not to understand. The language is impossible, though I take lessons in in.

Salomon was right. Music does flourish here. I would not have thought it. The few Englishmen I met in Vienna and the court were not promising. I thought them clever merchants, and wagers of war, but they pay for their music, this is a great thing I will never get used to. I am intoxicated with the freedom of going where I want, when I want. And being paid to write what I want.

For my new symphony they gave me riches — three hundred and fifty of their English pounds. And they liken me to Shakespeare; "he moves and governs passions at will". Salomon translates all my reviews, which are many and pleasing. I am overwhelmed wherever I go, my music has gone before me it seems, which must be God's work, not mine.

And there is another welcome from Mrs Schroter. I take great pleasure in her company. Would that I was not so old, and married, for she is a widow.

Magnani doubted that his book on Haydn would ever see the light of day. He was not sure if he wanted to show it to anyone, certainly not until he was sure of his reasons for writing it. But it was proof of his haul back from the abyss. He had a toe-hold on the direction of his life and there was a fresh lightness to his existence which might not last, could never last, but Magnani felt good these days, and that was enough.

'Take a few days off.'

Kaine greeted Magnani with these words as they commenced a stroll in the grounds. Their circuit of the institution was a daily habit, a ritualised time of chat for the two men.

'You deserve it,' Kaine said. 'Go up to Jacksonville. It's not much of a town but they have jazz clubs there. Sometimes players come down from the north.'

'Yes I know, I've seen that in the papers.'

'Tell you what, I've got to go up there shortly. I can make it on a weekend. It's time to take the begging bowl around again and we have a good sponsor there. Patricia's father actually. He's a tycoon of some sort. Got two fine kids. Two normal kids. We could go up in the car.'

'Will you be taking in some music, Wilbur?'

'No, I don't think so. These old bones might get to jumping again, and break themselves. Anyway if it was the modern stuff I'd spoil it for you.'

Magnani did not know if he wanted 'the modern stuff' himself. In fact, he did not know how he would react to re-entering his musical world, and it would be wise to find out sooner rather than later. He took up Kaine's offer.

They travelled on the last weekend of May. Kaine said the weather was still very tolerable, but Magnani found it very hot. He had bought some lightweight shirts and a tan coloured jacket which made him look like an accountant on holiday. The Brothers Lazurus would not have approved. Kaine still wore a winter suit of sombre grey which camouflaged the spills of his cigar. He had changed his panama hat for a homburg, which made him look even smaller than he was. It gave him an obsequious air.

'It puts the giver of money at his ease,' he explained. 'I suppose that makes me some kind of whore but I learnt early how to do things. There is a ceremony to go through when you are asking for money. The power of the image is paramount. Look too confident or smart and people get suspicious. In this hat and suit I look like a southern preacher. They like that, and give more. Assuages their souls.'

Magnani did not find much to inspire in the countryside. It was flat and green and cultivated. Kaine must have thought likewise for after an initial burst of talk he settled down into silence. Going to Jacksonville from Tampa was like taking a trip to Edinburgh from London. Magnani would never get used to the distances. They had started after breakfast and hoped to reach their goal by six that evening.

They were three hours late. The ancient car started to misbehave a hundred miles out of Tampa. First a thin line of a steam wisped from under the hood, then great gusts of it blew back, as if the car had turned into the Penn Flyer.

'Does this sometimes,' Kaine said, nonchalantly. 'Have to stop and let it cool off. He pulled the car over, got out, and disappeared into the steam. He waved it aside with his hat and opened the hood. Magnani warned him against burns as he went to take off the radiator cap, but the old man had done this many times before.

'No water left in there to burn me, Frank.' He was right. The radiator made a despairing gurgle and settled itself to cool.

'We'll have to fill it up regular now,' Kaine said. 'I keep a five gallon can of water in the trunk.'

'What if the engine seizes?'

'It won't. It's a tough old dog.'

They limped to Jacksonville on fifty mile waterings.

'I never take it out of the state in summer,' Kaine said, 'its been overheating for a time now.'

'How long?'

'Oh, about fifteen years, I guess. Twenty, maybe.'

Kaine drove into downtown Jacksonville. It was an open city that sprawled as much as it could for its modest size. Larger than Tampa, but nothing like the northern cities Magnani had experienced.

'All the music joints are along here,' Kaine said. 'They sometimes have good musicians, and you can get a decent room there.'

He pointed to an old hotel, the sign of which was beginning to glow in the fading light. 'The Fitzroy' it said, but the 't' was not illuminated.

'It's better than it looks,' Kaine said. 'I've stayed there a few times, when I was younger.'

'Where will you stay ?' Magnani asked.

'With the Parker-Stevensons. They wouldn't hear of an old man like me checking into a hotel. Tell you what Frank, I'll meet you outside the Ritz, say six o'clock Sunday evening. The car will be better going back at night. We should get to Tampa in the early hours. You can sleep on a few hours Monday morning.'

'Thanks.'

'Think your money will last out?'

'It'll be fine.'

Before setting out Kaine had thrust another envelope of notes into Magnani's hand. It was a strange way to be paid.

Magnani checked into the Fitzroy and was shown a room on the first floor, one alongside the faulty sign. He rather liked the pink glow it cast into the room. Kaine was right, the place was better inside. It had an old-world style to it, lots of polished wood and faded wall pictures. It was clean and the bed comfortable, and one night's stay took two thirds of his money. Magnani washed quickly and changed his shirt and went out in search of music. As he passed the bored desk clerk he was glad he didn't have to stay in hotels anymore.

He passed a few clubs, Joey's Juke Joint, Alberta's — which offered exotic girls — and the Treble Clef Saloon, the home of 'cool' jazz. The down-at-heel look of the area was familiar to Magnani, it seemed to be the lot of his music to inhabit decay. The Treble Clef looked the most promising. The others he knew would be geared to low quality music and high priced drinks served by professionally attentive waitresses. Magnani's solo state would be taken as a sign that he was a husband on the loose, or a commercial man looking for company, or someone who wanted to talk and was prepared to pay for it. He had been thought all three in his time.

A combo that had worked New York when he was there was at the Treble Clef, a three piece rhythm section fronted by a tenor sax player. He paid the cover charge and was shown a table in the middle of the room. He would have preferred a side one, where he could sink into the shadows and listen, but they were all full. A girl brought him his large whiskey, winked at him and left him the check. He drank half of it down and felt his stomach recoil. It had forgotten about drink at the institution. Kaine had never offered alcohol and, after the first week, Magnani had not felt any need for it. Despite his weaknesses, music was his only addiction. And he needed it now. He willed the combo to be good, and was impatient for them to start.

Magnani recognised some jazz types in the club, and the mix of night people that never changed in any club, in any country. Overhead two large fans whirred at half speed, limbering up for the summer. Many sat in shirt sleeves, something Magnani had not seen in wintry New York. The combo appeared, four men in their thirties, neatly suited and closely shaved. They had post be-bop written all over them. The piano led them into a fast 'Night in Tunisia' which needed more pieces to make it work. Magnani was disappointed, and ordered another whiskey.

The combo settled into a medium paced set. They were better when the tempo slowed. A fine version of 'Body and Soul' was the high spot. It had a well phrased melody line played by the sax and confident improvisation in the middle section. The piano came in with an obligato Magnani thought rather original, encouraging the sax to paraphrase Porter's melody. It was worth coming to town for.

As the whiskey hit and the combo stayed sweet Magnani wished he had his guitar in his hands, he could have sat in with this music comfortably. They were good musicians who probed the tunes intelligently but did not lose their audience or each other in back-waters of indulgence. The tables were polite and attentive, very different to the north. Magnani joined in the applause at the end of the first set. By this time he was a little drunk, and as mellow as the saxophone. The thought crossed his mind to go backstage and introduce himself, but he thought better of it. How could he explain the absence of his guitar?

The Treble Clef filled to standing room only, and not much of that. Magnani was joined at his table by a couple who quarrelled and kissed in equal measure. It was his luck to have them for the club was generally quiet, just a chink of glasses over the low murmur of talk. The couple thought the same about him.

The man glared across at Magnani whenever his girl said something to annoy him, as if Magnani had put her up to it. He wore a light blue suit and a red and white polka dot tie. Magnani felt his solitude accused but even they managed to shut up when the combo played the second set.

Magnani was now feeling the drink. He wished he had eaten first but responsibility to his body had never been one of his strong points. The club was a pleasant haze of music and people. He followed the runs of the sax in his head, and played them with his fingers on his imagined guitar. Whenever the waitress approached him he used her, until his change ran out. It was as well the hotel bill included breakfast.

Magnani was enjoying himself too much to notice how much he was annoying the couple.

'What's the matter with you, pal?' the man asked, 'you playing with yourself or something? Your hands ain't stopped moving under the table.'

His girl hiccuped, and giggled. Magnani looked at him blankly. There was a lull in the music so he brought the table and its occupants back into focus. For the last half hour he had watched the stage, the combo blurred into the lights but the sounds pin-sharp in his head.

'Ignorant as well, huh?'

'What's that?'

'He's drunk honey,' the girl said.

Magnani smiled at the man but it did not work. He had decided on trouble and the inebriated Magnani was the soft touch needed to spur his aggression.

'Go sit somewhere else,' the man said, 'you ain't wanted here.'

'Where?'

Magnani thought he was being quite meek but his drink was knocked into his face. He lunged back, and fell out of his chair. It was the end of his night at the Treble Clef. He was the innocent party, but he was a stranger and had to go. A large doorman ejected him, hustling him past the combo into the street.

'Best go home and sleep it off,' the doorman said, pushing him out firmly, but with less force than he might have used.

Magnani took his bearings and knew it was just a short walk back to the Fitzroy. But a rest would be in order.

Magnani came to an hour later, roused by the clubs on the street shutting up, and spilling their custom out. People milled around hailing taxis, some talking in groups, not yet ready to go home and face Sunday. Magnani was unnoticed as he got up and shook himself. He was still sluggish with alcohol but its worst effects had dissipated. With the bed at the Fitzroy firmly in mind he moved down the street, taking the studied, shaky care that all drunks take.

Johnson was standing on a corner with two other men, one white. They saw each other at the same time, and shared a disbelieving surprise. Johnson's eyes enlarged and flashed hatred and revenge. Magnani crossed the street as calmly as he could and heard Johnson's steps quicken after him. It was not far to the Fitzroy but he was not coward enough to run. He turned to face Johnson.

'Frankie, it is you. Jesus man, ain't this a thing?' His two companions stood a few yards off, watching the situation.

'I never did believe that shit about you fucking off back to England,' Johnson said.

'You disappeared as well, didn't you?'

'Just resting up, Frankie.'

Johnson touched his head. 'That was quite a dent you gave me.'

'You tried to kill me.'

Johnson flashed his teeth in a grin. 'I get like that sometimes. Didn't ought to have smashed my head like that though, Frank. I get headaches, lots of headaches. Real bad. And when I gets them think of you, baby. Little Frankie, Frankie the Limey.'

Magnani thought it best to keep talking but he knew there would no reasoning with Johnson.

'What are you doing now, Johnson?'

'This and that. You don't look like you are doing anything Frank, you in a state, man.' Johnson laughed his most dangerous laugh.

It was true, it was Magnani's fate to always look his worst when he met up with Johnson, who wore a charcoal-grey suit and a crisp white shirt.

'Look Johnson, that's in the past. Let's call it quits. You stuck a knife in me a few times, remember?'

These last words set Johnson off. Magnani watched for another blade but this time there was none. Johnson hurled himself at him, bringing him to the ground. But Magnani was better prepared than before, and the shock of meeting Johnson had rapidly sobered him.

He gripped Johnson by the lapels and turned him over. It was not hard to do, his spell in the institution had made him fitter than he had ever been. Johnson pummelled at him with his fists but Magnani blocked most of the blows with his forearms and worked some of his own into Johnson s midriff. He gasped and threatened to kill Magnani, but his threat was idle. There was an absence of fear in Magnani. The Kaine Institution had been a pleasant but ephemeral dream but now he was back in the real world, continuing a fight started in New York. A fight for his life. He felt other hands on him, there was a sharp pain in the back of his head as he pushed Johnson away. He heard Kaine's voice shouting at him; it was the last thing he did hear.

Kaine was tapping him gently on the cheek. 'Frank, you all right?'

The old man came into focus, his eyes almost touching Magnani, who had never seen a kinder face.

'Don't try to get up yet,' Kaine said, let your head clear.

Magnani looked around for Johnson but there was only Kaine, a few gawpers, and a policeman. The cop stood behind Kaine with his hands in his belt, one close to his gun, which he wore open at the hip. He spoke.

'I should take him in Mr. Kaine.'

'He was set upon officer, you've been told that. Man's got to defend himself. My assistant is a visitor to these shores.'

Magnani sat up on the sidewalk. Blood trickled from a cut inside his mouth and he was stiff around his ribs and kidneys. He thought to ask where Johnson was but realised the folly of that question.

'You know those guys?' the cop asked.

'No. They just came up to me. I think they wanted money.'

'Uh huh.' The cop scratched at the stubble on his chin. This had been a long Saturday night.

'All right Mr. Kaine, if you say so. Get him off the street now.'

To Magnani he said, 'maybe it would be better if you did't t come back to Jacksonville, son. It don't seem to like you.'

Magnani silently agreed.

Kaine helped Magnani to the car. 'Come on Frank, let's get you to the Fitz.'

'Wilbur, I don't understand. How are you here?'

'I was driving down the street. I had a whim to come down here. You got me thinking of the old days in Kansas City. Why not, I thought, I'll join Frank in the Clef for an hour. I thought you'd be there, it has the only decent music in town tonight. And the Parker-Stevensons had a dinner party. I was not missed.'

Kaine must have stepped past a sleeping drunk outside the Treble Clef and not realised it was him, Magnani thought.

'I took in the last set there and was heading back to the Parker-Stevensons when I saw you in a clinch with that black guy. Couldn't believe it at first.'

They drove the few seconds to the hotel. As Magnani opened the door on his side Kaine grasped his arm. 'It was him, wasn't it Frank. The one from New York?'

'Yes. It was him.'

'Hell, the luck of that.'

Kaine examined Magnani in the bedroom.

'You'll be sore in the morning but your bones are okay.' He probed Magnani's mouth. 'Don't need stitching, the lip's a bit torn inside. Try not to chew on it.'

Kaine took a powder from his pocket and mixed it in a tumbler of water. 'This will help you sleep. Hell, I feel like a real doctor again.'

Magnani drank the draught and lay back on the bed. Kaine settled himself in a chair and took out a book from his voluminous suit. He read a dog-eared copy of *Huckleberry Finn*, humming to himself in his uniquely tuneless way. He had carried Twain's book around with him for many years, and knew it as well as a Bible-belt preacher knew his Book.

NINE

Magnani and Kaine got back to Tampa a day late. Kaine explained away Magnani's injuries to the women as a street fall.

'The boy got so excited about the jazz he didn't see the steps. Fell right down them.'

They were satisfied by this but John Carr told Magnani by his look that he knew better.

It was a week of foreboding. The past had reared up to smash Magnani's fragile wall of security. Each day he checked the perimeter of the home with anxious eyes, expecting to see Johnson lurking there. Kaine tried to allay his fears.

'Forget it, Frank,' Kaine said, 'it was just bad luck. It won't happen again, and he'd never find you here, anyway. Hell, why should he look?'

'He's looking for me now. His face was full of hate, and Johnson is the kind of man who needs to keep burning. It explains his existence to him, even if it is so unnecessary.'

'Hate usually is, if you are on the outside of it. Who is Johnson, anyway?'

'Someone who hung around the New York jazz scene. He was a fixer, and drug dealer. An ex-drummer. Johnson was my first contact over here.'

'What was the original fight over?'

'I've never really worked it out. There was an edge between us which built up. But nothing else. Maybe it was because I was an outsider, and having some success.'

'And because you were white?'

'Johnson is mean enough to be a racist, but that would be flattering his motives. He never showed any concern for his fellow blacks, everyone was a mark for him.'

'Uh huh. Well, perhaps he'll get put away, or dead.'

'Perhaps.'

Magnani's work continued. The big band learned more numbers and performed them one Saturday in June before an invited audience of parents and local people Kaine had coerced into attending. Magnani conducted his twelve players as they tried to match rhythms with Ellington and Basie. He had erred on the side of caution and decided they would play along with the records. Carr had hooked up some speakers in the largest room. This way the culture shock would not be too great. Even so the audience was nonplussed by the end, a fact noted and enjoyed by Kaine.

'Ain't never heard no decent music before,' he whispered to Magnani. 'I reckon a few felt kinda tainted — all this monkey music.'

He winked and went on his rounds. There were rare visitors present; donations would have to extracted from them. The highlight of the performance was a drum duet shared by Wesley and Tony. It was frenetic and turned into a battle but it went down well. Magnani's time with the group was vindicated, and for a while his worry over Johnson lessened. But his unease had never disappeared since that night in Jacksonville. It was worse than the first time, for it proved his premonition of further contact with the man.

As the guests filed out, to be given tea and cakes on the lawn Carr motioned to Magnani.

'Can you come here for a second, Mr. Magnani?'

He followed Carr to a storeroom.

'What is it, John?'

Carr looked at him with his unreadable face.

'Man downtown been asking about you?'

'What man?'

'Black guy, snappy dresser.'

'Asking you?'

'Nah, I keeps my mouth shut — at all times. I was in a joint down on twenty third. I drinks there sometimes, when the missis is on me. There was this guy, from up north, asking some of the boys if there was an English guitarist working the area.'

'What was he told?'

'No-one knew you there. But if he asks in the record store, or a few other places, they gonna tell. No reason not to. You know this guy, Mr. Magnani?'

'I think so.'

'Is it to do with your trouble in Jacksonville?'

'What trouble?'

Carr s brows arched. 'I ain't born yesterday, boy.'

'Yes, it is. And it's about time you called me Frank.'

'He gonna bring trouble here?'

'I don't know. I hope not.'

'Wouldn't be good.'

'I'll sort it out John.'

'Huh. I'll tell you — Frank — that man had murder in his eyes.

I seen it before a few times. If you gotta skip I know people downtown. There's boats going from Tampa all the time — South America, Europe. All places.'

'Thanks John.'

'Okay. Only I wouldn't want any trouble here for Mr. Kaine.'

To run again. It pitted his stomach with distaste but this time there was another dimension. For the first time Magnani felt responsible for others. The children, Kaine, Joyce and even D. Bell, whose moods he had learned not to notice. They did not deserve to be touched by Johnson's world.

Magnani made excuses not to go into town. Before the next trip to the Bijou he feigned a migraine and kept to his room. That he might be accosted by Johnson when with the children was a risk he did not want to take. Johnson was the downside of his old life and he cared enough about his new one to keep him out of it, if he could.

In the evening Kaine asked him if he was well enough to take their usual constitutional. He said he was . They walked through air thick enough to cut. It was impregnated with a day's heat and the heavy scent of the bougainvillaeas. They were in full flow now, flashing their reds against the white walls of the buildings. Kaine wore a short sleeved shirt which exposed his thin, blue-veined arms. The veins reminded Magnani of the scars of the miners of his home town. His own body was free from marks, and healthier than it had ever been. He wore shorts bought from a store in Tampa and through the spring the sun had browned his legs and arms.

'Migraine gone, eh?' Kaine asked. 'Infernal things. I used to get a lot in medical school, though such things were poo-poohed in those days. Affairs of the head were not given much credence. Mister Freud was not very well known and his industry was in its infancy.'

'Is that what you think causes them — psychological pressures?'

Kaine shrugged. 'It's as handily a vague reason as any. That and inventing them.'

'Okay, I own up. I didn't think it wise to go into town.'

'Think he is looking for you?'

'I know he is. Carr had a word with me. Johnson is around.'

'I see.'

'It will only be a matter of time before he finds out I'm here. Tampa is not very big.'

'Guess not. There's always the police, you know. I'll vouch for you.'

'Thanks Wilbur, but no thanks. I appreciate my stay here, more than I can tell you, but it's best if I move on.'

Kaine looked closely into his face and Magnani saw how old the man was. 'Don't run, Frank,' he said. 'No-one ever can.'

'I know it, I know it well. But I don't want Johnson coming here.'

'What about the kids?' he question hurt.

'Joyce can take over the big band. All you have to do is stand there and wave a stick.'

'Don't sell yourself short, Frank. You've done a hell of a lot more than that. And you know it. I've seen you grow all the time you've been here. We all have, and the institution had gained. You've reintegrated Wesley — a minor miracle — and we are all made younger by your presence.'

'I could never have stayed here, Wilbur. I only have papers to be in America for six months. I'm beyond that already. And there's my music.'

'You made it here.'

Magnani was arguing in spite of himself. He looked to ease the path of his flight with reasons, but he loved Kaine's praise. He needed to believe it, but his mind was made up to go. It had been since Carr had tipped him off.

The drone of insects taking the last of the sun soothed and the heat was bearable at this time. Kaine had been right, Magnani had got used to it. They stopped to watch a small cloud of ladybirds rise up from the bougainvillaeas and go whirring over the grass. Magnani felt the attraction of belonging, of having an existence mapped out, with logical aims and steady progress. The antithesis of his life. He might have been looking for this in Haydn, an ordered history buried in respectful time to counteract the wild swings of his own existence. Since Jacksonville he had not written anything. That all seemed rather pointless now.

'I have to go Wilbur,' Magnani restated.

There was silence for half a circumference of the lawns. Magnani knew Kaine was chewing over possibilities and was relieved when the old man said, 'yes, I guess you do, Frank.'

He was also disappointed.

'You haven't come far enough down the road to stay. Another six months here and you would not leave, Johnson or no Johnson.'

Magnani cut him off before he could say anything more. 'Carr says he knows people on the docks. Says he can get me a boat out.'

'Yes. John is well connected.'

'I thought I'd sign on as a deckhand if I can't afford to pay my passage.'

'There will be enough money coming to you to do so. Better go soon then son,' Kaine said.

Magnani did the rounds with D. Bell. They checked on the dormitories at ten o'clock. There was no imposed curfew on the children but few ever wanted to stay up much past this time.

'They've had enough by then,' Bell said, 'burned up all their energy — just like regular kids.'

She led him through the girls' room, where Patricia tried to look alert and interested but could not prevent a yawn from spreading behind her hand. In the boys section Wesley snored, a steady thunder in E Major which no-one noticed. Tony sprung out of his bed to shake Magnani's hand. He had not done this for some weeks. Could Tony possibly know this was the last time he would do so? He forced himself to return Tony's steady gaze. They were almost eyeball to eyeball.

'Hi, Frank. It's hot.'

'Yes.'

'Is it hot, where you come from?'

'Rarely.'

'Why?'

'It's a different type of country.'

'Like Texas. I'm gonna go to Texas one day.'

'Yes, like Texas.'

Magnani extracted his hand, which was always difficult with Tony and continued his round. D. Bell turned out the lights and shut the door after him.

'Hmmph. Texas. Why did you tell him that?'

'Because he wanted to believe it, and there's no time to tell him anything else.'

'What do you mean, no time?'

'I'm leaving. Something has come up.'

'Jesus, that's sudden.'

'Yes.'

'Well, you came in with the wind, can't be surprised if you go out with it.'

They walked to the staff living room, a place rarely inhabited. Sometimes, after ten, there was a get-together for coffee and sleepy talk. Bell never attended. Tonight she joined Magnani. She percolated some coffee and gave him a cup. It was the first time they had been alone together.

'How old are you, Magnani?' she asked.

'Twenty nine, now.'

'You look older.'

She lit a cigarette, tossing the carton over to him. 'See what it says on that. Be happy, be lucky. Pathetic.'

'What, to be happy?'

'To read it on your cigarettes. They must think folks are dumb.'

Magnani decided to risk a confrontation.

'Have you ever been happy?' he asked.

He expected her to spit a curse at him but she did nothing but drink her coffee and drag deeply on her Lucky Strike.

'What's it to you?' she replied.

'I've been here six months and I've never seen you smile.'

'Don't believe in it.'

'This is work you need to smile at.'

'Are you going to dose me with your thoughts, just because you are leaving?'

'It's easier to talk knowing that, I admit it. But there's never been a chance before. You are always with the children, or you are not here.'

'You keep to your room a lot yourself. Carr tells me you are writing something in there.'

'I was.'

'About us?'

'No, not at all.' He was not sure if she believed him.

Bell slurped her coffee a little as she drank. He noticed for the first time the thin pencil of her moustache. It glistened with the coffee and made her look even sterner. But he no longer disliked his prickly colleague. She prevented the home from being other-worldly, she was real and brought the streets into the place. She lit another cigarette from the dying tip of the first.

'My second attempt to be happy.'

'See, you made a joke. Are you feeling all right?'

'Shut up. I come from Danville, Virginia. Not far from where Kaine sprung from.'

'Did you know each other, before here?'

'I said to shut up. If you are going to listen just listen.'

Magnani obeyed.

'I had one of them, one of the children. A Mongol. I wasn't married, never wanted to be married. He was a Polack sailor, can you believe that? As if they ever had a navy. We had a time together for a few months, before he blew. Left me with a swelling stomach and a job that didn't want me. That was all right. I went back to my folks and told them my man had got himself killed. Fell off his boat on a black night, I said. They were simple people. Then the baby came, worse than any here. You been punished, ma said. God has seen what you done and punished you.'

Bell thought about a third smoke but allowed her cigarette to die in her hand.

'Things were tough. Roosevelt was about to drag us into that war of yours and Danville was not a place to be different. I gave the kid up. To a place like this, I suppose. I never knew where because my father fixed it. Put a hole in his savings. I didn't do it for you, pa said, it's to keep the shame from your ma, and me now there's just my pension. I was not young. Past thirty.'

She paused, and pushed back a strand of her thin hair. Softened by the glow of the table lamp her face looked younger. Magnani glimpsed the girl Bell might have been.

'My father died soon after, and ma followed. They always did everything in pairs. Ma said I bust his heart, doing what I did. Not just having a baby, you understand but having a baby like that. Neither could stand the shame of it. For a time I felt dirty, and the more dirty I felt the more I slept around. There was always someone passing through, the war was a time of people passing through. Men liked me.'

Magnani's coffee cooled in his cup but he dared not reach for it.

'I passed out one night,' Bell continued, 'they took me to a doctor. That's how I met Kaine. He was visiting another doctor there to pick up a new kid for this place. When he offered me a job I was surprised, when I found out what type of place he ran I couldn't believe it. It was almost enough to make me think there was a God.'

Magnani found his voice.

'Kaine knows about your child?'

'Of course he does. No-one else though, until now. Every day I've worked here I've seen what I gave away, and was glad and sorry for it. That's how it should be.'

'Surely you don't see the home as a punishment?'

'Why not? I used to think my son might end up here. That would be the final twist of this thing.' She placed a hand over her heart. 'But I wouldn't know him, if his name was changed. As those girls say down at the Bijou, they all look alike. Bell's eyes were moist, a tear rolled out of one. It tracked down her cheek and rested at the corner of her mouth until her tongue snaked out to lick it away.

Magnani reached out his hand and put it over hers. She did not pull from him. 'I'm sorry for your trouble, D. Bell.'

'Yeah. That and ten cents will get you a cup of coffee.'

'What's your first name?'

She thought about this for a time.

'Daphne. I've hated it for as long as I can remember. They called me Daffy in school.'

'Why didn't you give yourself another?'

'D.Bell is good enough.'

More penance, Magnani murmured under his breath. He spoke up.

'The kids would like to call you by a name. You do good work with them, and have done for a long time. They like you.'

'I know I do good work. Kaine would not have me here otherwise. He's soft but he's no fool. But don't tell me I'm liked. That's a lie, even if its a kind one.'

The door opened and Joyce joined them. Magnani withdrew his hand before she could see it.

'Hello you two, is that coffee?'

Bell got up quickly. 'I'm turning in. I'm bushed.'

She left the room.

'That's D. Bell,' Joyce said, 'Miss Antisocial. She's been here the best part of twenty years and all I know is that she comes from Virginia, and can be very difficult to work with.'

'Yes, that's how she is.'

Magnani followed Bell's suit and excused himself, leaving Joyce to wonder what she had done.

The *Volos Star* did not inspire confidence. Magnani stood on the Tampa dock with John Carr, who pointed the boat out to him.

'There she is, Frank. Greek registered — they ask the least questions. Magnani saw a medium sized freighter of indeterminate age. Under its English name it had a duplication in Greek letters which made it seem from another world. Rust dappled its sides. eating away at the old green and blue paint. Its belly was fat and sagged low in the water, as if inviting the ocean to take it.

'Will that thing get across the Atlantic?' Magnani asked.

'Sure. It's average, for a tub. I been on plenty when I was younger.'

Carr had arranged everything. He knew who to see, who to ply with drink. A passage on the *Volos Star* had been fixed and Magnani would be its sole paying passenger. Carr had cautioned him about working his way.

'That's no good for you,' Carr said. 'You don't know the work and you don't know sailors. They is funny, knifemen and arsehole creepers a lot of 'em. And on a crate like the *Volos* they use a Moroccan crew — job's too bad even for the Greeks.'

At seven in the morning the day had already got up a head of steam. It was an armpit-trickling, pore-opening, hair sticking to neck kind of day, when the southern sun announced its four months of lordship over the land. Its ally was the flat, hot wind that stole in from Cuba or up from the Yucatan cauldron, to mock each over-heated body with useless caresses.

Magnani dripped with nerves and sweat. He had said his good-byes to the children on Sunday night, waiting until they were turned in for bed. It was better this way, they might be able to sleep him out of their immediate thoughts. Only Wesley seemed to take it in. 'No guitar now,' he had said solemnly, and recommenced the sucking of his fingers. There was amusement in the faces of Tony and Patricia, they thought he was joking, that he would be there as usual in the morning. Magnani knew he was cutting their trust with his caution, or his cowardice; he did not know if it was for them or himself that he ran.

Daphne Bell and Joyce saw him off on the steps of the home. He gave each a hug and whispered 'so long Daphne' in Bell's ear. There had been a brief meeting with Kaine after breakfast. The old man did not want to come outside. He handed Magnani his last enve-lope, which contained enough for his passage and two months living in Greece, according to Carr. Although he had left the guitar in his room Magnani found it waiting for him in Kaine's office.

'Weren't going to forget this, were you?' Kaine asked.

'It belongs to the institution.'

'Who would play it, son? No, you take it, it's part of you, not us. Take this too.'

Kaine gave him a copy of his beloved *Huckleberry Finn*, a new edition. 'Couldn't give you my copy, like me, it's disintegrating. Have you ever read it?'

'No, I haven't.'

'All life is in it. American life anyway.'

Kaine stuck out his thin hand and Magnani felt its swollen veins as he lightly squeezed it.

'Put Johnson out of your mind, Frank. He's over.'

'I know.'

'You can always come back to us, if you want.'

'Thanks. That means a lot.'

'Then you are richer than when I picked you up in Roanoke.'

'Goodbye, Wilbur.'

Magnani turned and went quickly out of the room, the guitar clutched in his hand. On the steps his belongings waited, packed in the sack.

The *Volos Star* floated out into the Gulf of Mexico. Once clear of the confines of Tampa it chugged down the coast line towards Miami and the Atlantic. It suited the sluggish gulf. Magnani leaned against a handrail and watched the *Volos* push a path through the waters. It was a tired push, achieved without any semblance of grace, just a rusty hulk going about its business.

He was given a small cabin aft of the bridge, one of two kept for the rare passenger. A Maltese cook, who doubled as steward, was Magnani's official contact with the crew. On boarding he had shaken hands with the captain, Peliades, who had offered his limp hand and promptly ignored him. This suited Magnani.

The cabin was large enough to sit in and trapped the heat like a steam bath. It smelt of diesel and former occupants.

'Nice here,' the cook said. He tapped the guitar. 'Musica. You play?'

Magnani could hardly deny it, but he put the guitar as much out of sight as he could. It would take more than two weeks to reach Piraeus and there was no challenge in the voyage and, as yet, excitement in his destination. He thought of Coleridge's painted boat and felt equally stuck, and mocked by his mode of transport.

He was to take his meals with the officers, but this turned out to be the first officer and engineer. The captain kept to his bridge, or more often his bunk. When Magnani did encounter him he smelt of ouzo and brooded past him like a Greek Ahab. To ply his life in such sterile surroundings would do this to a man, he thought. When the other officers got to know him a little they raised imaginary bottles to their lips behind the captain's back.

Magnani saw no sign of Carr's dangerous men. As he had forecast, a crew of Moroccans did the menial work, overseen by Greek officers. The cook from Valetta made the numbers up to eleven. The Moroccans went about their work with resigned surliness, broken by the occasional lightening of spirit. A sailor fell heavily over a paint pot and onto the freshly whitened deck. He stuck there long enough to make an outline with his meagre body. This made the Moroccans' day and their voyage, a precious break in their manual gloom.

They did not stop at Miami; the *Volos* skirted the Florida Keys and headed out into the grey Atlantic, charting a course that bisected the Bahamas. Magnani watched the spine of the Keys unfurl and thought of gangsters on the dodge, washed-out writers and other sundry failures. The islands looked flat, barren and hostile, perfect places for the *Volos* to sink. Magnani wondered if he now qualified to live on them.

The weather was fair every day. He was given a deckchair of which he made full use. His bronzing was complete. The *Volos* docked at Gibraltar to take on goods but Magnani did not disembark. His lethargy did not want to brush against the Englishness of the place. On the quayside he saw the Jack Tar and the Jolly Roger Tavern, and that was enough. They trawled across the Mediterranean, the *Volos* even lower in the water with extra cargo. In two more days they were off Piraeus, waiting for permission to dock.

Crossing the Atlantic, Magnani had read Kaine's gift, vegetable-like in the sun. He was as lazy as Huck's Mississippi. Once, when the slow movement of the *Volos* had jangled his nerves, he tried to play the guitar, furtively in his cabin. Its strings had stuck to his fingers and the sound he produced was brittle and life-less. Now he made himself look forward to Greece. He pushed it into his thoughts as the weather freshened and the journey's end appeared.

There was a touch of Meltemi seeping across from Turkey which eased Magnani's despondency and told him that he should be glad he was free. This was a shaky freedom, born of chance and accident more than design. It was a lonely, impecunious state, he had no idea where he would go or what he would do, but the breeze licked at his dreams, revived them and told him of possibilities. He knew more about ancient Greece than he did of its present state. Byron flickered through his mind, and mingled with vague images of warring Turks and Venetians, but he had no chronological grasp of the country. Yet he preferred this, his mind was as open as his ignorance.

No-one bothered him when he left the *Volos*. Hardly anyone noticed him. The first officer gave him his passport back and the cook brought him a last coffee. 'Coffee no good here,' he said, jerking a cheerful thumb at the mainland. Magnani walked down the gangplank to be gazed at by a bored customs man. It was all so different to New York, the difference between a spark and ember. Magnani said that he was on holiday and was let into Greece after a casual opening of the guitar case and a check of his money. In the customs shed a radio played, music that was more Eastern and

African than European. Magnani heard a reed instrument wail like a bagpipes trodden on and took to it in the first sixteen bars. He quickened his steps through the sleazy metal world of Piraeus.

It was a few miles to the centre of Athens. Magnani caught a bus that a tobacco seller pointed out to him. The weather was hot but without the humidity of Florida. Not that it would have bothered him, he was fully broiled now, as Kaine would have said, The language would be a problem, a fact which hit him hard as he looked at the street signs. Some had English equivalents to their Greek letters, many did not.

He found a hotel in a dusty side street that looked cheap enough for him, Athen's answer to Al smiled at him with a face cupped in both hands. He listened to the same music Magnani had heard on the dock. It was loud and reverberated up the wooden staircase, strident woodwind battled with a racing percussion: it was the only life in the place. After a charade of hand waving and slow speech Magnani obtained a room at a price which embarrassed him, if he had worked it out right. Now he understood Carr's optimism for cheap living. Unlike Al, this hotel man carried his sack and showed him up to his room, which was small with a large bed. The man, who Magnani thought was called Caliph, or something like it, patted the covers of the bed avidly, causing small clouds of dust to rise up from it, and speckle silver in the sunlight. The room was not clean but Magnani liked it. There was none of the menace of New York.

Magnani began to feel good without knowing why. There was a heavy silence here, breached by distant traffic and people noises, but not broken. He could hear the music from the lobby below but this too blended into the calm. He was in a different world and felt it strike a chord with his character in his own southern background. After a quick wash in warm cold water Magnani realised the reason for his changed mood. He sensed there would be no rush here, the occasional panic of movement perhaps, but no rush. There had been none since he had stepped off the *Volos Star*. As he sank onto the mattress Magnani realised he had not even craned his head in the bus to find the Acropolis.

TEN

Magnani slept well in his lumpy bed, undisturbed by the attack of bugs. They left a stitch of bites across his back but a tepid shower cooled their itch. He forgot them as he determined to atone for his disinterested arrival in this ancient world. If he stood on tiptoe and looked over rooftops the Acropolis could be seen. The Parthenon drew the eye upwards and the early morning painters' light etched the ruin in sharp relief. Magnani saw a perfectly formed rectangle fronted by eight pillars, and was not disappointed.

It was a good day, cloudless and bright and not over busy. There were scatterings of tourists but not enough to spoil. The Parthenon had been built to impress, and with its heart exploded, shot at, or stolen, it still did. Magnani reached it quickly, climbing the narrow streets in sandals acquired for the Florida beach. He slipped a few times, unused to gripping such smooth stone with leather, but did not lessen his step.

Sitting between two pillars he caught the murmur of talk within. This place trapped words and took the imagination to older days. If Magnani had been alone he might have dared the gods and played the guitar, so fine were the acoustics. A few tourists glanced down at him and took him for a Greek.

He stayed on the hill for several hours, looking down on the massed development of Athens, noting the green parts and gauging the city in his mind. Sometimes the honk of a car or the squeal of tyres carried up to his perch. When the sun softened and his stomach gnawed he descended. He found a café near the hotel where he ate moussaka and drank a local wine, blood-red from Crete. He did not know what he ate but after a suspicious prodding of the aubergines decided that it was good. He bought a tourist map at the café and thumbed through it at his table. It was the kind with cheerful sketches and arrows, colourful and almost useless.

As he entered the lobby of the hotel Caliph spied him from his cubby-hole. He took the map from Magnani's hand.

'Go to the islands,' he said, 'here, and here — and here.'

He stabbed a grimy thumb at names which were strange to Magnani. 'Good here, peace here. Not like Athens, or Cairo — my home.'

Caliph's English had improved overnight, as if he had dusted it down for his new guest. 'Plenty people come work here,' he

- 151 -

continued, lots of Egyptians like me. Soon Athens she crumble again.'

He laughed at his prediction and slapped Magnani good day.

Magnani stayed at Caliph's place for three nights, planning a rough route for himself. He would go north, following Caliph's thumb to the port of Volos, he owed the old *Star* that much. Volos was the gateway to the Sporades Islands, which attracted Magnani for what the map described at their 'pine-clad shores'. Blindly he imagined a mix of Sweden and Africa. At a bureau he bought tickets that would take him to the island of Skopelos, which Caliph said was little known and less visited by foreigners.

To celebrate his plan of action Magnani drank two bottles of ouzo with Caliph. As the Egyptian's only foreign guest he was pampered. He was shown how to mix the drink with water to make a glass of cloudy potency, a kind of Greek schnapps. He had never liked it but here it blended better with the heat and the olive oil.

'Come,' said Caliph, when the ouzo was finished. 'I shut up the place. And I take you somewhere my friend, like we have in Cairo.'

"Somewhere" was a brothel, the back room of a bar where girls sat waiting. Caliph entered with a knowing wave of his hand, showing off his night world to Magnani. The girls were friendly and bored. When they did not smile they were pretty but when they did their teeth revealed years of neglect and hinted at a future in which a price might have to be paid. They were arranged among ornate cushions and were heavy with jewellery and excess weight. With warning bells ringing in his ouzo-soaked head Magnani allowed himself to be led away by one of the girls. Caliph flashed his own imperfect grin, approved the girl and shoo-ed them away. He thought he was offering a manly kinship.

The girl was Leila, another Egyptian. Her English ran to her name and a range of sexual invitations. It was sufficient and made things easier. Magnani refused the murky wine she offered but availed himself of everything else. Leila drained the tension from him expertly and he remembered her almond-shaped eyes and tiny voice, and the graceful movements which belied her bulk.

He used the key Caliph had given him to re-enter the hotel. His host was nowhere to be seen; he had melted into the soft night for another assignation.

The train to Volos was slow and the journey long. Once again Magnani arrived at the end of the day. The hotel recommended by

Caliph was just off the harbour, close enough to catch the bustle of boats and the chat of people about them. A sunset of fleecy orange soaked the darkening sky and reflected on the sea, to bathe the moored caiques. Volos itself was an unattractive working town built around the curve of a bay, the Aegean stretching away from it, to the island Magnani sought.

From Volos a ferry service plied the Sporades, serving locals and tourists alike. As Caliph had predicted the latter were in short supply. Magnani was in a country not much changed for centuries, more people had come to conquer than to visit.

At five the next morning he was drinking coffee with the fishermen, waiting to leave. The ferry was little more than a launch but it braved the high swell resolutely, causing stomachs to lurch in unison. Aboard were a few island people and a man bringing his family back to his birthplace. Magnani stood as far forward as he could, leaning into the elements and enjoying the voyage. It was everything his time on the Volos Star had not been. He was invigorated and scoured of worries as his mind leapt over the sea to Skopelos. His instinct told him he would be all right there. He would finish the book and rework his relationship with music; this premonition of certainty dashed over him like the spray forced from the sea.

They passed a number of small islands, some no more than rocky outcrops topped with clusters of green olive trees. Each tantalised with hints of his destination. They stopped at Skiathos, largest island in the Sporades chain. It conformed to the map's description, with large areas of it was pine forest and generous beaches. Magnani thought of disembarking but stuck to his original choice.

Skopelos was quite different. They chugged into a compact harbour fronted by a café, its chairs empty and waiting. A group of people stood ready to greet the launch. Fishermen lolled in small boats and a lone cat sat on the edge of the quay, in anticipation of scraps. The arrival of the launch would be the main activity of the day here: if this was the rush hour Magnani knew he must like the place.

A small girl with a squint stepped in front of him as he disembarked. She said something to him in Greek but turned it into English on seeing his incomprehension.

'Room? You want a room?'

Beyond her Magnani saw others about to approach. He settled for youth and nodded his head at the girl; she led him away from the quay, up steep cobblestoned alleys.

Skopelos was a squat island, a smaller companion to Skiathos, with the main town at one end, built up in layers around the natural harbour. Magnani struggled after the girl with his sack and carried his guitar with shy pride.

This was Maria Karefelas, oldest child of Dimitri and Soula. For the next six months Magnani was to share their house. Dimitri Karefelas was a carpenter and like most of the islanders, a part-time fisherman. He had built a guest room on one side of his house and Magnani was its first occupant, arriving before it was quite finished. Maria led him to a pleasant rectangle of a room which caught the light and was simply furnished with a wooden bed and pine furniture. There was not yet a door and a gap led to the family section of the house, with a thin curtain as division. Maria ushered him through, into the kitchen. Magnani was struck by the difference. His room was empty and clean and still smelled of new wood; it was geared towards city Greeks. The Karefelas kitchen, however, was a hive of small children and grandparents, of cooking and the occasional chicken.

Dimitri Karefelas was on the fringe of forty, an upright man, strongly built with unflinching sea-grey eyes and a tangle of salty black hair. His wife Soula was small and self-effacing, appearing from behind her husband to meet Magnani. But she ruled the house, flitting about her kitchen like a nesting bird. Maria was the only Karefelas who spoke English so she became Magnani's go-between, though he determined to learn as much of their difficult language as he could. The rent was absurdly small, adding greater longevity to Magnani's money.

'Come eat,' Maria said, tugging at his arm. He was put to sit next to granny, who smiled at him with a face notched with wrinkles. Magnani saw the youth in her eyes, and the strong yellow teeth. She dug him in the ribs and chuckled, encouraging her husband to do the same. These were Soula's parents. Granny had broken the ice, and the family bubbled into life as it sat around the table. Magnani experienced Greek kindness for the first time and felt welcome, and safe.

From the first day getting up very early was a delight for Magnani. He had learned to do it in Tampa, but never to like it, it was hard to break the nocturnal habits of a jazzman. But on Skopelos he changed. To stretch and to look out of Dimitri's unpainted window frame ensured his mood would be a good one, and that a long, clement day lay before him. He looked forward to his life on the island, it would be a place of firsts.

The Karefelas house was two thirds up the hill and from it most of the harbour could be seen, and part of the coast. It was rocky and indented with small bays, few of which could be reached on foot. Magnani saw a community of white houses gathered together in tiers, sometimes merging into a confused mass. And he would learn that the islanders behaved as if they were one. There was a strong identity here, as if his own Welsh terraces had been scrubbed clean of coal and grey days. Magnani would recognise the same concerns and petty jealousies, the gossipy talk of idle moments and the same inquisitive caring. He wondered if this life was as much under threat as his own peoples' but knew change would come in the guise of progress. He was himself a herald of it.

In the morning the light was uncannily sharp. The wood smoke drifting from chimneys did not challenge it. Magnani was able to pick out detail on the hats of the fishermen as they bobbed in the harbour boats and the grain of the quayside tables was clear gold. The light gave Magnani the feeling of being in control; one saw clearly so one thought clearly. This was a very basic logic but his new world was one of the senses, of sight, smells and touch. The people of Skopelos liked to touch, to enhance talk and make their points. He became adept at deciphering hand actions and learned never to raise his thumb to anyone. From the terraces below his room wafted up smells of plants and herbs he did not know, but they fused with the view to stimulate and encourage. For him this was a far less alien place than America.

He allowed himself a week to explore the island. Skopelos was served by a bus that ran more on some days than others. When there was a demand, and no fish, a fisherman drove an aged blue and white Mercedes, left in Volos by retreating Germans. It put Magnani in mind of D. Bell and her counterpart. He shared the bus with farmers and their animals, and stray travellers who followed unbeaten tracks. That there were few of them suited his sense of isolation. He knew he was in part a selfish interloper using the island for his own ends, but he needed the safety of an unknown language and a people who were equal in their ignorance of him. Magnani wanted the qualities that Kaine's children had begun to instill in him to be further nurtured here.

He found a beach which the islanders called 'Paradise'. They had good reason. A track of grey dust led down to a small stretch of pebble and sand, flanked by giant pillars of rock. A cliff overhung it heavy with pines, which impregnated the air with their resin. The sea was deep turquoise and Magnani swam in it most days. Often

he was the sole disturber of the water, although fishermen sometimes chugged past and waved. When he had integrated well enough
to use Dimitri's bicycle he became one of the minor sights of the
island, going to swim in Paradise when wise men slept.

Magnani obtained a small table in the town. With Maria laughing
and encouraging he hauled it up the steep streets to the house,
where it became his place of writing. It was just large enough to hold
his Haydn papers and a few books. When he wrote it wobbled a
little but he learned to match it with the rhythm of his pen. Bouts
of writing were offset by his visits to the beach, strenuous hours
linked easily with idle ones in long days.

Soula Karefelas assumed Magnani would eat his meals with her
family, more as a hospitality than a service, though he often breakfasted in a harbour cafe. There he learned his first Greek, accumulating words from fishermen returning from their lobster pots. With
Maria to help him the words grew into phrases then short sentences,
and doors were unlocked. Magnani became social, and even a little
popular, something he had never been before.

As Magnani rejuvenated his research, insights into Haydn came
more freely. To sink into another time in this timeless place was
natural and the book he thought spent took on new life. When
Magnani walked in the early morning and felt the heat surge from
the ground that had trapped it overnight he knew he was better
placed to empathise with the composer's own communing with
Nature. The fug of New York nights and the dripping heat of
Tampa was absent, and for intensity Skopelos could not manage
much more than the slap of dice on a backgammon board. But
Magnani's thoughts here were intense, for he had a unity of purpose. Haydn saw nature as the confirmation of God and recharged
his hope and his music from it. Perhaps Magnani could do the same.

In a few weeks Magnani was able to bury Johnson in America and
as he progressed on the book he felt able to pick up the guitar again.
He exercised his fingers in early evening, sitting in the window frame
of his room, or going beyond the stony edge of the house to play on
the cliff top. His performances evolved into a local eccentricity in
Dimitri's street. Children peeped around corners and giggled behind their hands. Older people watched him for a while, decided he
was harmless, and left with a polite wave of condescension and a
rub of the head. Magnani could not believe how public he had
become.

When he thought his hands were making the right connections
with his head and the fretboard of the guitar he ran through his book

of arrangements. And he matched the pace of his writing in the mornings by composing short pieces of music. Magnani tried to mix everything he had learnt in a style he could call his own. The guitar was not an ideal instrument to write with but he scored parts for small combos the best he could. His melodies were strong and the style harked back to a generation before his own.

Magnani aimed high. He tried for the lyrical smoothness of early Lester Young, added the lusty, full-blown quality of Coleman Hawkins and pushed the works along with the insistent rhythms that had captured his soul as a boy. Styles perfected by guitarists like Eddie Lang and Freddie Greene, men little known publicly, but players who leant their personalities to every outfit they were part of. Magnani wrote for himself and anyone else who might want to listen — his friends perhaps. And he had a few friends now, just enough to fill a small table in a club but one more table-full than he had ever had.

Sometimes Dimitri and the grandfather sat solemnly before him, and tried to make sense of his noise. For Dimitri it was not entirely alien, he had heard echoes of jazz on his trips to Athens but the old man was locked into his own musical heritage, one long-formed and impenetrable. Magnani's music might have come from the moon. To please him Magnani picked up lines he heard on the cafe radios. To mimic it in ignorance was easy enough, he worked flamenco patterns into eastern scales, hit a simple repeated theme and let it roll around with little control. The old man was not fooled, but he was delighted by the attempt and praised the counterfeit music with a raised glass, and a slap of his wife if she passed.

When he did not write or play or swim Magnani fetched up in Spiro's cafe. He visited others in the town but settled on this one. Spiro lived in a world of dead chickens. His cooking revolved around them, they hung from hooks over his charcoal grill, plucked, gutted, trussed, waiting their turn on the coals. Magnani sat amongst burning fats and woodsmoke, at first alone, then joined by Dimitri and a growing number of islanders. By mid evening faces glistened with wine and heat and old men played backgammon, thrusting their dice and markers savagely onto their boards and smacking their crusty lips in anticipation of victory.

In Spiro's Magnani was introduced to an island musician, an eighty year old who played the fiddle with a dexterity that belied his age. With this one Magnani became an occasional floor show. He laid down rhythms on the guitar which approximated those he heard on the radio and let the old-timer solo away. They became quite popular and Magnani teased himself with thoughts of being back in the business again. And he liked playing for no money.

The island had finished its preparation for high summer. Shop and café front had been painted for the influx of city Greeks and the scattering of foreign tourists. These were mainly German men, from Westphalian peasant stock who now made cars in Dusseldorf. They became a two week sight, rumbling from café to café, expecting the war to be forgotten, and oblivious if it was not. Magnani was thankful to be taken as indigenous.

He wrote to Pearson and Kaine and received replies surprisingly quickly. Kaine's was more note than letter. Magnani saw the old man clearly as he read his upright handwriting, thin letters with elaborate loops written on yellow paper.

Everything is quiet on the Kaine front. The kids still look for you and I shrug when they ask me if you will be back — will you? How's Greece? A slow delight I bet. Watch out though, Frank, it might creep up on you and silt you all up. The women send their regards, and Carr says that Johnson has skipped town.

Kaine

Pearson talked about gigs and also asked about Magnani's return. It was expected that he would be back. 'We cleared out of Kansas after a while,' Pearson wrote, 'the big city has more of a hold on me than I thought.' With a different pen Eileen had written briefly. She told him to take care and put her usual solitary cross under the words.

Magnani increased the hours spent writing as it gained pace. Each chapter he completed added to the weight of the manuscript and made it easier to go on. He knew the book would be finished by summer's end. Now he wrote when the day was at its hottest. He liked the silence that descended on the town like a cloak, stifling industry and talk. Although Dimitri's house was cool, with thick stone to keep out the sun, he placed his table as near the window as he could, to catch any sliver of breeze.

Looking down at the harbour, and the lazing alley cats at the foot of the house, Magnani wrote his way to Haydn's last days. The cats were his confidants, scrawny bundles of fur and half-wild. They treated people with the disdain that was accorded them, and when a page would not come he watched them lounge away their days. The cats' sloth contrasted with his energy but there was a synthesis between his life and their own. He liked their presence and fed off constancy; sometimes they offered him a languid eye in return.

As Magnani wrote Haydn's demise, so his own life renewed. Haydn, Skopelos and its people were cathartic and he thought often of Pearson's exhortation to return and play, and Kaine's open door. They offered the comfort of a second chance and he loved them for it. By early September Magnani had arrived at the final page of his book. He wrote as neatly as he could, but with trembling hand. It was hard to believe he had achieved the stack of paper on his table. Three inches of it lay there, white but worn at the edges. He bent to his task and did not notice the table wobble, or the cats squabble outside.

Age is truly upon me. I know how firm its grip is each time I am shaved. I hate it. At first I watched the man's hand for any sign of tremor, and the razor caught the morning gleam, a cold light on the steel that I had fight not to shrink from, though Thomas is expert and I am safe in his hands. That is it. To be in another's hands, it is what I fear. But I am old, older than most, and should not complain. I am too near God for that.

The house shakes. How close the French hurl their missiles. Soon we will be overrun. Am I selfish to wish that I had not lived to see it? So be it then. I have not been out, not since I heard my Creation, almost a year ago. That was a good night. They shouted 'Long live Haydn!' as I entered, and I had conceit enough to enjoy it. Salieri was there, I noted him, though he would not meet my eyes. And Beethoven, he is no longer young, at least not for our trade. I wondered if he is as deaf as they say and pray not. At the end he kissed my hand and gazed on me with that so-proud face. There was torment in him, and loneliness, but I could say nothing as people gathered around me. But the kiss was good.

Napoleon is in the city, Vienna is his. But at least his infernal noise is stopped. I sleep very badly and his cannon did not help. Some nights I thought they were inside my head, so much did they shake me. And now the Corporal rings my house with a guard of honour. Life is indeed strange.

When one is an invalid one sometimes takes a long time to realise it. I have been one since that first shave, three long years ago. My life has been a healthy one but this offers little comfort and has ill-prepared me for my plight. I linger, and fear losing my dignity. In recent years my brothers have paved the way I must tread.

The spring is in full bloom, I can smell it through the open window, and servants put bunches of it into the rooms. French is carried on the wind but this is a good time of the year....

Magnani had little money left. He had eked it out but even on Skopelos it was finite. There was not enough to return to America, should Pearson fix his work permit. In a second letter the drummer was full of talk of new engagements: 'folks is asking about you Frank, they remember those nights in New York. I got good contacts now, we'll get you back in. Don't worry about that, just come.'

He asked Dimitri about the possibility of work on the island. The carpenter scratched his head and laughed, 'Why do you want to work?'

'I have no more money.'

Dimitri's face clouded for an instant, then reverted back to its customary optimism.

'Few here have money,' he said.

Magnani knew his situation would be hard to explain. The fact that he had come to Skopelos made him rich in Dimitri's eyes, and with what passed for pay on the island it would be impossible to save anything. Even if he could work.

Thoughts of working a passage back to New York came to him but he also dreaded leaving Skopelos. It had been a gorgeous respite and the spirit of the place and its people had recharged him. Yet he felt he had to leave. Skopelos was not his home and to stay, even if possible, would be denial of his self and his talent. And a victory for Johnson, and all Johnsons. Magnani would become Kaine's silted-up man.

There was another possibility. To go home, back to that Welsh valley so far away in life-style and distance. He had not been there more than twice in five years, and those returns had been short and fraught. In the family house there was an air that he was different, which made Magnani uncomfortable. There was a gamut of reactions to be run, and too many stubborn personalities with which to clash. His mother was grateful for the guitar, it had saved him from the pit. But his father distrusted it, and his role as a musician. It had led his to solitary, unWelsh ways.

The time was not right for him to go home. It would be a defeat, a prodigal son returning broke, and minus his guitar. There would be 'I told you so' in his father's eyes, glad pity in his mother's. And with his rush to London as soon as he was old enough he knew little of working in his own country. What jazz there was stayed in the docklands of Cardiff. In the valleys he remembered the buds of rock and roll flowering in Teddy Boys' hearts, and phoney songs that dripped with honey. Magnani wrote to his parents as a sop to his dereliction of them. 'I am seeing the world,' he wrote, 'will try to get home by Christmas.' They would know as well as he that this was a vain hope.

He decided to try to get a boat New York bound. After much persistence Dimitri told him that this might be possible. Many of the island men had been to sea, it was the one way of earning enough money to furnish a house, and take a wife.

'I have an uncle in Salonika,' Dimitri said, 'he knows that life. He might be able to help you.'

Magnani spent his last days on Skopelos preparing for his return. Word came from the uncle that a place could be found for him, as replacement for a sick deckhand. The shipping company wanted to save on wages, would take a chance on Magnani, on the uncle's say-so. Soon he would be on a boat like the *Volos Star*, a tub just as slow and dreary.

'Don't worry,' Dimitri said, 'my uncle told them you have been a sailor for years, an old hand.'

Magnani's face dropped. 'Why did he tell them that?'

'Why not? It is for a short time — one voyage. Surely they will know you are no sailor, but by then you will be in America, for free.'

It would all depend on Pearson being on the dock to meet him.

As each day drew him nearer to leaving, the island tried to hold him. He swam in Paradise for the last time. Floating on his back on a warm autumn morning he sucked in the scent of the pines and contemplated the wide sky. It was taking on more blue for the winter. Now he would love to spend it here, he was closer than he had ever been to the heart of a place. Each gulp of air satisfied, each search with his eyes brought a confidante, each familiar landmark increased his conspiracy with the island. He would always be in its debt.

Magnani took the long road back to the town. His eye was taken by a hilltop church. On each trip from Paradise it had flashed its white dome at him, one of the many which dotted the high places of the island. He rode his bicycle as far as he could towards it and walked the rest of the way up a winding track overhung with bushes.

It was a church built to hold very few. Magnani entered its gloom, blind for the minute it took his eyes to adjust. Then the flickering candles took effect and the small windows threw in their share of light, faint shafts which criss-crossed the interior. He was in a damp quietness, a remarkable cool that enveloped him, as if it was meant to. The candles were fresh and he wondered who had lit them. He had seen no-one on the way up, and it was the only access.

On the walls of the church faded mosaics traced the island's history. He saw Greek women cower beneath invading Turks, their hands wrung over their faces. The artist had captured fear and lechery well, even on the pitted plaster eyes glared out at him. He traced the paintings with his fingers and felt a tactile connection with the past. He sat in the church for a time, saying his farewells. When the chill began to seep into him he got up to leave, but stopped at the door to light a candle, on impulse. Magnani had no religion and hardly knew what the candles signified, but he felt the need to light one. He hoped he was burning away his miserable past.

Magnani left Skopelos on a Friday, on the early morning ferry. Dimitri and his family accompanied him to the quayside, a trail of sorry faces. Each regretted his leaving, and Magnani loved them the more for that. He had donated his writing table to the Karefelas household and had managed to buy small gifts for Maria and Soula. Magnani shook hands formally with the grandfather and added a light embrace with Dimitri. The women stood off a few yards, shy and polite again.

'Come back,' Dimitri said, 'you have added to our lives.'

'You have given me mine back,' Magnani answered, and was on the launch before Dimitri could react. He took his place in the prow and did not look back.

The journey to Salonika went by in a slow rush, hectic connection-making then full stops at nowhere. The usual hubbub of travel washed over Magnani and did not penetrate his thoughts. They were on what he had left and what he was going to. He had been happy on Skopelos, he touched it and smelt it and wondered that it was there each day. This happiness would be tested by his second attempt on New York.

In Salonika there were two days to kill, and just enough drachmae left to kill them with. In his last days on the island Magnani had earned his supper with music, playing each night with the violinist and his friends from the mountains. He was their amateur but each rigorous night prepared him for his re-entry into a place of failure.

Magnani found a cheap hotel. The smell of pines and charcoal still in his nostrils was soon pushed out by the diesel wafting up from the docks. He was on his own again and found he did not like it. What he had once thought his natural state no longer measured up. First Kaine and then the islanders had shown him that it was bred on selfish conceit, and his music had struggled against it, not in alliance with it. Perhaps in time, he had gained a spark of wisdom.

He met Dimitri's uncle at the arranged place and received the papers he needed, instructions and a clasp of the hand. His helper was concerned not to be with him any longer than was necessary and Magnani realised Dimitri had asked a big favour on his behalf. He was to board his vessel the next day.

Early Sunday evening was heavy, slung with low clouds and sultry with the aftermath of summer. The heat was unwilling to let go, and a restless irritation was in the air. Magnani was trying to shrug this off when the earthquake struck.

He had been strolling on the long curve of Thessalonika that faced the sea, the one attractive part of the town. As he walked back from the sea front the ground began to throb under him. It was as though the movement was inside him. Hands sifted through his organs and sought to rearrange them. There was instant dizziness and he wheeled like a drunk amidst other whirling people. The throb turned to vicious shaking. An apartment block opposite bulged its midriff, spewing masonry onto the road. It shuffled sideways and plummeted down, and all around it other buildings were dancing to destruction. Magnani began to run with the others.

'Go to the park!' he heard someone say, an English voice, clipped and straining to resist panic.

The road cracked as he ran over it, a streak that opened into a metre gap. A car turned over as its wheels stuck in it, the driver's eyes white inside. Magnani fell several times on his lurching run, his vision blurred by dust. His flight carried him to a small clearing of grass where hundreds of people lay hugging the ground. He did like-wise. How it moved under him, the seething guts of an angry earth that pulled his breakfast from his stomach. He vomited amidst wailing women and wide-eyed men. Magnani had found the safest place but thought his piece of ground would erupt at any moment, rending and hurling its occupants skywards. Towards the centre of the town buildings still fell, thumping their way to the ground, the taller ones split like saplings.

Yet Magnani's fear was vague, he felt as he had in the alley with Johnson. Dislocated. A clouded sense that he was dreaming, and not really in this place, not in danger. When the noise lessened and the ground seemed straight he dared to sit up and wipe speckles of vomit from himself. Next to him a young man trembled like a leaf; they were all leaves, shaking with shared shock. The Englishman stood up and dusted his cream jacket. He wore a tie with cricket bats on it and had a whisky hue to his cheeks. Even the quake had not paled this. Magnani was able to smile at the tie, English normality in the midst of hell. Crazy normality.

'Are you all right, old man?' the man asked.

'Yes,' Magnani answered, not sure if he was.

'Good show. I'm off. Got to see what damage has been done to the office. Blasted nuisance these things.'

He strode off, seemingly oblivious to the chaos around him. Magnani tracked him with his dazed eyes as he pushed firmly through the Greeks, and wondered at his race. As he struggled up he felt his stomach kick again. The feeling would stay for some days. His nervous system tried to pre-guess another quake and each tremor that came in its wake set off alarms.

The earthquake was more than a nuisance for thirty-five people. These perished in the initial destruction, crushed in their buildings, or by them. Most were dug up in the following days. As he passed through the torn city Magnani saw the legs of one couple protrude from the rubble. He guessed what had happened. Like him, they had been walking from the sea front, and were caught by the building on the other side of the street. They were well dressed, the man in a charcoal suit and highly polished Italian shoes, the girl in a blue floral dress. Their Sunday best. People gathered around them, pointing and crying. Some shrank back from the bodies then drew near them again, and lamented with greater vigour. A rescue truck bumped down the uneven street carrying men with inadequate equipment. Forlorn rescuers who knew they were too late. Salonika was a place of grief, and it was not lessened by familiarity. Each generation bore this, and a hundred minor quakes to link the chain of bitter memories.

There was another, lesser shock waiting for Magnani in his hotel. He passed staff busy with brooms and pans, clearing up fallen plaster and broken fittings. The building had not suffered major damage but his guitar had. It was crumpled against the wall of his room, pieces of wood in a plastic case. He did not bother to disinter the fragments. It joined the rest of the debris in the street below, hurled there by a disconsolate Magnani.

He sat gingerly on his bed, dust rising about him. After some minutes of torpor he roused himself and checked the rest of his belongings. The Haydn manuscript was still intact, and legible, if a little gouged along one edge. Magnani repacked his sack and decided to go straight to his boat.

The docks were well outside the epicentre of the earthquake. One gantry tumbled into the water was the sole witness to the devastation. People here were too busy to ask Magnani questions and he no longer had the guitar to mark him out as he made his way through the crowds of seamen and dockers. He boarded his boat without fuss. A Greek first officer checked his name against a list and took his passport without opening it. The man was more concerned to be out of the harbour before any further disaster struck.

Magnani was a hand on the *Aegean Queen*, out of Piraeus. She was larger than the *Star*, but like it in every other way. As the crew came on board Magnani felt completely lost. He did not know whether to blindly copy their actions or admit to someone he had no idea what to do. But he managed to find the bunkhouse and was waved to an empty berth by a man sprawled on his back, a Spaniard who jabbered at Magnani in a patois of Greek, Spanish and English. Most of the crew were here, talking about the earthquake. By their faces Magnani knew none were from Salonika.

A mate appeared to bark out orders. Magnani followed the Spaniard, doing what he did. On deck this man described the actions of the earthquake with his hands, and whistled through his serrated teeth. He gestured to Magnani to take hold of a rope. As he pulled he took a last look at the lacerated skyline of the city. Large holes had been punched in it, especially on the upper slopes. Rows of houses came an abrupt end and the air was still heavy with disturbance.

Magnani felt the diesels throb under him and the Queen came to life, adding to the queasiness in his stomach. It was a sad and hectic leaving but it was his body that had been shaken, not his resolve. The loss of the guitar invited him to regain his own. His determination to bite at America again was firm, and he flexed his hands against the coarse rope in anticipation.

ELEVEN

Horizon flattened into sky, two shades of blue divided by a blurred line. The sky was wide and for ten evenings Magnani had watched it, when he could get on deck. The blue dome collected his thoughts and gave him some respite from his seaman's toil. It had been an uneventful voyage, as flat as the sea, with no change in the weather. A few times a cloud formation had threatened then dissipated to featureless blue again. Each day grew longer and increased his expectation of America. He had played his first night a thousand times in his head, his head was ready for it, but his hands suffered in his work. The more he tried to protect them, the more they were buffeted. His right palm had a rope-burn across it, and his nails had been mashed. Part and parcel of manual work but dangerous for a string player.

Magnani had cabled Pearson about his arrival. 'I'm coming over almost penniless,' he wrote, 'without a guitar. It will help if you can be there.' He knew his entry depended on someone vouching for him, and proving that he had a job waiting, and providing him with a union card. His friendship with the drummer would recommence with three very large favours. And he did not forget the money Pearson must have paid to get his guitar out of hock. Yet Magnani still looked forward. His last year had been full of new experiences and he had grown because of it. He felt the calm of Skopelos would always be with him, steadying, holding his feet on firm ground. If he could weather the first few weeks in New York he might have a chance. And then he might look for a publisher for his book, and think about Tampa.

All this seemed far away as Magnani laboured with the Spaniard. They painted a section of deck with grey paint, covering the rust for another few years. No-one bothered him much. There was none of the camaraderie he had imagined existed amongst sailors on the *Aegean Queen*. They went about their work knowing they must repeat it every day. Most wanted to be elsewhere.

'Men are on boats because they can't do much else,' the Spaniard said. 'Forget about loving the sea. That's easier to do when you live near it, not on it.'

It seemed to Magnani that most of the seamens' lives were as grey as the Atlantic.

His day consisted of simple maintenance tasks. He was not expected to do anything else. Bits of the *Queen* were cleaned in futile exercises, and once he was called below decks to help mop up sea water that had been let in by a defective pump. He filled buckets in the slimy depths of a half-empty hold, smelling the vessel's decay, and hearing the scuttling of rats in the gloom. Even the long scrubbings of deck were a relief after this. The days dripped away.

The *Queen* was not far off New York. Magnani could see its magnificent skyline that had inspired so many, helped, seduced, suckered and spewed out so many. The city was lighting up, a mass of pinpricking lights, as if the stars were dropping onto the ocean. A dirty Staten Island peered out of the gloom. It was almost dark, they were stealing in at night, like unworthy visitors. But the *Aegean Queen* was on time, arriving when Magnani had told Pearson it would. He had packed his sack, wedging the manuscript at the bottom. It stood waiting by his bunk, ready to fly with him.

Magnani felt ready for anything. His nostrils caught the scent of the great city, repulsed it and craved for the air of Skopelos, then caught it again. It would not go away. It was the smell of massed people, their lives and industry. Adrenalin surged through him once more. This place was real and could not be avoided. His fate was here, it lay some where amongst those streets and had eluded his grasp that first time.

He received his passport and a few dollars from the first officer — the captain he had never seen close up. In his pocket was Pearson's letter offering him work. With sack slung over his shoulder and black woollen hat on his hat he looked the one thing he was not, a regular seaman.

Pearson was in the Immigration Office with a man Magnani did not know, a bald-headed man with a grey fuzz of sideburn down each cheek. Magnani felt like an inmate being visited in prison. There was a desk and a walkway between them, and all the bureaucracy of America. Pearson and the unknown man conquered the latter. Magnani's passport had been greeted with a mute frown, its pages flicked over with rejection, if not contempt. The official looked Magnani over and his eyes said 'you must be joking.' Magnani could only smile, and wave discreetly to Pearson. Pearson's companion introduced himself to the official, who was young and bored. The man placed a hand on the uniformed shoulder and drew the official out of Magnani's earshot. From the other side of the walkway Pearson offered upturned thumbs of encouragement, which he thought very British. Magnani stood there helplessly. The strength he had been nurturing since that night Kaine picked him up counted for nothing here. He was in on the indulgence of a young man who had worked a long shift in a hard job. He watched as Pearson's man walked the official up and down, hand still in place on the shoulder. Next to it the man's collar looked white, though it was really grubby, and stained with his day. Magnani turned away and did not turn back until he heard the thump of the stamp on his passport. He had been granted a three month stay, subject to certain conditions. As always, these involved money, and had been taken care of. By his friend Pearson.

They were shy of each other at first and Magnani could not greet the drummer with the innocence he offered. Pearson introduced him to the other man.

'This here is Danby, Frank, our union man. It took some time to swing it but we got lucky. A few of the guys talked up for you — you was remembered and Danby here did the necessary arranging.'

'Thank you,' Magnani said.

Danby waved a laconic hand. 'S'all right. If you get regular work you should be able to get an extension on your permit. Just play good.'

'I had to give you an address for you to stay at, Frank,' Pearson said. 'You're at Buen Vista again.'

Pearson looked healthy. He had slimmed down twenty pounds and his face was leaner, emphasising his wide smile. His was a good welcome, he kept patting Magnani on the shoulder, as though to check his presence was solid. They had clasped hands for a long few seconds.

This time there was not the drudgery of a long walk. A Yellow cab was waiting to take them across the city to Buen Vista. Magnani was excited, but calmer than his first heady arrival here. Sights were expected this time. The cab weaved its way through narrow dockland streets, competing with a hundred other horns and hasty travellers. They headed to the night glow, where people lived. It was late autumn, almost a year had passed. The city was settling itself for another hard winter, its sky dirty with clouds and the tall buildings sunk in shadows. Magnani's body huddled up against the chill, and longed to be back in the sun.

As they entered Harlem Magnani saw more people on the streets. Pearson's people. Groups of black men gathered here, to brood through their workless days and while away the nights. On the sidewalks he glimpsed the myriad racial types. The people of Skopelos would have been amazed, so many countries represented here, in the city of rush.

Magnani was content to sit back and let Pearson talk. When they dropped Danby at a corner he became more garrulous. He had big plans for playing together, for playing the music they liked.

'Everything is loose here, Frank. The music can go any way. Be-bop guys are all changing — have to change, some of them. Might be a chance to get into something big.'

Magnani smiled agreement. He did not like to ask about his guitar, and Pearson did not mention it.

At Buen Vista girls played on the street near the door. They saw Magnani's white face in the taxi and laughed at him. Two gyrated hula-hoops around their hips, whipping up a storm of rhythm. They licked their lips at Magnani and mouthed unheard words. They were ten year old women welcoming him,

It was waiting for him in the living room. Polished and resting on a stand, it shone out a greeting, the mahogany burr catching the light. Eileen stood behind it, a smile of welcome on her face. She came to him and hugged him, ignoring his discomfort. He remembered her smell of freshness, and images of their short times together came to him.

'Frank, I can hardly believe it.'

She pressed slender hands into his shoulders.

'You're back.'

'Like an old penny.'

'Pearson shined up your guitar, and put new strings on it,' she said.

'The kind you like, man. It's ready to burn,' Pearson added.

They stood before him in expectation. He wanted to react with open love for his loyal and forgiving friends but his deeds of the past were in his mind. So he dropped his sack, sat down and took up the guitar. He would rather have done so in private but he knew this was what they wanted. A piece he had worked on in Skopelos came to him. He stroked his way through the changes smoothly. Pearson whistled.

'Hell man, you ain't lost a thing. Didn't I tell you honey?'

The guitar was joy in his hands. It was like coming home to a loved one, breaking out of a cell: regaining hope, cementing within his grasp that which had been slowly coming back to him. Magnani might have been alone. For some minutes he ran around the fretboard he knew so well. Where he had to fight against the inadequacies of his Tampa model this instrument cajoled every move. Pearson handed him a glass.

'Have a shot of this, Frank. Eileen got some good malt from the club.' He boomed out a laugh. 'You in a world of your own with that thing.'

Reluctantly Magnani put down the guitar and drank with his friend. The whisky was strange and with the first sip he knew he did not need it anymore, neither to play or to live. It tasted of staleness and burnt opportunities.

'How much did it cost to get the guitar from Mo?' Magnani asked.

'Don't worry about that now,' Pearson said. 'Wait 'til you are working. I've fixed up a few sessions with some of the boys.'

Eileen busied herself in the kitchen.

'She's cooking up something real nice for us, Frank.'

'You should have children Pearson. You are a born father, and you've done far too much for me.'

'Maybe we will have kids, me and Eileen. We been kinda close lately.' Pearson dropped his voice. 'Don't think I'm too old do you Frank — I won't see forty no more.'

'Of course not. Now's the time.'

'Hah!' The answer pleased the drummer. He poured himself a long shot but Magnani did not drink his.

'You know Frank, about me and the lady, I don't know why, but we been doing all right since you checked out. You brought us luck, boy.'

'Any news on Johnson?'

'Same as before, man. He just dropped out of sight here. Been that way since you left. Probably got hisself dead somewhere.'

'Perhaps.'

'You ain't still worried about that dude, are you?'

'No, I'm not.'

'Good — he's yesterday.'

'What about Gaines? I haven't kept in touch with the scene.'

'No. Greece is a long ways away. You must tell us about it, Frank. Eileen is always on about your travelling.'

Pearson was getting mildly drunk, a happy intoxication that he controlled. 'Yeah, Gaines,' he continued, 'he's not around either, least not playing. The man's sick, Frank. Had some kind of stroke I heard. His left side is all froze up.'

'I'm sorry to hear that.'

'Yeah. He wasn't my kind of people but he had some music in him, and that's something.'

'Yes.'

'You got it too, Frank. It pours out of you, man.'

'Pearson, shut up and finish your drink, before it starts talking for you.'

They ate Eileen's meal of soul food and chicken. It was easier to be with her each minute. Magnani sensed an acceptance between them that their small play was history, a result of unsteady lives colliding. These lives had now focused elsewhere. Eileen had forgiven his manipulation a long time ago; Magnani had not let himself off that hook but felt easier about it. As he ate he wanted to be at the guitar again, there was an edge of anticipation about playing which gave him the necessary tension to create, but it was not fraught or jagged. And he had places to go if it did not work out, and people to help.

Magnani did not stray from Buen Vista in the next few days. Pearson had a week remaining of an engagement at the Famous Door and Eileen worked there as a waitress. In the evenings Magnani was left alone to work on the guitar, to the backdrop of the nightsounds of Harlem. He got used to the chatter of its streets, the blasts of jazz and salsa that came through the window. He retrieved his book from the sack and worked through it, as he had always done, but adding the music he had written on Skopelos. These were intense days when he played until his hands complained, and raised a blister on one finger, something he had not done since the early playing days. He was proud of it. While he played Pearson and Eileen slept.

The blister gave him a reason to take a break and get out. Magnani took a bus downtown and walked around the city. At midday he was in Times Square, watching the neon signs revolve, claiming miracles. There was not much light here, oncoming winter and the shadows of massed buildings saw to that. The Square was seedy but attractive. Magnani mingled with the aimless and the wide-eyed, new arrivals to the city. The Square was a magnet that drew from its own myth. People came to be in the heart of New York, and watch the neon dreams, and the New Yorkers watched back. They preyed on the bustling loneliness of their world. Once, they too might have been wide-eyed. A man not much older than Magnani stepped in front of him, and stuck out a hand for money. He gave him one of his few dollars, which was snatched out of his hand before he could change his mind.

He walked down to theatre and club land, checking out the places he had played. There were two less. On Forty-Seventh street and Fifth Avenue Brentano's caught his eye. The old bookstore pulled him inside and made him think of his own thin work. But as he looked at the shelves of names he found he no longer questioned his audacity in thinking he might join them. Writing had begun as a safe relief from the present but now it had merged with it, helped locate his life and make him question how he was spending it. His dead musician Haydn was a strange ally of Kaine and Pearson. They had all helped push him onto a firm path.

On his way back to Buen Vista he stopped off in a bar. He sat on a tall stool in its gloom and drank a beer. A few other afternoon people with nowhere to go did the same, idlers of time, like he had been. There was a newscast on the bar's television. It reported on the politician Kaine had told him about, Kennedy. He was like the old man had described, prominent teeth and a permanent tan, but there was a spark in him, perhaps, that went beyond mere political showbusiness.

'We stand on the edge of a new frontier,' Kennedy said, and you wanted to believe it. And to believe that he meant it. It was where he was, Magnani thought, at the edge of a new life, even a new self. He watched Kennedy's eyes exhort the watching millions. It was film of a broadcast the previous evening. Vote for me, the eyes said, trust in me, put your hopes on me. America was gearing up to go to the polls the next year. Political machines were churning in preparation.

'Whadya think of that guy?' the bartender said to a slumped barfly.

'I think he's a commie. He likes waps and niggers, for Christsake. And he wants to give our money away, to all them bums. He's unAmerican.'

'S'right, Joe,' the barfly said, holding out his glass. 'An' a nancy-boy. He smiles like a girl.'

Magnani smiled also, at the memory of Kaine. "un-American." He had used that word. This was a repulsive, attractive country that throbbed with energy, but he felt it was going horribly off the rails. Yet he determined to see more of it, this time.

Pearson was waiting for him when he got back.

'Frank, where you been?'

'Just out for a walk around, taking the air.'

'Do you feel ready to play tonight? A few of the fellers are getting together. I know it's sooner than we said, but why not? That's how you did it the first time. Shit, I remember you falling into Stein's still smelling of the ocean.'

Magnani rubbed his blister.

'Yes, all right,' he said.

'Just like that. You are changed, boy. Where's all the worry and the I don't knows gone? I love it.'

Magnani made up the rhythm section with Pearson, a bass and pianist. An assortment of reeds and horns would get up with them through the night. The Famous Door was closed to the public this evening. Twenty musicians sat around drinking, studiously ignoring Magnani but examining his playing carefully. He knew that his brief fling with New York was remembered by some, and his peers had come to see if he was worth re-admitting to the inner temple.

The club was much the same. Its decor cried out a little louder for an uplift and whatever colour the walls had once been they were now the colour of smoke. The nicotine yellow of a thousand nights. Obligatory fans pumped around the heavy air, oblivious to the cold outside; here it was always hot.

Magnani sat on the left side of the stage, using the amplifier Pearson had borrowed for him. It was strange to hear his chords come out of the speaker. He did not feel as close to the guitar as he had on the island. There he had wrought out every sound himself with his hands on the wood. Here electricity was an intermediary although his sound took on a richness of tone that went some way to reassure him.

It was not an easy start. Cole Eyles, a rising young pianist, took them into 'Round Midnight', a skilful arrangement that emphasised the smouldering melody of the tune. Chuck Booker played trumpet, with a smooth West Coast sound which Magnani thought worked, despite the scorn of some New York players. They thought it the watered down stealing of their own ideas. Booker played well, his blond hair flicked back over his forehead and hanging low over his collar. He made the tune ache.

Magnani comped along steadily, letting the music get in his alcohol-free body. As discreetly as possible he had left all drinks untouched on his table, winked at by the abetting Pearson. As yet there was no hard edge to anyone's playing for no-one had to prove anything, apart from Magnani. This was not a cutting session. He took his first solo on 'Chelsea Bridge', a minor ballad that offered many possibilities. The band eased back, edging his playing to the front to give him plenty of space to work in. Starting with a few trusted figures he soon moved into what he had developed on Skopelos. After a few choruses he included echoes of the music he had heard on the island. He had the club's attention now as he built up a series of fast octaves that Wes Montgomery was making fashionable, though Magnani did not know it.

The empathy in the band nurtured his efforts. Pearson shuffled out the beat with his brushes a soft insistence on the skins that

Magnani locked onto, and Eyles embellished with intricate chording. They took the tune as far as it would stretch before Booker restated the head and breathed out the melody once more. There was a ripple of applause from the floor and Magnani knew he was back, grasping the first rung of the ladder again. That most slippery rung, which bars the way to the higher ones, or leads gloriously to them.

Magnani stayed on stage for several hours, acting as sideman or leading a scaled down four piece. There were consummate musicians around him and he enjoyed them. His freshened senses were able to draw on his experience, use it, and enhance it with innovation. But there was a certain irony. The raw hunger of his audition with Gaines was gone. Jazz was an old friend now, not a terrible, addictive task-master. And he was in control of himself, that he knew as he took a short break. Magnani had reached that point down Kaine's road.

In a break he sat with Pearson, who bubbled with Magnani's triumph. 'What did I tell you, what did I tell you,' the drummer said every few minutes. Magnani wondered what his friend's reaction would have been if he had failed. Other musicians nodded over to him in muted compliment. There were disparate personalities here. Some were ugly, one man who played like an angel would win no award as a human being. A few too many were hopeless junkies, and others moved sideways through their lives, as Magnani had done. Hiding behind their talent until it withered or burnt out under the strain. Yet he felt in tune with them, despite the change in himself. These men were a threat to no-one and gave pleasure to many. And they inhabited a world Magnani understood more now that he had been away from it. He was breaking a mould by returning. Few musicians left the top flight of jazz and successfully returned. Lips went and touch deserted players, and the reasons for laying off in the first place had the knack of recurring.

Magnani saw a desperate longing in the men here, they were excluded from a mainstream existence by the skills that drove them. And took over them. Some were haunted by the fact that they could have belonged, could have been normal Joes, but knowing they were hooked on what they did. A masochistic life-style that could diminish and destroy, but whose bitter lessons fuelled their art. And that was enough, it had to be enough. It had been for Magnani until Kaine had opened a door. He played out the rest of the night without losing his touch, if anything it grew surer as he met the music of his fellows.

Magnani accepted one drink at the end of the session and went back to Buen Vista with Pearson, being slapped along the sidewalk by the effusive drummer. Neither man felt the cold and the city was less alien to Magnani. He could never be at home in its stone corridors or get used to its bustling ways but it did not threaten so much.

As Pearson went in to join Eileen Magnani was already in his makeshift bed. Before playing he had been glad Eileen was not there, now he was sorry she had not been. She had needed to sleep on her one night off. He heard Pearson rummage around in the bedroom and imagined him sinking into bed beside her. It was imagination tinged with envy but not the worthless jealousy he had once felt. The drummer deserved to be with her. A year ago Magnani had traumatised her life, unloaded his problems onto her, almost wrecked her relationship, then run away. A typical Magnani sequence. Now he had learnt to think of others he hoped he might never do this to anyone else. Maybe one day he might even put others first. Like Kaine had done all his life, and Pearson also, in his laconic way. And it was not lost on him that they were happier than he had ever been. Kaine's worldly tiredness did not detract from this fact, there was still an indefatigable core of goodness in the old man. It was a state Magnani had always shied away from, for it seemed out of his reach.

He woke thinking of Kaine, and the institution. Without getting up he reached for his notepad and wrote him a letter, resting the pad against his knees. He briefly sketched his Greek months and his re-introduction to jazz, but said nothing about the earthquake, or the loss of the guitar in it. The last line said he would be going back to Tampa, to the home. He gave Pearson's address and placed the letter in an envelope before he realised the import of his words.

Going back. And he had just made a triumphant return to his craft. Yet it was this success that had cleared his mind. Music was a first love that would never die within him, and his work on Haydn had been something to hold onto when all else was crumbling, but neither was his life's blood. Working with Kaine's children had placed a quality in his mind that would not fade, and which he did not want to fade: it was a secure feeling. A year ago he thought what could be achieved on a stage, though rare and fleeting, was worth the price paid. But it was too easily thwarted by the life that jazzmen seemed doomed to lead. The faces in the Famous Door last night told him that another twenty years of cool loneliness was not for him. He was not strong enough to face it, or perhaps had become too strong. He wanted to be always able to play, to even write again, but he wanted his role in Kaine's home more. It was this less fragmented role for which on life the island had prepared him.

In the next few days Pearson busied himself with Magnani's career. A union card was procured, presenting Magnani with a debt for lapsed dues. His bill with the drummer was mounting up and he had not the heart to tell him that he would be going down to Tampa as soon as he had earned enough to pay him back.

Magnani became part of a new quartet with Eyles and Pearson, and a bass player from Toronto called Laskins. It was an easy coming together, a meeting of kindred spirits, led by Eyles but egalitarian, with none of the commercial constraints of Carlton Gaines. They rehearsed above a pool room opposite Buen Vista. Magnani worked out arrangements with Eyles to the click of china balls on green baize, and smelt the canning factory in the cold mornings. They quickly gathered together a collection of standards and original compositions. Eyles was a melodic yet spare pianist who did not cram every space with notes as Gaines had. This suited Magnani well. He bounced ideas off the pianist and there was a good natured rivalry between them that led to interesting counter-point. On the growing reputation of Eyles they were engaged at the Farrago, a new club trying to gain an identity on the New York jazz scene. They were known as the Eyles Four.

Eyles had a solo engagement to fulfill in Paris in the new year so the quartet would be short lived. In this time Magnani hoped to save enough for his needs. And he would not have to disrupt the group.

The Farrago was bright and decidedly unseedy. It was not typical jazz country but the place had a lightness of spirit that matched Magnani's new state of mind. His musicianship reached high spots most nights at the Farrago. It was the friendliest outfit he had played in since Paris and he almost thought he was wrong about this world until he realised Laskins was using drugs. The bass player disappeared in breaks to return beaded in cold sweat, with eyes glazed like cherries. And there was the shaking, apologetic smile as he took his spot behind the bass. He still played well, with a warm, gliding touch on the strings. Magnani thought of Filigree and it crossed his mind to talk to Laskins but Pearson warned him off the idea. 'Can't do nothing, man. Can't say nothing, not when they that far down the road. Like telling a man with the blues to snap out of it — makes them worse every time. Maybe Laskins will pull through, it ain't rotted his playing yet.' This was the drummer's practical side, which had enabled him to survive.

Magnani knew he had made the right decision. He told Eileen about it on the quartet's seventh night, the first time she had come to hear them play. She sat at a front table and tapped her slender hands to the music. Magnani felt her pride, and warmed to it. He managed to talk to her alone in a break, relating his plans as Pearson entertained college aficionados of the quartet. From that table Magnani heard the drummer mention his name and knew his friend would be heaping him with praise.

Eileen was not surprised by his decision. 'Pearson will be kind of upset, he has big plans for you and him,' she said.

'I know, I don't know how to tell him.'

'When are you thinking of going?'

'I can pay Pearson back in a month. Best to go then, the longer we play together the harder the break will be. And Eyles will be splitting up the quartet then anyway.'

Eileen stirred her Martini with her cocktail stick, making small eddies against the glass. Her ice-cubes looked like miniature icebergs in a green sea.

'Will you be all right down there, in Tampa?' she asked.

'Of course. I made good friends there.'

'And here.'

'Yes. I'm lucky. Eileen about our... about us... Do you...?'

'Let's not talk about that. It was a few nights of madness, that's all. No-one knows about it, so no-one gets hurt.'

'You got hurt.'

'No more than you. You've changed since then Frank, changed a lot. Ease it out of your mind,' she said. 'I have. Pearson and me are real close now,'

'I know it.'

'Frank, down south, did you meet someone, a girl maybe?'

Magnani smiled at the visions of Kaine's ladies.

'No, not in the way you mean. But I met a situation.'

'You might get lonesome.'

He did not tell her how numbingly lonely music could be.

'I'll have too much to do. Besides, there is plenty of time for me to meet someone, a good looking talented man like me,' he jested.

'Don't leave it too late. Time kind of creeps up on you, Pearson always says. And you need to be with someone, Frank.'

Pearson joined them, placing a hand on Magnani's shoulder and fondling Eileen's cheek with the other. 'Hey buddy,' he said sternly, 'you making out with my woman?' He flashed his double tier of pearly teeth. 'Ain't this guy something though honey, coming back to us and playing like he does — the wizard of the fretboard.'

'Eileen nodded.

'Come on Frank,' Pearson said, 'we gotta play the next set.'

The drummer hoisted Magnani to his feet, a middle-aged man perpetually young, with enthusiasm too natural to be trammelled by life.

They drew healthy audiences to the Farrago. Other musicians in town came to see them, the ultimate compliment for a new outfit. Eyles arranged a recording session for the quartet in their third week, giving Magnani's music the chance of permanency. This month in New York was a paradox; never had he been so close to success, yet he was about to close the door on it and enter Kaine's open one. He did not waver. The better he played, the more secure he felt about letting the guitar take second place. Magnani did not fully understand it but knew enough to go with his instinct, which had never been a stronger one. 'It is fate,' Dimitri would have said.

They planned to cut four sides, three original numbers and an arrangement Eyles had written for 'Here's That Rainy Day', the Jimmy van Heusen ballad. Theirs was a cool approach, relying on the quiet empathy of four musicians rather than frenetic soloing.

'I want to get the mood of this city on a Sunday afternoon,' Eyles explained, 'recovering from Saturday, fat, lazy, licking its wounds — and not looking forward to Monday.'

This suited Magnani and to his satisfaction there was also a healthy slice of the blues in the quartet's playing. They met at two in the afternoon and worked until six, and were back on stage at the Farrago by nine. They had mornings to sleep but some days Laskins did not manage this. He turned up with fuzz on his face and rings around his eyes, as if a barman had pressed glasses into their sockets. But apart from Friday, when he dozed in between takes, he did not let the quartet down, and nothing was said.

Eyles's agent Tom Pantel, who was not trusted even by Eyles, did the fixing. He was a busy, bearded little man who flitted around like a magpie, procuring deals, and work for himself. Pantel arranged two days of recording downtown and told them it could be a forerunner to an album of material when Eyles returned from Paris. No-one believed him but they were all pleased with the opportunity to get their music down. Pantel was surprised by their relaxed attitude. He liked to describe to his clients the magnificent futures that lay ahead of them, drawing a golden carrot before their eyes, and around their contracts.

The quartet licked its music into shape, and each member was satisfied by it in a week. Saturday was declared a day off and Magnani took advantage of it to get out of the way of his hosts and nose around the city. The Manhattan shops amazed him. It was the first time he had taken the trouble to look at them; usually his eye was caught by music and book stores. He walked through the age of innovation; invention galloped along on the back of capitalism here, and displayed itself in windows. He saw record players that offered the new stereo sound, machines that washed and dried clothes in one, even blankets that were warmed by electricity. His parents would have liked one. Advertisements were everywhere, garish slashes of coercion in massed ranks to assault the eye. Magnani passed a large billboard in the shape of a new jetliner, flying over London with a beaming load. He visited Brentano's again and made a mental note to look up publishers, and send his manuscript to one of them before he had time to change his mind.

The weather was turning colder, threatening to break into winter any day. To herald it the breath of walkers was white, and bodies well wrapped up. Magnani realised he might never experience the city in summer, the seething swelter he had identified so much with jazz — hot horns and pounding drums, pressure cooker music for pressure cooker lives. Then the solace of a soft ballad to recharge bodies, millions of massed bodies. If ever a place had proved stress could be creative, it was New York.

He rode the subway back as darkness fell, sharing the yellow glow with people returning home to the suburbs. He found Nina's and ate there, pleased he could do so without worrying about Johnson.

On Sunday the quartet used their Farrago engagement to run through their recording numbers one last time. It was a relaxed night. Only true jazz lovers came out on cold Sundays, and they worked to these, a receptive, almost quiet, audience. Magnani's mind had stopped seething, he knew where he was going and what he was doing, and was doing what he wanted.

They breakfasted together in the morning and began work in Ace Studios at ten, watched by Pantel in the recording booth. He looked like a gnome behind the thick plastic window, and chewed on a cigar that emphasised his size. Monday morning could not have been a less natural time to play but they warmed to their task and completed four good takes by mid-afternoon. Magnani sank everything into his playing, knowing this might be his one stab at posterity Laskins did likewise, perhaps for other reasons.

Pantel deemed himself pleased and cancelled Tuesday's session to save money. They were shunted out quickly to make way for a teenage singer who came in with an entourage. Pearson chuckled at the circus and nudged Magnani. 'We in the wrong music business. Look at them dames with that kid. He must trap them with that grease on his hair. Ain't it something though, piled high like the waves down on Coney Beach.'

Magnani told Pearson he was leaving that night, at Buen Vista. They were mellow with good food and Pearson had drunk Magnani's share. As he began to lay out their future in his exuberant way, smashing all problems with his words , Magnani cut him short.

'When Eyles leaves for Paris I'll be checking out too, for Tampa,' he said.

At first he thought the drummer had not heard him. Pearson poured himself another beer and placed the empty bottle on the pile in the waste basket. A small mountain of green glass. He took a long draught and looked at Magnani.

'Come again, Frank? No I heard you the first time. Hell, have you planned this all along?'

'No. But I decided on it a while ago. I know it's crazy, when we are doing well here but it's something I have to do. I want to go back, and take up where I left off.'

'In that old guy's place huh? You right, it is crazy.'

'Am I letting you down again, Pearson?'

'I'm disappointed Frank, can't say I'm not, I thought we'd go on as a unit, but I don't think you are letting anyone down. When were guys like us 'sposed to be normal? Eileen was saying to me that you are a different kind of guy now, I can see it too. And that's what is making you go, I guess.'

Magnani handed Pearson a bundle of notes.

'What's this?'

'Three hundred dollars. I've saved it up from our Farrago money. I owe you more, much more, but it will have to do for now.'

'Man, I don't want it.'

'But you have to take it, Pearson. We couldn't be the same friends if you didn't.'

Pearson reached for the notes and pressed them into a roll. He saluted Magnani with it and stuck the bills in his top pocket. 'You are changed, boy. Perhaps I'll buy Eileen something special with this dough.'

'Yes, do that.'

Despite Pearson's unselfish acceptance of the news there was a quietening in the evening. When Eileen got back from her work they were both asleep in their chairs, without further addition to the glass mountain.

Magnani remembered his dream that night, and wished he had not. The fight with Johnson was the peak of many tight spots as an adult, but he had not known the naked terror of childhood again. Not the type that softens the will until it is jelly, and movement is frozen for fear of increasing the threat, and the body rejects all messages from the brain to run, and the desire to let out panic in a scream is great.

In sleep Johnson came to him again, wielding a guitar like an axe and grinning madly. He awoke on the floor, fallen from his chair. It was a cold seven o' clock and he was in the real world again. He dressed, made himself a pot of coffee, and forgot about the dream.

Magnani sent Kaine another letter but still the old man did not reply. There was now the seed of a doubt in his mind. It was almost Christmas, and the quartet geared itself up for the season, and its own end. Pantel said their record would be out before the new year. He came to the club one night with an acetate in a brown paper bag.

'It's all here, guys,' he said, 'and it will get you noticed. Hey, its the end of the decade, almost, things are jumping again. And people are not so uptight, have you noticed that?'

They eyed him dubiously but he did not notice. Like all good agents Pantel had the capacity to believe his own promotion. He was almost a politician.

'The man is an asshole, but he might also be right,' Pearson said when he'd gone. 'Maybe there will be a time for jazz.'

'I'll take some copies over to Paris,' Eyles said. And they all laughed.

In the Farrago, at least, it was a time for their jazz. Audiences remained steady, and they had built up a reputation. Each man had played well most nights, a tight unit of sound that pulled together. Magnani was going out playing the way he wanted to, and had not failed this time. In the middle of a hot number he thought of Vermont, and shivered.

They were in the middle of a first set when Kaine showed up, with D. Bell. Magnani blinked at them as they walked in. Kaine pushed his way to the empty front table with D. Bell in tow; she was flustered, and looked away from the stage. If he could have taken his hands from the guitar Magnani would have rubbed his eyes. But it was them. Kaine half raised a hand and smiled his wan smile.

Kaine clapped hard when the quartet finished and stopped only to stretch out a hand to Magnani, who clasped it, then clasped the old man to make certain of his presence. Kaine was a frail body of bones in his arms.

'Thought I wasn't going to write back, huh?' Kaine said. 'I felt like seeing New York again, been a long time since I was in this town.'

'I can't believe you're here.'

'I wanted to hear you play, Frank. Hell, if you are coming back to us it might be the last chance I get.'

'Is it all right, me coming back?'

'I said it always would be, didn't I?' Kaine pressed his veined hand over Magnani's. 'So, we have a lot to talk about, but not tonight. Tonight I want the music. As you can see I talked D. Bell into coming.'

As Bell's eyebrows raised Kaine hastily added. 'The old car finally gave up and the ladies would not let me come alone.'

'Hello, D. Bell,' Magnani said. He thought better of calling her Daphne,

'Hi yourself, Magnani. You look like you are doing good here.'

'The quartet's working well tonight.'

Magnani saw Pearson watching them from the bar and beckoned him over. 'This is Pearson, another one-name person. I've told you about this man, Wilbur.'

'Indeed you have.'

'Laskins and Eyles wandered over to the table, attracted by the age of Kaine, and the noise he was making. Magnani introduced them and their table swung. He did not drink but was intoxicated by the way Kaine had appeared, a wispy, white haired man dancing into the club and back into his life, setting the seal to his decision and perhaps to the rest of his life. Magnani watched Kaine entertain the quartet, a slight figure in an ancient suit telling the boys about the early days of jazz. They listened and laughed and Kaine was the youngest boy among them. Magnani was able to edge D. Bell away to the bar as the break stretched far longer than it should have.

'It was Kaine's idea,' she said, 'just appearing like this, I could hardly contain him on the bus up. Let's surprise Frank, he said. He's been planning it for weeks, his last adventure, he called it.'

'How's the home?' Magnani asked.

'Much the same. Kaine is ageing quickly though. Until tonight, that is. He's young again tonight, like I never saw him before.'

She lit a cigarette and blew smoke upwards. She still had a severe hair style, as if someone had placed a bowl over her head and cut around it. But she was no longer severe to Magnani. Daphne was reassuring and there was a bluff welcome in her nonchalant face. The memory of their talk had not faded for either of them.

Eyles joined them. 'Come on Frank. We've been dogging it to long.'

And Magnani played. He entered a mood he had felt when he watched that horn player on his first New York night, what seemed a lifetime ago. But this time he was a participant and the crowd sensed there was a special buzz on the stage. There was a subtle cessation of talk as people left their tables and stood at the front to receive. Laskin's eyes lost their glazed-cherry sheen and were animated again. They came to life like lizards anticipating heat, and the quartet was hot. Pressure cooker music. With Pearson pumping out a solid beat they went for fast numbers. Without horns they could not offer Kaine the sound he remembered but they compensated with the passion of one fiery heart, which bled its music all over the stage. Despite the throng in front of him Magnani seemed always to be able to see Kaine. He nodded to him sometimes, then screwed up his eyes for another solo.

He saw his life as he played, as if all his experience was translating through his fingers onto the fretboard. But Magnani was no drowning man; he had never been more alive. Eyles moved to a rhythm role, knowing that he must give centre stage to Magnani. And Magnani could play anything. The guitar was part of him, he did not hold it so much as be joined to it. Every idea he played was heard in his head beforehand, a split second of creation that sparked the fuse. Was this how Haydn did it, how they all did it? At one point he watched the progress of his fingers as if they belonged to someone else. They ranged in patterns along the fretboard, yielding clusters of notes or fast runs, or a burst of small chords to accentuate his progress. His concentration was intense, but he was still able to step outside it, and enjoy his own playing.

In the audience a man moved in the shadows of the far tables. A man in a white suit, and black shoes as sharp as glass, a blood-red shirt and pink tie. Carrying a fedora with a brown satin band in his hand. He undulated through the abandoned tables to press through the people at the front, and stand at Kaine's table. Kaine did not notice him.

The quartet was playing Charlie Parker's 'Hothouse'. Magnani traded phrases with Eyles, each man scaling great heights of control. Their virtuosity cut through to the nerve of the audience, notes tingled spines and moulded each set of ears to receive. Only the ears of the white suit were closed.

Through the sweat that ran off his forehead Magnani could hardly see the faces in front of him but he could hear them. Voices surged with the music, tied to it by enthusiasm and need. He was urged to go on, to get even better. Music entered people entirely and they joined Magnani in his search for conclusions.

The quartet finished the number. Kaine saw the man for the first time, leaning his hand on the chair next to him. His detachment struck the old man. He looked again at the black face and memory tugged at him. It was a determined face, with eyes fixed by malevolence. Snake eyes in a smooth suit. And Kaine knew who it was. He stood up to warn Magnani, who was mopping his face with a towel.

Johnson dropped the hat to reveal the gun. It glinted silver in the stagelights, and people shrank away from it . A girl's scream alerted Magnani. He looked up through the parting crowd as the bullets struck. They splintered through the guitar and lodged in his chest. For seconds he felt them tickle there, like insects nudging his skin. Then the hammer blows of pain, pounding him to the floor. And people whirling, coming to him, or going away. He heard Pearson's 'Frank, Frank' but the voice was thin and reedy, and shook like an old record. He saw the whites of Johnson's eyes as he was wrestled down to the floor. There was blood on his face from somewhere, dripping down into pattern of his tie. It was a face snarling with madness.

Kaine held Magnani's wrist and pawed at his shirt. He felt the warm flow through it and saw where the bullets had entered, and knew there was no hope. Magnani focused on Kaine's face and tried to smile, to tell him it was all right. But the words would not come. And the old man started to fade, to swirl away from him until just his eyes were there, twin specks of brightness, far stars moving ever further from him. Magnani wanted to follow them but could not, then they too were gone, and life had gone with them.

★ ★ ★

Pearson gave up Buen Vista to Kaine and D. Bell, insisting they stay there. He checked Eileen and himself into a nearby rooming house. 'We must share our grief,' the drummer said. And there was grief. The sharing of emotion Magnani had so needed in the last years of his life was instigated by his passing. Kaine and Pearson swopped their brief histories of the guitarist.

Magnani's guitar was sold to pay for his funeral. Pearson wanted to keep it but Kaine said it was better this way. 'Let it be played by someone,' he said. The killing made a quarter of a column in the New York papers, rather more in the jazz journals. One paper carried a picture of Johnson.

Magnani was buried in the small plot of a Harlem church. Other jazzmen were there, some without headstones, some with graves trampled into the ground: epitaphs to a perilous and unkind profession. At the service Eyles played one of Magnani's compositions on the piano, and there were small nods of approval as the chords echoed on the cold stone.

'See, Eileen,' Pearson said, 'Frank was right. He always said you gotta die on the way up, he always said that. The dude is made, man.'

He held onto Eileen to keep the choke from his voice. Their hands dug into each other as they shared very different memories of him.

In Magnani's belongings Kaine found the Haydn manuscript. The music written on Skopelos he put in the keeping of Eyles. He read the manuscript propped up in Pearson's bed. Magnani was on every page and Kaine understood him better with each chapter; a lonely and bitter young man who researched the past for solace. Kaine's sadness was heightened, for he knew Magnani had been close to belonging, to having the guts to share himself and his talent. He had truly left his island, to make himself and others happy. Happiness. He recognised how elusive a quality this had been in Magnani. He had known on that Virginia station, for he saw himself in the Welshman.

Kaine finished the manuscript by dawn and slept with its pages on his chest. A deep, untroubled sleep in which he dreamed of the closeness of death and did not fight it. He woke glad that Magnani had left his mark. Later in the day he sent the manuscript to an old college friend of his, a publisher.

Kaine wrote in detail to the address he found in one of Magnani's notebooks and hoped his words would help. But there had not been enough money to send Magnani back to his homeland, and no-one had crossed over for the funeral. Then, with D. Bell he took the train back to Florida, heading away from the cold but taking the gloom with them.

'This is how I met him,' Kaine muttered, 'he was getting off a train.'

'I know,' she said. She wondered how much longer Kaine could go on now. He fumbled for his pipe and stoked it up, sucking it into life with hollowed cheeks. His hands had the glassy touch of age, loose-skinned, almost translucent. But his eyes still defied. Kaine sat back and smiled.

'What's making you do that?' Bell asked.

'Just thinking about Frank's big band. That was something, you know. Such choice anarchy. Perhaps I could continue the music, what do you think?'

'He'd like it.'

'Pearson told me at the station that folks are talking a lot about that recording he made. Recognising Frank's gift.'

'Do you really think he would have come back to Tampa, if his music was taking off?' asked Bell.

'Yes. He was ready for us. He was ready for life. That's the shame of it.'

Kaine gave up on his pipe and put his hands behind his head, dozing as they travelled deeper south.